A Kiss from the Marquess

The Duke's Lost Treasures
Book 2

LANA WILLIAMS

ARE YOU SIGNED UP FOR DRAGONBLADE'S BLOG?

You'll get the latest news and information on exclusive giveaways, exclusive excerpts, coming releases, sales, free books, cover reveals and more.

Check out our complete list of authors, too!

No spam, no junk. That's a promise!

Sign Up Here

www.dragonbladepublishing.com

Dearest Reader;

Thank you for your support of a small press. At Dragonblade Publishing, we strive to bring you the highest quality Historical Romance from some of the best authors in the business. Without your support, there is no 'us', so we sincerely hope you adore these stories and find some new favorite authors along the way.

Happy Reading!

CEO, Dragonblade Publishing

Chapter One

London, England, May 1876

NORAH WRIGHT STARED in disbelief at the director of the Museum of Antiquities. "What do you mean he's not here?"

The stocky, middle-aged man adjusted his round spectacles and cleared his throat. What little grey hair he had was swept over the top of his balding head in a failed attempt to hide it. Someone should tell him he needn't bother.

"I'm terribly sorry, Miss Wright. I do realize this is the second time his lordship has failed to keep your appointment." Mr. Stockton pulled his pocket watch from his waistcoat and popped open the lid as if checking the time would somehow bring his employer to the museum. "I can't imagine what's keeping him."

Norah scowled. She had a suspicion of the reason—the fact that she was a woman. Over the past six months, she had encountered more than her fair share of prejudice from men. As a petite blonde, men seemed to assume she didn't have a thought of her own, nor could she function without their assistance.

However, she shouldn't jump to conclusions. That the mysterious Simon Webb, the Marquess of Vanbridge, had failed to meet her a second time was no reason to make assumptions. Perhaps he had a valid excuse, though she was highly doubtful of it.

Leo Stanton, the Earl of Marbury and her soon to be brother-in-law, had warned her that the marquess was a bit of a recluse and rarely attended social events. Marbury had offered to send a message to Vanbridge on her behalf, but this was something Norah wanted to do on her own.

Since it was a business matter for Vanbridge's museum, she'd been certain he would keep the appointment. When he hadn't shown up for the first meeting, she'd relented and used Marbury's name when making the second one, not that it had done any good.

"Why would he agree to the meeting if he had no intention of keeping it?" Norah asked, holding tight to her patience.

"It's not that he doesn't intend to keep his appointments. More than likely, he simply forgot."

"My time is just as important as his." Norah patted her reticule, which contained the carefully wrapped items she wanted to show the marquess to see if he would display them in his museum. "I even brought the artifacts with me."

"Oh?" Mr. Stockton's brows rose with interest. "I would be delighted to examine them. I'm certain I can make the proper arrangements for you if they're of value."

"No." Marbury had advised her to talk with Vanbridge. No one else would suffice. "I must speak directly with the marquess. These artifacts will not be stuffed in a corner or placed on a dusty shelf."

"I can assure you that I—"

"No, thank you." Norah had only just retrieved the items from the previous museum that had "displayed" them. However, she'd had trouble finding them, despite knowing exactly what she was looking for. How could anyone else possibly view them? That was not what she'd had in mind when she'd started this quest.

Her father, David Wright, had died nineteen months ago while digging in a shaft for treasure on Oak Island in the wilds of

Nova Scotia. The items in her reticule, along with a journal her father had kept, were the few items of David Wright's they still had.

Norah intended to find a museum willing to display the artifacts and share her father's story of treasure hunting to honor his memory. Never had she realized how difficult finding the right museum would be. The men in charge made vague promises of displaying the pieces but never followed through. Her father's artifacts were merely more items in a building filled to the roof with random relics.

That simply wouldn't do.

Norah wanted a special exhibit to honor David Wright's years of work. Seeing how poorly the two other museums had treated the display of the artifacts made her even more determined to see it done properly. She was not about to hand over the items to another museum employee who wouldn't follow through with her request.

"I must speak with the marquess personally."

"Of course." Mr. Stockton's lips tightened with displeasure.

Norah lifted her chin, not caring if this man thought her a meddlesome female. She knew what she wanted and intended to get it. While she wasn't the dutiful daughter that Ella was or the sunny one like Lena, this was something she was well-suited to do. Something she *needed* to do.

With nowhere else to go, Norah and her sisters had arrived in London a few months after their father's death to meet their estranged grandfather, the Duke of Rothwood.

However, they had been less than welcomed. The duke had cut all ties with his only child, Lady Bethany, when she'd chosen to elope with David Wright. Unfortunately, their mother had died six years earlier, having never reconciled with her father.

It had taken Norah and her sisters months to convince the duke to finally lower his defensive walls and allow them to truly become part of his life. While Norah could use her grandfather's name to convince the marquess to aid her, she preferred not to.

"The only thing I can offer is to make another appointment," Mr. Stockton said with reluctance. "I will make certain his lordship is aware of it. Perhaps I could send a message to remind him of the meeting."

The way the man's brow puckered as he mentioned the latter suggested even that might not bring the marquess to the museum.

Norah considered her options. No purpose would be served in making another appointment. It would be a waste of her time. She could think of only one option. If the marquess wasn't going to come to her, she would go to him. She chose to ignore the voice in the back of her mind that reminded her women didn't pay calls on men. Especially unmarried ladies to unmarried men.

But this was a business matter, she told herself. Society's rules didn't necessarily apply.

"Thank you for your time, Mr. Stockton. I will be in touch if I require further assistance."

"You're sure you wouldn't prefer to leave your items with me?" He eyed her reticule with what looked like longing. "I can promise to see them safely displayed."

"No, thank you." Norah forced a smile. "Good day."

She stalked out of the office on the fourth floor of the building with her maid and a footman following. Her grandfather insisted both servants accompany her unless one of her sisters did.

Ella, her eldest sister, was busy planning her wedding and her new life as the Countess of Marbury. Of course, Ella continued to encourage Norah to find a husband as well. That had been the entire reason behind them coming to London.

But Norah wasn't ready for marriage. She'd only started to enjoy her new life and wasn't prepared for that to end. Not after seeing how narrow her mother's world had been. And she had yet to meet a man who made her reconsider. The conversations she'd had with various gentlemen since their first ball nearly a year ago only confirmed her opinion. They either flirted and flattered outrageously or spoke of how important they were.

She had hinted to Ella that she wasn't interested in marrying yet, though it had fallen on deaf ears. Was it so wrong to want to relish the taste of freedom she'd experienced thus far? London was far from perfect, but there was much to see and do here compared to Oak Island, where she'd been raised.

Lena, her younger sister, insisted she was done visiting museums for the time being, although she appreciated Norah's efforts to see their father's artifacts displayed. Ella did as well. While Norah valued their support, she wanted—needed—to be the one to do this for her father. To make a gesture to show how much she loved, supported, and believed in David Wright and his work. And she had.

It was just that life on the remote island hadn't been easy. They'd lived an isolated existence that focused on her father's efforts to the exclusion of all else. One that she had started to resent when their father died. If only she hadn't chosen the morning of his death to quarrel with him—ironic given that she was considered even-tempered and the peacemaker of the family.

Guilt had her rolling her shoulders as they descended the stairs. The disagreement with her father was a secret she kept from her sisters. Had that argument contributed to his death? Had it made him careless or distracted and therefore caused the accident that had taken his life?

The worry made her desperate to find a way to honor her father and his work. It was the only way to make amends.

Norah glanced about the museum as they went, her frustration mounting. She'd been so certain this was the right place for the sort of exhibit she had in mind.

The Museum of Antiquities had been open for less than five years. It had a fine reputation, and she could see why. Each exhibit told a story, and that was exactly what she wanted for her father's artifacts.

Not one exhibit spoke of pirate treasure, which would make her father's exhibit special and unique rather than one of several. That was the reason she and her sisters hadn't been there the previous year when they'd toured so many museums in search of their father's missing journal.

The house had been the former residence of the late Marquess of Vanbridge, the uncle of the current marquess. Located on Parker's Lane near Lincoln's Inn Fields, its exterior was nondescript—a four-story townhouse of neoclassic architecture. The first two levels of the white stone building had arched windows and a narrow wrought-iron fence that lined the front. However, it was the interior that had one looking about with admiration.

The curving stairs of the residence looked as if they floated, lending an other-worldly atmosphere. Arched passageways echoed the exterior, and the golden-colored paint, along with an impressive amount of natural light, brought a rich look to the inside, making visitors feel as if they'd entered a special place— and they had.

Several rooms were set up to mimic an actual archaeological site. One held the 3,000-year-old sarcophagus of an Egyptian king along with many artifacts that had been found in the burial chamber. Another held Greek statues and décor that made one feel as if they had wandered into an ancient Grecian home. Yet another contained a plaster model of the Temple of Vesta in Italy.

Norah had been so fascinated by the museum that she'd already toured it twice, the second time with her sisters. She appreciated history, and by the look of the museum, she had to assume the Marquess of Vanbridge did as well, as he'd been the one to design the displays. That level of attention to detail and creativity was exactly what she wanted. Vanbridge honored the stories of the discovery of the relics as much as he did the items themselves, another reason Norah wanted to speak with him directly.

Unfortunately, he no longer spent much time there. In Norah's opinion, his absence was beginning to be reflected in the rather dusty displays and numerous cobwebs. The director didn't seem to bother with those issues. Was it any wonder she didn't trust Mr. Stockton to see her artifacts shown in the proper manner?

Although the marquess was a member of the Royal Geological Society along with Marbury, he rarely attended meetings or social engagements. The Society focused on matters of exploration and sharing information among its members. He didn't feel the need to bother with polite Society or anything that went along with it, according to Ella's betrothed. The idea nearly made her shudder. How did he spend his time without friends and gatherings to occupy him?

Norah might value history but had no intention of immersing herself in it. Still, she had a certain curiosity about the man who had created the unique exhibits. And she was determined that today would be the day she satisfied it.

"Shall I advise the driver we're returning home, miss?" James, the footman, asked after he assisted her and Dorothy inside the carriage.

"No. Please have him take us to the Marquess of Vanbridge's residence."

James paused with his hand on the door, watching her as if he hadn't heard her correctly. "Miss?"

"I do believe it's in Mayfair."

James heaved a sigh as he shared a look with Dorothy. "Yes, miss. I believe you're right." He closed the door slowly, continuing to watch her as if hoping she'd change her mind.

Norah glanced out the window as the conveyance rolled forward. A tingle of nerves simmered inside her at the idea of going to the marquess's home. She dearly hoped neither Ella nor her grandfather found out about the meeting.

This was only business, she reminded herself. Yet her nerves refused to settle.

SIMON WEBB, THE Marquess of Vanbridge, turned the oddly shaped stone in his hand to better catch the light and make out the faint carvings softened by time. He copied the markings as precisely as he could onto the paper on his desk.

He muttered a curse as the skin on one of his sore knuckles split open again. Boxing this morning had been particularly brutal, but he had no one to blame except himself. The ache in his shoulders and arms was a welcome one. Especially now that his body was strengthening.

A punching bag was his only target at the moment, though his valet, Miles, had offered to serve as an opponent in addition to his teacher. Simon wanted to improve his skills and technique before he took on the former infantry soldier, as he had no doubt Miles would easily defeat him.

Simon didn't need any more reminders in his life that he was less, especially when it came to sports and other physical activities. He liked to think the adult version of himself was much healthier than the younger one but didn't care to test the theory.

The physical activity of boxing was supposed to improve his mental clarity and analytical abilities. To allow better concentration and focus. Damned if it didn't seem to be working. He also had more energy, something he appreciated after being rather sickly in his youth with one ailment or another.

Simon had been third in line for the marquess title and never expected to inherit. Never wanted to. However, the death of his uncle and cousin nearly a decade ago had changed Simon's path from studying to be a solicitor to suddenly inheriting a title.

His own mother and father had died in a carriage accident when he was seven. As an only child, he had been left hollow with grief and terribly alone. Perhaps that could be blamed for his frequent illnesses. He'd gone to live with an elderly aunt and uncle on his mother's side, but they'd been ill-prepared to deal with a young boy and had returned him to Eton as quickly as possible. When Simon was twelve, they'd both succumbed to influenza, leaving him alone again.

His Uncle Theodore, the previous marquess, had taken him in. Luckily for Simon, his uncle shared Simon's father's love of history, though it was the only thing they had in common.

Uncle Theodore had gathered a significant collection over the years. It seemed an easy decision when Simon had inherited to turn the former residence and its artifacts into a museum. He could think of no better way to honor both his own father's memory and that of his uncle's.

Doing so gave Simon a reason to focus on his own passion for history. He was far more interested in the past than the present or the future. Neither of those held any appeal.

A strange noise caught his notice, causing his pencil to halt mid-air. It almost sounded like voices. Yet that couldn't be, he thought with a scowl. He never had visitors, and the staff knew to be quiet at all times so as not to interrupt his work.

There it was again. Puzzled, he straightened in his chair just as the door to his study opened.

"My apologies, my lord." Fletcher, his butler, bowed with a stately yet dramatic grace that spoke of his years on stage. "But it seems you have a caller." He was obviously flustered by the unusual occurrence, as was Simon. He never had callers, nor did he want them.

Simon waved his hand in the air, the pencil still in his grip. "Send them away." He looked back at the carvings without a second thought.

"Yes, my lord." The door closed behind the servant.

A peaceful silence descended as Simon returned to his work. However, it didn't last long. Voices soon echoed in the entrance hall again. Simon released a frustrated sigh, then started drawing again only to hear another knock.

"I'm terribly sorry, my lord." Fletcher bowed again after opening the door. "The caller insists on seeing you. At once."

Before Simon could refuse, the door pushed open farther, revealing a lady. A beautiful, petite lady dressed in a deep blue gown that reminded him of an ancient Egyptian figurine made of lapis lazuli. The vibrant blue was one of his favorite colors. He blinked in surprise as he jerked to his feet, certain he didn't know her. He couldn't imagine why she was calling but ran a hand through his hair, suddenly aware of his disheveled appearance.

"We had a two o'clock appointment at the museum, my lord." Was it his imagination or did her tone hold a hint of steel? She dipped into a brief—very brief—curtsy, as if she resented having to do so.

"Oh?" He frowned and glanced at his desk, thinking to check his calendar, only to remember that he didn't keep one. As he considered her reprimand, he vaguely recalled a meeting regarding new artifacts. "Was that today?"

"Yes. And, also, two days ago."

"Hmm." He shook his head. "You'll have to make another appointment. The week after next would be best." Whether he'd remember was doubtful. His absentmindedness was a bother at times. Though he often jotted down things he wanted to remember, finding the piece of paper on which he'd written them was a struggle.

She smiled, but it wasn't especially friendly. "I'm afraid that won't do." She glanced around with interest, causing him to follow her gaze, wondering what she saw.

His study was like most others, lined with books on one side and a fire burning in the hearth on the opposite. A bank of mullioned windows was behind his massive desk, providing the light he needed to work. Papers and books were stacked on the polished surface in a haphazard manner, along with a lamp.

However, his study differed from ones he'd seen in that there was only one chair before the fire and none before his desk.

He didn't have visitors.

A long, red leather couch stood near the bookshelves because he sometimes fell asleep reading there. Mrs. Fletcher, the housekeeper, had placed a brightly woven blanket on the end of it in case he did. A sideboard stood to one side of his desk with crystal decanters filled with amber liquid, though he rarely drank.

The woman glanced at the butler as if expecting him to depart, then strolled forward as she continued to look about the room.

Fletcher started to go only to pause, then, with a shrug, walked out, leaving the door slightly ajar. He'd served as butler for the past five years but didn't always know what was proper.

Simon's stomach tightened as the lady continued toward him, though he couldn't say why. He easily dismissed the sensation. The only women who'd been in his study were servants. Was it any wonder the lady's presence pushed him off balance? Still, he found himself checking his tie and tugging on the hem of his suit coat, realizing he should've gotten his hair clipped a week ago.

"I am Norah Wright, and I have some artifacts of my father's, David Wright, that I would like to show you." She paused briefly to study a hand-painted clay vessel sitting on a shelf.

The name was familiar. After a moment's consideration, he remembered receiving a message from the Earl of Marbury about Wright's stolen journal. Simon hadn't been of any assistance as he hadn't come across the missing item.

However, the mention of artifacts never failed to catch his attention. "What kind?"

"Those from a treasure hunter who spent decades digging on Oak Island."

He frowned as he tried to place the location. "In Nova Scotia?"

"Yes." Her bright smile suggested she was pleased he was at least familiar with it.

"I read something about his search, but that was some time ago. Pirate treasure is not my area of interest."

Miss Wright now stood before his desk, and he drank in her presence. She was small in stature, barely coming to his shoulder, and had curves everywhere a woman should. Her heart-shaped face was smooth, her features even. Her eyes were what caught him. They were blue, but rather than cornflower bright, they were stormy, like the sea on a cold winter's day.

Brows a shade darker than her hair arched above them. Her narrow nose tipped up at the end and her lips were full. She appeared confident and intelligent.

And truly beautiful, he realized. Her face had the sort of symmetry sought after in statues and paintings.

"I'm sorry?" she asked, one brow raised.

He frowned, wondering if he'd said the words out loud. Perhaps he was alone too often, as Mrs. Fletcher continually suggested.

"Nothing." He rubbed the back of his neck as embarrassment prickled it. He liked being alone and saying his thoughts out loud was only one of the many reasons. "Wright never found much of anything from what I remember. What sort of artifacts do you have?"

She tightened her lips, her displeasure at his statement obvious. "A copper coin from 1713, three links of a gold chain, and a stone with strange markings on it."

"Markings?" He eyed the reticule she held, hoping she might have them with her.

"If you would've been at the museum today, I'd have shown them to you."

He was intrigued more by the stone than the other items. Puzzles of that sort, like the one on his desk, were what he truly enjoyed. He reached out a finger to run along the carvings of the stone he was currently studying, the motion settling him slightly. "Unfortunately, those aren't enough for an exhibit."

A flash of annoyance crossed her face. "So I've been told. But I have a few ideas to expand them." She stepped close and bent to examine the carvings he'd been attempting to decipher. "What is this from?"

"It came from South America and is most likely Incan. But its purpose is unclear as of yet."

She looked up at him, her eyes round with wonder. "Fascinating."

"Yes, it is." Her interest softened his reserve. "The carvings remain a mystery, but I think I'm getting closer to understanding them," he said as he rubbed at the lead smudges on his fingers.

"That must be quite rewarding."

"Indeed." Before he thought better of it, he opened his desk drawer and pulled out a small clay statue. The figurine of a short man with a large nose and tall headdress fit easily in the palm of his hand. "It was found with this."

"Oh, my." She took the relic with care, turning it over, running a gloved finger along the rough surface.

A ripple of awareness ran along his skin at the reverence in her tone and expression. To think she appreciated the small statue as much as he did was more appealing than it should be.

"How old do you think it is?" she asked as she handed it back with care.

"Perhaps as much as a thousand years. More research is needed."

"I look forward to hearing what you discover." Her warm smile sent his pulse skittering. "The displays at your museum are wonderful. So creative and unique."

"Thank you." He wasn't above finding her compliment flattering, though it wouldn't change his mind.

"They're exactly what I'm looking for. Something that focuses on what it's like to search for treasure using the artifacts I mentioned."

To Simon's surprise, he was somewhat intrigued. Hadn't he always imagined what it would be like to go on a treasure hunt? Museum visitors might appreciate that experience, as well.

Though doubtful whether it was possible with so few artifacts, he found himself agreeing to meet Miss Wright at the museum the following day. He had the feeling he would remember the appointment after having met the captivating lady.

Chapter Two

"NORAH, PERHAPS YOU should reconsider." Ella rose from a chair in the drawing room at Rothwood House, her expression troubled, as Norah prepared to leave for her appointment with Vanbridge. "I have to wonder if the marquess is correct. Father didn't find much. I don't see how the few items we have could be made into an exhibit."

Though her sister's tone was gentle, Norah had the urge to stomp her foot in protest. "I thought you agreed with me. That you supported this idea."

"I appreciate your wish to honor Father and his work. Truly. But you've already done what you can."

Without success. Though unspoken, those two words rang in the air between them. What she'd managed wasn't enough. Not when the heavy weight of guilt still sat on her shoulders.

"I'm not certain why you're so adamant about an exhibit," Ella continued. "We often share Father's efforts with others, so he won't be forgotten. He doesn't have to be remembered with a public display."

Norah turned aside in frustration only to turn back. "Telling a few acquaintances about him isn't the same. It's not enough." With the marquess's hesitation to agree to her request echoing in her thoughts, she'd shared her frustration with Ella after returning home the previous day, though she hadn't mentioned where their meeting had been held. Ella would not approve.

Her idea had to work. There was no alternative. Not when she couldn't think of any other way to make amends for what she'd done. How could she hope to assuage her guilt if she couldn't share Father's efforts with as many people as possible?

Though she'd had the artifacts with her the previous day, she'd decided against showing them to Vanbridge. She'd wanted more time to think of a way to convince him to create an exhibit. Hence the reason she'd discussed it with Ella, hoping her sister might provide additional ideas.

Instead, Ella was casting doubt on her plan. Yet she couldn't share the reason she had to do this. How could her sisters forgive her for what she'd done when she couldn't forgive herself?

"We have Grandfather to think of now, as well," Ella said, adding to Norah's upset.

The duke's dislike of their father had softened but only slightly. His Grace preferred to act as if David Wright had never existed.

Of course, Norah, Ella, and Lena didn't agree with that but did their best to avoid speaking of their father in their grandfather's presence.

"The exhibit isn't about Grandfather." Norah didn't like to argue, but she couldn't let this go without trying harder.

"No, it's not." Ella sighed. "I just don't want you to be disappointed if the marquess doesn't agree."

"I won't. If he refuses to create an exhibit, I will set aside the matter." That promise made Norah all the more determined to convince Vanbridge to aid her.

The marquess was an intriguing man—tall, dark, and sinfully handsome with broad shoulders and a slender build. His wavy brown hair had been carelessly brushed to one side and was long enough to curl over the collar of his suit coat.

His green eyes were warm and gentle with flecks of gold. Long lashes often swept down to hide his thoughts. With a Roman nose, high cheekbones, and dark brows, his attractive appearance was enough to make her look twice. Or three times perhaps.

The cautious watchfulness in his demeanor was also appealing, though she couldn't say why.

"Very well," Ella said with a smile, pulling Norah's thoughts back. "If those few items were enough to convince Father to keep digging for so many years, they could capture the interest of museum visitors. Why don't I accompany you? Between the two of us, we might sway the marquess."

Ella had stood by their father in every possible way, especially after their mother's death. She'd helped to organize his notes and maps, raised Norah and Lena, and tended every aspect of their lives.

Norah was but a shadow compared to her strong, steadfast sister who moved through life with purpose and determination. Norah felt selfish in comparison and definitely less. Less worthy. Less clever. Less devoted to family.

All the more reason she needed to attempt this on her own.

"No need." Norah forced a smile. "I know how busy you are with wedding preparations."

Ella pressed both hands to her cheeks as a delicate blush crept into them. "Only a few more weeks. I can hardly believe the day is nearly here."

"Nor can I." Her sister's happiness outweighed Norah's concern for how different their lives would be without Ella living under the same roof. She would miss her terribly. Ella had been their rudder for so long, and Norah and Lena had come to depend on her. But that worry would have to wait. "I will advise you of the outcome upon my return."

"I look forward to hearing good news."

Norah appreciated the offer of support and smiled as she walked down the stairs, catching the lyrical notes of a harp drifting through the house. Lena was playing this morning, the light-hearted piece suggesting her younger sister was in good spirits.

"I'll return in a moment," Norah told James and Dorothy, who waited in the entrance hall. She hurried down the corridor toward her grandfather's study and peeked in to see if he was inside. She'd made a habit of sharing bits of her day with him when possible, to help strengthen the tenuous bond between them, especially with Ella leaving soon.

Not long ago, this door had remained firmly closed with Davies, the butler, guarding it whenever her grandfather was within. The Duke of Rothwood had gone to great lengths to keep Norah and her sisters away from him—out of his study and out of his heart.

Bless Ella for her persistence in wearing him down. It had taken months before he'd had a true conversation with the three sisters and even more time for him to come to care for them.

"Grandfather?" She hated to interrupt him. In fact, she still felt a pang of nerves when she did, as she remembered all too well the scowl he used to wear if they so much as looked at him when they'd first arrived.

"Good afternoon, Norah." He gestured for her to come forward. His white hair was combed neatly to the side, his fine wool suit coat fit perfectly, and his tie was knotted precisely. He appeared every inch a duke. "Where are you off to this afternoon?"

"I'm going to the Museum of Antiquities."

He frowned. "Didn't you do that yesterday?"

"Yes, but today the Marquess of Vanbridge is meeting me to discuss a possible exhibit." Norah held her breath, knowing he wouldn't be pleased. While she rarely mentioned her father, she hadn't wanted to hide her idea for an exhibit from the duke. She knew he'd hoped the topic was over and done given her lack of success with her previous attempts.

"I see." His frown made his disapproval clear. "I can't think Vanbridge will be of much help. He knows little about pirate treasure."

"Yes, but the exhibit would be one of a kind in his museum.

And I like the stories he tells with his displays."

"Hmm. He's a different sort of gentleman, always keeping to himself. Though he's a member of the Royal Geological Society, he rarely attends any meetings or lectures. I would caution you from placing too much faith in him."

"I will certainly keep that in mind."

"Who is accompanying you?"

"James and Dorothy," Norah said. He was a stickler about safety after the events involving the theft of their father's journal the previous year. Thank goodness, they'd recovered it.

"Are you working on anything exciting?" she asked, hoping to distract him. His tidy desk held only a handful of papers. It looked far different than Vanbridge's with its papers, drawings, and books stacked here and there, not to mention a rock or two.

"I'm reviewing proposed legislation to amend the poor law." He scowled. "It doesn't do enough, in my opinion."

His words made Norah smile and reminded her that he was a good man. Unable to resist, she rounded the corner of his desk and pressed a kiss on his cheek. "Thank you for caring. More needs to be done to aid the less fortunate."

He stiffened for a moment at her gesture before a small smile came over his expression. He patted her hand, which rested on his shoulder. "Indeed, it does. We should consider more charitable activities, as that is certainly easier than trying to amend laws to aid them."

"Excellent idea. In fact, if Vanbridge is agreeable to an exhibit, perhaps we could make the unveiling a charitable endeavor. Special tickets could be sold to unveil it. The proceeds could go to The City of London's Orphanage." The charity was one of several her grandfather generously supported.

"I suppose that is possible." Despite the lack of enthusiasm in his tone, his expression suggested he liked the idea.

"I shall keep you apprised of the situation." Norah bid him goodbye and took her leave.

In a short while, she was climbing to the offices on the fourth floor of the museum once more with her servants, hoping Vanbridge remembered the appointment this time. At least she was managing a lot of exercise with all the stairs she'd gone up and down this week.

As per usual, Mr. Stockton sat at his desk on the landing with several papers before him and a pen at the ready.

Norah would've thought he'd spend more time among the exhibits. Then again, she knew little about running a museum. No doubt there was a tremendous amount of paperwork involved.

The director's eyes widened in surprise at the sight of her, and he slowly stood. "Miss Wright. What a pleasant surprise. You've changed your mind about leaving the artifacts with me, eh?" He rubbed his hands together as if he already knew that to be the case.

"Actually, I'm meeting the marquess." Yet her stomach sank. It was obvious from Mr. Stockton's reaction that Vanbridge wasn't there. Now, what did she do? Venture to his residence again and show him the artifacts there? She feared he might put them in a drawer and forget them.

"I'm terribly sorry. His lordship isn't here." He glanced over his shoulder at a door to one side, suggesting that was where the marquess's office was located. "Nor do I expect him today. He always advises me when he's coming, you see."

"Does he?" Norah sighed. She'd had high hopes he would keep their appointment this time. That he'd felt the same connection she had when they'd spoken. Apparently, it had been one-sided. How disappointing.

"Always." Mr. Stockton eyed her reticule. "Perhaps it would be best if you left the items with me. I'll be sure to share them with the marquess when he comes in."

"No need. I'm here now." The deep voice had Norah spinning to see Vanbridge had indeed arrived.

How he wasn't breathless after climbing all those stairs, she didn't know. His broad shoulders filled out his suit coat nicely.

The wave in his hair suggested it was freshly washed. His scent drifted toward her, a mix of bergamot and the woods, and was very appealing.

The realization of her attraction was alarming. She'd met numerous gentlemen over the last year but had never felt this hum under her skin, as if her senses were somehow attuned to him.

Then again, if she'd found someone who caught her interest, how perfect that he was a reclusive gentleman who avoided social engagements. She wouldn't be tempted to deepen their brief association. And Vanbridge's obvious preference for researching history was yet another strike against him. She wanted a husband who cared more for her than whatever he found carved on a rock or buried in the ground.

The admission nearly caused her to grimace, making her feel even guiltier because of what she'd said to her father before his death.

While she would like to eventually marry and have a family, that would be several years from now—after she'd filled her life with experiences and activities that she hadn't been able to enjoy while living in a remote area.

However, she wasn't averse to a minor flirtation with the handsome marquess. Especially when their association would be so brief.

"My lord." Norah dipped into a curtsy, pleased when Vanbridge bowed. He hadn't bothered to do so yesterday. No doubt he'd forgotten. "I'm so pleased you're here."

He appeared nonplussed at her warm greeting. She shouldn't delight in throwing him off balance, but she did.

The marquess cleared his throat, then nodded at Mr. Stockton before gesturing toward his office door. "Shall we have a look at what you brought?"

"Yes." She smothered the unexpected urge to say something flirtatious. She never did so normally. Not when doing so might cause an unwanted suitor to have unrealistic expectations.

Vanbridge unlocked his office door and held it open for her.

Norah stepped inside, eager to see this version of his workspace. Her expectations were met with disappointment. Nothing showed his personality. Not like his personal study had.

Only a simple desk and chairs were in the room, along with a pleasant watercolor on one wall. At least there was a chair before his desk here. She took a seat and adjusted her skirts before setting her reticule carefully on the floor.

The marquess started to close the door only to stop, making Norah wonder if James had frowned at him. The footman was rather protective of Norah and her sisters.

After leaving the door partially ajar, Vanbridge rounded the desk and sat, looking over the empty surface as if he expected something to be on it. Those small moments of uncertainty brought forth an urge to aid him, as if he needed a friend to guide him.

How silly. He was a marquess, not a young boy, and older than her own twenty-two years if she were to guess. No doubt those moments of hesitation were caused by how rarely he went out in public. He seemed to feel the need to think through what he should do before he acted. If only she didn't find that so appealing.

Resisting the urge to wave a hand before her suddenly flushed face, she drew a slow breath instead and reached for the reticule only to halt. She needed to state her argument for the exhibit carefully. Handing over the artifacts without a proper explanation wouldn't do.

"May I tell you a story?" she asked.

He looked at her for a long moment, his green eyes steady. "Yes."

The simple reply after he considered the question released a flurry of butterflies inside her. Heaven forbid if this man ever graced a ballroom with his presence. The ladies would swarm him.

She shoved aside the ridiculous notion and gathered her

thoughts. This was important, and she needed to take care with not only what she said but how she said it.

"Over twenty-five years ago, an adventurer met a lady and shared his dream of finding buried treasure on a remote island. The lady was so intrigued by the man and his passion for the quest that she gave up everything to help him pursue it." She drew a breath to ease the well of emotion that filled her as she considered just what her mother had given up. That wasn't her concern today. "But the story began long before that.

"In January of 1698, Captain William Kidd worked as a Scottish privateer. He and his crew overtook an Indian vessel, the *Quedagh Merchant,* said to have 15,000 British pounds onboard. Kidd captured the ship and took the loot, causing a protest to arise throughout the British Empire. Upon learning he'd been accused of piracy, Kidd sailed for New York with the hope his influential friends there would aid him. After all, he believed what he'd done was legal. But he was arrested anyway."

"What happened to the treasure?"

"Excellent question." She smiled. "He hid it for safekeeping before his arrest so he might use it to barter for his freedom."

Norah pulled out a booklet from her reticule and handed it to him. "Perhaps you've seen this publication printed in America that details the life, trial, and execution of Kidd."

"I can't say that I have. Pirates aren't a focus of mine." His frown concerned her. She would much rather his interest was caught.

"I understand," she said. "But that's exactly why this exhibit will be perfect for us both."

"How so?"

"A different sort of exhibit could bring new visitors to the museum. And you would provide a fresh view on my father's artifacts rather than adding them to any pirate-related items the museum already has."

"Hmm." He read the headlines on the front page of the booklet, then met her gaze with a raised brow as if intrigued. "This contains letters from Kidd's wife?"

"Yes, along with other documents regarding the proceedings. My father thought it quite interesting." Norah paused while he reviewed the booklet before she continued. "Kidd eventually revealed the location of the treasure, hoping it would help his case. Instead, it was used as evidence against him at his trial. Although Kidd insisted on his innocence and that he was merely acting on his duties as a privateer, he was found guilty and hanged in 1701."

"I have the feeling the tale doesn't end there." Vanbridge's gaze held on her as if she were his latest find, and he was eager to find out more.

Her mouth went dry, and her entire body tingled at the sensation. It didn't help to remind herself that it was her story he was interested in rather than her.

"You're correct. Before he died, Kidd insisted there was yet another treasure. A much larger one that he'd buried."

"That's the one people are still looking for today."

"Yes. However, he took the secret with him to his grave. But clues still surfaced." She withdrew a newspaper clipping to hand to him. "An elderly man who lived in New England and was considered a recluse and mute surprised his neighbors on his deathbed by not only speaking but sharing his life as a sailor aboard Captain Kidd's ship. He alleged to have helped Kidd bury four million dollars in gold on a secluded island east of Boston."

Vanbridge's expression turned doubtful. "If that were true, wouldn't the sailor have claimed it for his own?"

"He said he never dared to speak of it or take it for fear of enduring the same fate as his captain."

"I suppose it would be difficult to insist on one's innocence and yet be found with plunder."

"In 1795, three young men started searching on Oak Island for treasure. Since then, many, including my father, have also searched." Norah withdrew the copper coin and handed it to him. "My father found this in a shaft he dug that he believed led to the

Money Pit, where the treasure supposedly is."

Those long fingers were nearly graceful in their movements as he turned it over to examine both sides. "Finding this might convince me to continue looking as well."

"He also found a significant amount of coconut fiber on the island."

"There could be multiple uses for it," he said, his tone skeptical. "Possibly as dunnage for ship's cargo. Or even making rope."

"Or perhaps caulking a ship's hull." She paused with a smile. "What's interesting is that Father found it deep underground in the shaft he believed led to the Money Pit."

Vanbridge's brows raised as he processed the idea. "That *is* interesting."

Norah pulled out another carefully wrapped item and laid it on the desk. "These gold links were found at a depth of ninety-eight feet in that same shaft."

"From a watch chain, most likely." Again, those long fingers of his manipulated the item to examine it. "Strange that it was found so far underground."

"Indeed. You can see why my father was convinced something significant happened on the island." She retrieved a large piece of folded paper and carefully opened it. "This is the most intriguing find. It's a copy of the markings on a stone found in 1803 by another searcher approximately eighty feet down in a shaft that later collapsed. The stone is just over two feet long and about a foot wide."

"Odd markings," the marquess said as he studied the triangular shapes, dots, squares, and circles. "Have they been interpreted?"

"Not as of yet. Some think it a cipher of sorts."

Vanbridge sat back in his chair and studied the items on his desk for a minute before looking at Norah. "What is it you hope to accomplish with an exhibit?"

Norah shifted to the edge of her seat, hoping she could convince him. "To help people understand why my father searched all those years. To show them he had reason to and might've been successful if the shaft hadn't collapsed on him." She swallowed against the lump in her throat as grief threatened to take hold. Now wasn't the time for tears.

"And perhaps to allow them the thrill of discovery," she continued, "even if it is from the safety of a museum rather than on a remote island in Nova Scotia."

Vanbridge folded his arms over his chest as he stared at the items again. "There isn't much to show."

"I realize it will be a challenge. But it's the story behind these artifacts that needs to be shared. You're the perfect person to create such an exhibit."

"I would have to do some more research, but I admit to having a few ideas. Nevertheless, I can't promise many people will venture here to see it." His brow puckered. "Unfortunately, attendance has been steadily declining."

"A new exhibit might change that." She fisted her hand on her lap, hoping he would agree.

"Hmm."

"I would be pleased to help promote it. In fact, I would like to suggest we host a party for the unveiling. A fundraiser for charity."

Vanbridge immediately shook his head. "I don't do parties." He said the word as if it were foreign on his tongue. "Nor do we have the staff for such an event."

"I'm not suggesting a ball or anything. This would be smaller, perhaps fifty guests. I'll take care of the details. You need only prepare the exhibit with the same care and attention that you used with the other exhibits." She looked at him expectantly. "What do you think?"

"As long as I don't have to attend." He shifted in his chair as if uncomfortable.

"You have to be there. The Earl of Marbury will come, of course, as well as numerous members of the Royal Geological Society."

"I nearly forgot Marbury and your sister are soon to be married."

"Yes. I hope my grandfather will attend the unveiling, though I can't promise that." She bit her lower lip, nearly certain it would be impossible to convince him to go.

"The Duke of Rothwood?"

"Yes." She held her breath as she watched him mull over the possibilities. "Think of the benefits the exhibit and gathering could provide for the museum. We'd like to raise funds for The City of London's Orphanage. Perhaps some of the children could be given a special tour of the museum as well. Please say you'll do it."

SIMON FEARED HE was sunk as he looked into Norah Wright's stormy blue eyes filled with such hope. How could anyone refuse her anything? He sighed, thinking perhaps all was not lost. "I don't see how my presence would benefit—"

Miss Wright shook her head before he could complete his argument. "I need you." Her eyes widened as her cheeks flushed a delicate shade of pink. "I mean, we need you there. At the party. That's what I meant."

He studied her uncomfortable expression, trying to understand what else she thought she'd implied. He reviewed the conversation and latched onto the part where she'd said, *"I need you."*

His body flushed just like her cheeks. He wasn't accustomed to being around women. The few interactions he'd had at social functions over the years had been painfully awkward, something he'd been relentlessly teased over. The subtle remarks and innuendos used by members of the *ton* were often lost on him.

Based on Miss Wright's embarrassment, her comment had merely been a slip of the tongue.

He frowned as the thought of kissing her took hold. Blast it.

The last thing he needed right now in addition to an exhibit to plan was a woman to distract him. He had research to complete and carvings to analyze. He flexed his still healing hands, realizing another bout with the boxing bag was in his future.

He forced himself to meet her gaze. This was business. Nothing more. After all, she was Rothwood's granddaughter and, therefore, no one with whom he should dally. Not that he dallied with anyone.

His lack of experience with women covered the entire realm of female companionship, from flirting to the bedroom. It was one more area of his life where he felt completely out of depth. He'd even failed when his late cousin had taken him along to a brothel, resulting in even more ribbing.

Simon was meant to be alone. Of that, he had no doubt. The loved ones in his life had been taken from him. Forming an association of any sort would only end in heartache. He'd had more than his fill of that.

"I would rather not attend." He heard the surly note in his tone, not so different from a lad told to eat the vegetables on his plate. He couldn't help it. The thought of going to any gathering put a knot in the pit of his stomach. People would want to speak with him when he had nothing to say.

"I would be there with you if that is of any reassurance."

He stared at her for a moment, realizing it did help, much to his surprise. "I will consider it," he offered with reluctance.

"Thank you. Now then, how soon will the exhibit be ready?"

Relieved to return the conversation to the exhibit, he considered the work that would have to be done. They settled on holding the unveiling in two weeks.

"Thank you, my lord," Miss Wright said as she rose. "I can't tell you how pleased I am that you've agreed." Her beaming smile had him catching his breath. "I look forward to seeing what you create. I'll be in touch in a few days to confirm some of the details. You won't regret this."

Unfortunately, he already did. But he was certain he could

find a way to escape the unveiling.

One bright note was that he'd be seeing more of Miss Wright. That was enough to have him smiling even after she departed.

Chapter Three

"WELL, MY LORD?" the butler asked as he closed the door behind Simon when he returned home from the meeting.

"Well, what?" Simon was confused by the servant's question as he handed him his hat and gloves.

"Will we be having any visitors today?"

"Of course not. Why would we?"

"That's what you've always said but look what happened yesterday." Fletcher swept his hand through the air in a grand gesture that nearly had Simon rolling his eyes. "A lady visited. *A lady.*" The man's voice rose with the repetition of the term, echoing in the entrance hall much like it might in a theater. "How was I supposed to know what to do with her?"

Simon knew very well what he'd like to do with Miss Norah Wright. If she hadn't made that remark about needing him, he wouldn't have these crazy, inappropriate thoughts.

In fact, he'd considered walking home just to try to work off the unsettling feelings, but Jarvis had been waiting to drive him and had looked so crestfallen when Simon mentioned walking.

Simon had carefully selected his servants, having pensioned off his uncle's staff soon after inheriting the title. He'd wanted a new start in a new house after Uncle Theodore's death. He hadn't liked the idea of the servants comparing him to his uncle. Besides, many of them had been elderly.

This house was smaller than the previous residence that had been turned into a museum and not as cold and formal. It reminded Simon a bit of his childhood home. There was also the added benefit of not needing as many servants.

Fletcher served as butler. His wife, also a former actress, was the housekeeper. Simon's valet, Miles, acted as footman, when necessary, as did Jarvis, who also drove the carriage. They had a cook, a daily maid, and Alice, another maid who lived there. Alice was a mother with no husband, something frowned upon by most employers. Her young lad was only two and lived there as well.

Simon knew they were a rather odd collection—misfits of a sort, including himself. He'd come upon the Fletchers first, through a family friend. They'd needed positions, as aging actors weren't in high demand. Fletcher suggested the role of butler might suit him rather well and thus far it had. Although in hindsight, that was most likely because they never had callers. Mrs. Fletcher insisted she had played the part of housekeeper and mother often enough that she was certain she could bumble her way through it.

Thanks to the Fletchers and their acquaintances, the rest of the staff had soon followed.

"I don't believe the lady will be calling again any time soon," Simon told him. Future meetings would be at the museum. The realization was rather disappointing.

"But what if she does?" Fletcher shook his head. "I need to know my lines if that happens. Please provide some direction as to how to refuse entrance to a lady."

"No other ladies will be calling, so there's no need to worry." Simon started toward his study, eager to sketch out his idea for the exhibit, only to pause. "However, if Miss Wright happens to visit again, be sure to show her in."

Simon ignored the butler's shock and continued to his study, his thoughts firmly on Norah Wright. The story of the lady's parents intrigued him almost as much as the lady herself.

Her heartfelt determination had proven irresistible, and her argument had been valid. He would like to draw more visitors to the museum, even if he didn't plan on attending the unveiling. The lower attendance number Stockton had noted in last month's report of the museum's affairs was concerning.

That reminded him of a clay pot he'd noted missing from the Inca display. He needed to ask Stockton where it was the next time he ventured to the museum.

Thank goodness he could rely on the director to take care of running the place. As much as Simon enjoyed examining artifacts and designing exhibits, he had little interest in the business side. Stockton had been with him for several years and was reliable, even if he lacked the knowledge of history that Simon had.

As he entered his study, he easily pictured Miss Wright standing before his desk. She was a distraction he didn't need. Women had no place in his quiet world. Thinking of her would only lead to embarrassing himself, much like he'd managed to do so often in the past. The sooner he worked out the details of her exhibit, the better. But first, he intended to do a little more research on Oak Island.

The urge to surprise her with a worthy design brought a smile to his lips. It would be a challenge to create something interesting with so few items. But given the public's curiosity about treasure hunting, why not allow them to have a taste of it? He was eager to show Miss Wright what he had in mind.

Then he caught himself and shook his head. Hadn't he decided he shouldn't—couldn't—waste time thinking of her? Somehow, he needed to find the fortitude to remember this was business. Nothing more.

"I'M SO PLEASED you can come," Norah said as she spoke to Lady

Havenby, a former friend of Norah's late mother's, at the Hayfield Ball five days later.

Norah had been doing her best to spread the word about the unveiling party for her father's exhibit in addition to the invitations she'd sent. It was only a week away, and she could hardly wait. "The proceeds will benefit The City of London's Orphanage."

"I wouldn't miss it."

Upon Norah and her sisters' arrival in London, the duke had asked Lady Havenby to introduce them into Society. She'd assisted them with ordering new gowns, along with all the accessories, made certain they received invitations to the proper functions, and advised them on how to navigate the curious stares as well as the gossip.

The latter had been rather entertaining, as Lady Havenby enjoyed gossiping herself. She seemed to know everyone and everything.

"If you think of anyone else who might enjoy the party, please invite them," Norah said. "The museum is wonderful, and the cost of the tickets will go toward a deserving cause. Have you visited?"

"I can't say that I have." Lady Havenby smoothed the skirt of her crimson silk gown with its black braiding and fringe along the edge of the draped overskirt. Her attire was always the height of fashion, which was why it had been so helpful to have her assist them. "Isn't that the one the Marquess of Vanbridge oversees?"

"Yes, that's right." Norah hid a scowl at the mention of his name. She'd sent him two messages to suggest they meet to review the progress on the exhibit, but he had yet to respond. She worried he'd forgotten his agreement, though Mr. Stockton assured her in a message that the marquess was working diligently.

"Have you met him?" the lady asked.

"Of course. We discussed the artifacts and the exhibit."

"Truly?" Lady Havenby's eyes widened with surprise. "He

tends to avoid people and rarely comes to social engagements."

"I spoke with him at the museum. He seems…nice." Nice was too tame of a description considering her attraction to him.

"Poor dear. He didn't seem comfortable at the few functions where I've seen him. He had a difficult childhood, you know."

"Oh?" Norah knew she shouldn't encourage the lady to gossip but dearly wanted to know more about the marquess.

"He never thought to inherit since he was third in line. He was an only child, and his parents died when he was young, so he lived with an elderly aunt and uncle on his mother's side. A few years later, they died as well. Quite tragic."

Norah's heart squeezed at the thought of a younger version of Vanbridge alone in the world. "That is terrible. So much loss."

"Another uncle, the previous marquess, took him in after that. But the marquess and his only son died when their boat sank while crossing the Channel." Her gaze narrowed as she stared across the crowd. "It must've been nearly ten years ago that the current marquess inherited."

"He has no other relatives?" Norah couldn't imagine life without her sisters.

"A female cousin, the daughter of the late marquess. But I don't believe they're on speaking terms. She was aghast when Vanbridge turned the family home into a museum." Lady Havenby studied Norah. "I do believe you've met the Countess of Mendenhall."

"Yes, I have." Norah refrained from saying she didn't care for the lady. How terrible to think she was Vanbridge's closest relative. She often wore a bitter expression, as if someone put too much lemon in her tea. But she had reason to be unhappy if she'd lost her father and brother so unexpectedly.

Grief was difficult to bear. Norah knew from personal experience, having lost both her mother and father, though at different times. At least she'd had her sisters to help endure the pain.

"I shall try to be more understanding the next time I speak with her." Only too late did Norah realize what she'd said. "I didn't mean—"

Lady Havenby chuckled. "If you found her abrasive, you're not alone. It's difficult to act kindly toward someone like her. But she has endured her share of tragedy. She's older than Vanbridge by several years and was already married before he inherited. That didn't keep her from expressing her unhappiness about the museum, along with his letting the entire staff go and hiring his own."

"With her already settled, the decision to turn the house into a museum must've been easier," Norah said, then deliberately changed the subject. "I'm surprised more people don't visit. The exhibits are unique."

"Not everyone shares your appreciation for history, my dear." Lady Havenby patted Norah's arm. "You and your sisters are unique in that."

"I suppose we are." Norah enjoyed learning about the past and thought much could be discovered from it. But she didn't have any desire to immerse herself in it like her father or Vanbridge. Life was meant to be lived and enjoyed in the present.

"There's Ella," Lady Havenby said with a smile. "She looks so happy, does she not?"

Norah turned to look at her sister, who approached with the Earl of Marbury. Ella truly glowed with joy and was even more beautiful because of it. Norah's heart lifted at the sight. "Indeed, she does."

For well over a year after their father died, Ella had been worried over their future. Norah hadn't realized just how worried until the pinched expression had eased from her face.

Norah hadn't understood the burden Ella felt to make the right decision for the three of them until later. Coming to London to knock on the door of their estranged grandfather, the Duke of Rothwood, had been a huge gamble.

"Lady Havenby. How lovely to see you." Ella pressed a kiss to the older woman's proffered cheek.

"And you, my dear. I was just telling Norah how happy you

look." She nodded at the earl. "Marbury."

"Good evening." He bowed in greeting.

"Do I?" Ella glanced at her betrothed with a smile, her eyes full of love. "It must be because I am."

Marbury tightened his arm where her hand was tucked beneath his elbow and shared a private look with her. "We both are," he said.

Norah smiled, pleased they had found their way to each other. It hadn't been an easy path. Especially since Marbury was the son of the man their mother had jilted at the altar when she'd eloped. Life was often complicated.

"Norah, I thought you'd be dancing." Ella glanced at the gentlemen standing nearby as if she intended to find someone with whom Norah could partner.

Norah bit back a sigh. Her sister had been relentless of late, trying to push her toward one gentleman or another. Norah's suggestion that she was in no rush to end the freedom she was just beginning to explore had been ignored. She supposed she needed to try to explain again at some point.

"Perhaps I will later," Norah said. "For now, I've been doing my best to spread the news of the unveiling."

"Does Vanbridge have the exhibit prepared?" Marbury asked with interest.

"I wish I knew for certain. He hasn't answered my messages."

"Shall I reach out to him?" the earl offered.

"Allow me to make another attempt first." Norah wanted to do this on her own. Involving Marbury might encourage him to take over in an attempt to help. Norah didn't want that.

However, what if the guests arrived at the museum and the exhibit wasn't ready because Vanbridge had forgotten?

Come tomorrow, she would visit the museum to see how it was coming along. This event was too important to leave in the hands of the absent-minded marquess.

THE FOLLOWING DAY, Simon stood back and wiped his hands on a rag as he studied the effects of his efforts. The display was unconventional. Perhaps too much so. Yet...

He liked it. Would Miss Wright? That remained to be seen. She'd sent several messages, and he'd finally responded with the hope of keeping her away until he made significant inroads on the work. In truth, he was rather nervous about her reaction. He didn't want to offend her by suggesting her father's efforts lacked results.

Rather, he hoped to place the visitors viewing the exhibit in the footsteps of a treasure hunter. To experience the confined space in which David Wright had worked for so many years. To make people wonder what might be found if they dug a little deeper. To suggest questions more than answers and create a sense of wonder in those who experienced it.

He'd done a fair amount of research on Oak Island to learn more than what Norah Wright had shared. He also wanted to verify her information. After all, he couldn't create an exhibit based on one person's account, regardless of the artifacts in her possession.

The interesting thing about Oak Island was that something had happened there. Something significant. But what exactly remained to be seen. There were so many differing theories, from treasure Marie Antoinette had deposited there to Captain Kidd doing so, and it was impossible to find a common thread to give a definitive answer.

The island was a puzzle, and he liked puzzles. He hoped those experiencing the exhibit did as well. With so few artifacts to display, he thought this was the best way to show them.

The sound of a throat clearing behind him had Simon turning to see Stockton standing near the doorway with a puzzled look on his face as he glanced around the roped-off area. "How much longer will this mess need to remain?"

Simon followed his gaze to the pile of dirt, buckets of water, plaster, and tools that sat on a large canvas cloth. "I'm nearly done."

"Truly?" The man's doubtful tone matched his expression. "What is it supposed to be?"

Unease filled Simon as he looked back at the exhibit. He'd thought it obvious. Was the display so far off the mark? An all-too-familiar feeling of uncertainty washed over him, something he'd experienced often in the years after his parents' deaths. Back then, it had been an almost crippling experience. One that had made it difficult to function and had made him the object of much teasing by his peers.

He wished he could say he'd outgrown it. Each time he thought he had mastered the feeling, it came creeping back. Even now, his skin was prickly, and a tight ball of tension formed in the pit of his stomach.

The unveiling party was less than a week away. Should he think of a better way to show the items? He'd been so certain this had been the right one. He tossed aside the rag and ran a hand through his hair as he considered his options.

"Oh, my." The feminine tone had Simon looking to see Norah Wright standing in the doorway just behind Stockton, her servants nearby, and her gaze riveted on the exhibit. Her eyes were round, and her mouth formed a perfect O as she took it in.

"I'm terribly sorry, Miss Wright," Stockton began with a pointed look at Simon. "As you can see, the exhibit is far from being ready for—"

"It's perfect."

Simon stiffened. Had he heard her whispered words correctly? As he watched, she walked forward, ignoring the pile of dirt and other items he had used to build the exhibit.

Then she cast her sparkling gaze on him, her expression one of wonder and excitement, before she looked again at the display.

"It's just as I remember." She reached out a gloved hand to

touch the dirt wall he'd created using a mixture of mud and plaster to build three sides of a shaft that ran from the floor to the ceiling. Rough-hewn timbers were placed evenly apart as if holding the earth back. A pickaxe and shovel rested nearby.

In the wall about eye-level, Simon had half-buried a replica of the coin she'd given him. A copy of the stone with its strange markings was waist-level.

"You were in the shaft?" he asked.

"When we were younger. But only the ones that weren't overly deep. Father dug several, trying to find the Money Pit. Mother insisted the deeper ones were too dangerous for us children." Miss Wright walked to the nearby display case, which held the other items she'd given him.

Printed signs above the case provided a timeline of events. Some were connected to other discoveries, and some were solely David Wright's. Hopefully, that left the observer to decide for themselves whether the events were related.

The sailor's story that Miss Wright had told him was posted in large print. The display case held the original coin and the publication she'd given him of Captain Kidd's trial. An artist he often worked with had copied some of the pages to make them look like the original documents so they could be viewed separately without anyone having to touch the original.

He'd also had maps drawn of the area as well as of Nova Scotia and had pinned them to the wall.

"It's so much more than I could've hoped for." Miss Wright blinked back tears as she looked at him again. "Unbelievable. I can't wait for my sisters to see it."

Simon cast a glare at Stockton, not appreciating the man's doubt. The director's apology to Miss Wright on Simon's behalf was unacceptable. Simon expected a certain level of support from the director. "You may go."

"My lord, I only thought—" he began.

"We will discuss it later."

"Very well." With a stiff bow, Stockton departed.

Simon turned back to Miss Wright, trying to think of an explanation for the incident, but her focus remained on the exhibit, much to his relief.

"This is amazing. I am so honored by the work you've done." She reached out to touch his arm, as if she'd forgotten her servants stood nearby.

Only then did he realize he was still in his shirtsleeves. Her touch burned, even through her gloves. Thoroughly unsettled, he stepped away to retrieve his suit coat from the back of a chair and shrugged into it. Should he apologize for his state of undress?

"Did you do it all yourself?" she asked.

"Not everything."

She turned to look about the room. "How do you think the unveiling will be done?"

"A curtain will hang in the doorway. If you'd like, you could say a few words in the outer room. Then you and your sisters would pull aside the curtain and lead the way into the exhibit." He pointed to the replica of a shaft. "People can start here and gain a sense of what it might be like to stand in one, then move on to the other items before exiting the display over there." He pointed to the far wall where an archway led to the next room.

"You've added so much more to it than just the items I provided."

The remark had him studying her expression to see if that was good or bad. Unfortunately, he couldn't tell, though she was obviously pleased overall with the exhibit.

"I know there are differing ideas as to whether there's any treasure buried on the island, as well as who hid it there," he said. "Why not present what we know and allow the visitor to decide what they want to believe?"

"My lord, you are brilliant." Norah's beaming smile had him smiling in return. "Ella and Lena are going to love it as much as I do. How can I ever thank you for this?"

"Perhaps by allowing me to remain home the evening of the unveiling."

She laughed, seemingly unaware he was serious. The lovely sound washed over him like rain on a parched desert. "That's not possible. Everyone will want to speak to you about your work and my father's. He would appreciate this very much, as well." She blinked several times.

Concern shot through him at the thought of her crying. He had no experience with tears. He stepped forward to touch her arm, uncertain what to say to comfort her. To his surprise, she placed her gloved hand over his for a moment, the connection again sending a sizzle over his skin, leaving goose pimples in its wake.

Then she released him to move toward the display case and examine the contents more closely. "I have received acceptances from nearly forty people already. I wouldn't be surprised if well over fifty attend."

"Oh?" He knew he should think of the news as a good thing, but the thought of all those people made him uncomfortable. Crowds were normally something he avoided. He never felt as if he belonged.

"Do not worry. I have the refreshments in hand. We'll offer champagne, of course. Can you show me where the refreshment table should be placed? We'll have music as well."

By the time Miss Wright departed, Simon's head spun. Her excitement and the details she'd planned were a force, much like standing on a cliff near the sea in a gale. It was almost enough to make him consider attending the party. Bemused, Simon went up to his office to update Stockton and to give him a piece of his mind. No longer would he allow anyone to cause him to doubt himself.

"My lord." The museum director jumped to his feet the moment Simon reached his office. "I am terribly sorry for the misunderstanding. You see, I—"

"If you ever speak disrespectfully to me again, you will need to find yourself a new position. Do I make myself clear?"

"Of course, my lord. Again, my apologies." Stockton's gaze

fell on something past Simon's shoulder. "If you're done with the supplies, I'll have Emerson clean up the area."

Simon turned to see a thin man near his own age dressed in a modest brown suit standing behind him. "Emerson?"

"He replaced Wallaby," Stockton said. "I'm sure you remember me telling you that several days ago."

"It's a pleasure to meet you." Simon shook the man's hand, ignoring Stockton's question because he didn't remember anything of the sort. Was his memory so poor or were his listening skills the problem? While aware of his absentmindedness at times, moments like this were highly disturbing.

Hadn't he just told himself that he wouldn't allow anyone to make him doubt himself? Yet once again, the unsettling feeling washed over him, making him wonder what else he'd forgotten.

Chapter Four

NORAH PRACTICALLY BOUNCED on her toes with excitement. "I do believe we're ready."

The night of the unveiling had come even more quickly than she'd expected. The preparations had taken up many of her days, but she'd enjoyed every minute. Especially the time she'd spent with Simon, though they'd always been properly chaperoned. He looked so handsome in his black evening attire.

"You have thought of everything." Simon glanced around the area where the refreshments were being laid out, and numerous liveried footmen stood ready to serve them. Musicians were setting up in another room. His gaze shifted to her, causing her to smooth her white, elbow-length gloves along her gown.

She'd worn one of her favorites, a shimmering blue-green satin with an elongated bodice that she hoped lengthened her small stature. It annoyed her to be the shortest of her sisters.

Her pale hair was swept up into an elegant coil with three long ringlets left to brush one shoulder. The overskirt was a shade deeper and draped into a modest bustle in the back. The neckline of the gown was one of the more daring she owned. In all honesty, she'd selected it with the hope of catching Simon's eye.

Had she succeeded? It was impossible to tell for certain, though she liked to think his gaze lingered on her already this evening.

"I hope so." Worry that a detail had slipped past her was concerning, but she released the unease as best she could. If she'd forgotten anything, it was too late to fix it. The guests would start arriving within a half hour. "What truly matters is the exhibit. That is the cake of the evening. Everything else is frosting."

Simon smiled, something which never failed to cause her stomach to dance. First, the smile lit his eyes. Then his mouth slowly curled upward, one corner at a time, as if he wasn't used to the action. His careful thoughtfulness made her wonder how he did other things, such as waltzing.

However, it was unlikely she'd ever know since he didn't attend balls. In fact, she was sad their time together was coming to an end. After this evening, there would be few reasons for them to see one another. She liked him in spite of, or perhaps because of, his idiosyncrasies. He was so different from the men she'd met since coming to London. She'd had true conversations with him on a variety of topics rather than simply listening to him talk about himself or enduring him outrageously flirting.

"Let us check the exhibit one last time," she suggested.

"Of course." He followed her up the stairs to the next level where a blue velvet curtain hung over the arched entrance. "Do you have a speech prepared?"

Norah worried her bottom lip. "I do, though I'm not certain it does the exhibit justice." She drew aside the curtain and sighed with satisfaction. "Then again, I do believe it speaks for itself."

The display more than honored her father's work. She might not have been the best daughter, but she liked to think this helped to make amends. Her sisters would appreciate it as much as she did.

Simon joined her in the exhibit area, then stepped forward to adjust the map as if it wasn't perfectly straight. He seemed as determined as she was to make everything perfect. He'd added several more items, including lanterns—rusty, well-used ones— similar to what her father had used. They added to the setting with their warm glow and also provided more lighting for the artifacts in the locked display case and the posters on the walls.

"I can't thank you enough, Vanbridge." Norah placed a hand on his arm, wanting him to know how appreciative she was of his efforts.

"The pleasure has been mine." He briefly touched her hand, the gesture catching her by surprise. "Why don't you call me Simon? Vanbridge still makes me think of my uncle."

"Simon." She took a deep breath as she looked into his eyes. A spell seemed to fall over them as they stood in the quiet room, the curtain giving them a small measure of privacy. "If you'll call me Norah."

"Norah." He drew out the syllables slowly in his deep voice. It was the most erotic thing she'd ever heard.

Her gaze fell to his lips, wondering what she could do to convince him to kiss her. He was too tall for her to simply lift on her toes. Or was he?

She took a step forward to stand directly before him. Unable to resist, she brushed an imaginary piece of lint from his lapel, then placed both hands on his suit coat. Though numerous layers of fabric separated them, she could still feel the heat of his body.

His gaze swept over her face, as if he were curious what she intended. To her dismay, his hands remained at his sides.

Norah was perplexed. How did she get him to kiss her? She'd had two kisses last summer from two different men. But neither had been to her liking. One had been taken before she'd been prepared. The other had been moist and limp, like kissing a fish. Neither had made her long to repeat the experience and served to confirm that she wasn't ready for marriage.

Somehow, she knew kissing Simon would be completely different. But apparently, she'd have to take matters into her own hands.

Though nervous, she could practically feel the ticking of a clock inside her. The guests would soon arrive. This might be her only chance, especially when she didn't know if she'd see him again after this evening.

"Simon?" she whispered.

"Yes?"

She licked her lips and swallowed hard, summoning the courage to ask for what she wanted. "I should very much like for you to kiss me." Heat flooded her face at the admission, and she watched him closely for his reaction.

"Hmm." His gaze dropped to her lips.

Norah rose onto her toes, hoping to encourage him. Their breath mingled as Simon eased closer. Norah's entire body felt light, weightless, as if she were drifting in space like a hot air balloon with only her hands on Simon to anchor her.

Then the distinct sound of footsteps on the stairs on the other side of the curtain caught her ears. "My lord?"

The air left Norah's lungs in a whoosh, leaving her feeling as if the balloon had been pricked, sending her flying back to the ground and sorely disappointed.

"Unfortunate," Simon whispered, then stepped away to pull back the curtain. "What is it, Stockton?"

"The guests are beginning to arrive."

"Thank you. We'll be down directly." Simon continued to hold the curtain as he turned back to Norah. "Are you ready?"

No, she wanted to say. Not until she had that kiss. But how could she protest when he acted like nothing was amiss?

Instead, she nodded. "Of course." This was for the best. After all, she wasn't looking for a romantic entanglement.

Norah led the way out of the room, still wishing they'd had two more minutes. Simon's whispered word echoed in her mind. *Unfortunate.* Perhaps she wasn't the only one who regretted the interruption.

SIMON WATCHED NORAH from across the room as she reviewed final instructions with Stockton. If only they'd had a few more minutes, he would've kissed that lovely pink mouth of hers. To his surprise, he realized how much he wanted to. Would he have the chance to do so again or was it a moment lost forever?

Yet it was so much more than that. Norah was clever and intelligent. He enjoyed their conversations. When he was with her, he didn't feel inadequate or out of place.

"Vanbridge."

Simon startled at the sound of his name to see the Earl of Marbury approach. "Marbury." He extended his hand, pleased to see him.

"It's a pleasure." The earl shook his hand. "You haven't been at the Royal Geological Society meetings of late." His dark hair was clipped short as usual, and his hazel eyes were warm as he handed a footman his hat and gloves.

"My time has been taken with several projects of late," Simon replied. While that was true, he needed to make more of an effort to attend at least one or two of the meetings and lectures held each month. Mrs. Fletcher would certainly be pleased if he did. She often told him he spent too much time alone at home. "Perhaps I'll be free for one in the coming days."

Marbury was one of the few men whose company Simon enjoyed. He knew him from their university days, though the earl was two years older. He was intelligent and listened to others' opinions rather than just sharing his own. His broad shoulders and thick chest were something Simon envied, though he'd been pleased when Miles, his valet, insisted his suit coat be let out in the shoulders for this evening. Boxing was proving to have numerous benefits.

"I'm somewhat surprised to see you here this evening," Simon said as he watched another carriage arrive through the window. "I read the article you wrote last year on Wright's work. You cast him in a rather unfavorable light."

Marbury grimaced. "I did, indeed. However, there's a story behind that. Perhaps next time we cross paths at the Society offices, I can share it. Did you see the additional article I wrote regarding the reasons why he continued his search?"

"I can't say that I did."

"I'll send over a copy." Marbury turned as two blonde-haired beauties entered the museum. They both smiled at Marbury and walked directly to him.

One of them greeted Marbury as she took his offered arm. "Leo."

Simon could only stare in disbelief at the two ladies, struck by their likeness to Norah. Feeling a presence at his elbow, he glanced over to see she had joined them. "How many of you are there?"

Norah laughed, then looked at her sisters. "May I introduce you to the Marquess of Vanbridge, who owns this wonderful museum. Vanbridge, these are my sisters, Ella and Lena."

"It is a pleasure to meet you," Ella, the lady who held Marbury's arm, said. "I cannot wait to see the exhibit you've created. Norah refused to tell us a thing about it."

"She said she wants it to be a surprise," the younger lady, Lena, added with a smile. "I rather like surprises."

"I hope this is a pleasurable one," Simon said.

"This Miss Wright has agreed to become my countess." Marbury shared a tender look with her.

"Congratulations to you both." Even Simon could see how much the pair cared for one another.

Before they could speak further, more guests arrived. Simon stepped back, relieved Norah and her sisters, along with Marbury, were there to greet them. While he recognized many, that didn't mean he wanted to speak with them.

Within the next fifteen minutes, the entrance hall and reception room filled with people. Simon soon felt the familiar uncomfortable feeling he experienced at social events. He made an effort to speak with a few acquaintances, including Viscount Worley, but did his best to stay out of the way. He much preferred the attention be on the Wright sisters.

The three were a vision separately, but together were even

more stunning. They looked remarkably similar with pale blonde hair and heart-shaped faces. There was no denying they were sisters who held a deep affection for one another.

Norah was the shortest of the sisters and the most beautiful, as far as Simon was concerned. She glowed with happiness as she spoke to friends, clearly in her element. Ella appeared more poised with an elegant yet reserved demeanor. She and Marbury seemed to be connected at some fundamental level as they frequently glanced at each other across the room as if sharing thoughts.

Lena was a restless soul, searching the room yet not seeming to find what she looked for. She gestured with her hands when she spoke, her body often moving as well. Yet she was watchful at times, as if drawing in the energy of those around her.

As interesting as the sisters were, it was Norah who drew Simon's eye time and again. He forced himself to look away, knowing it wouldn't do for anyone to catch him staring.

With a sigh, he checked the grandfather clock in the adjoining room and realized it was almost time. He made his way to Norah, who spoke with an older woman, doing his best to ignore the rising tension caused by so many people in the small space. To his surprise, Norah seemed to immediately sense his presence and looked at him.

"Shall we proceed?" he asked.

"Yes." Her beaming smile caught his breath, her excitement impossible to ignore. She looked back at the woman to whom she'd been speaking. "If you'll excuse me."

"Of course." The lady nodded, her gaze shifting to Simon with far too much interest.

Norah gathered her sisters, then the three went partway up the stairs and turned to face the crowd.

"Good evening, ladies and gentlemen." Norah's voice echoed in the entrance hall, easily gaining everyone's attention. "Thank you all for coming. Tonight, we have a story to share with you."

Her brief speech lasted only a few minutes but touched on all the important points—the charity, her father and her sisters, the museum, and the exhibit.

Simon was dismayed when she mentioned him specifically, expressing her gratitude for his assistance with the evening's events. He dipped his head in acknowledgment as a round of applause sounded, his body tightening with nerves.

Then Norah invited the guests to return to the museum soon to view the other exhibits. Her sisters added their appreciation to everyone for coming, then the three led the way up to the exhibit.

Simon followed but stood to one side so he could see Norah's sisters' reactions. The ladies waited for the guests to join them before the curtain. Norah's eagerness was palpable as she placed a gloved hand on the curtain.

Simon's stomach knotted, and he wished he were at home in his study where he didn't have to worry about anyone's reaction to the exhibit. Then Norah's shining blue eyes met his, and he suddenly realized he wouldn't have missed the moment for anything.

"We invite you to follow in David Wright's footsteps and search Oak Island for treasure." She drew back the curtain and hooked it to one side, her gaze shifting to her sisters.

Simon watched them as well, hoping he'd done their father's work justice. He wasn't sure he would've had the perseverance David Wright had, digging for decades only to find so little. Yet, from the research Simon had done, it was clear the activity on the island hinted at something. Even he was tempted to see what other information he could unearth.

Norah's sisters stilled, staring at the display as if hardly able to believe their eyes. The crowd gave an audible gasp before breaking into applause.

Then the three ladies took each other's hands and moved slowly forward. Ella reached out to touch the gold in the dirt wall with a gloved fingertip before turning to whisper to her sisters.

Simon dearly wanted to know what she said. The younger

one, Lena, wiped her eyes. He couldn't help but smile.

Then the crowd pushed forward as if the Wright sisters' reaction made them more curious. Simon remained to one side of the doorway watching the guests' reactions as they filed through the exhibit, pointing at and discussing the items displayed.

"Well done."

Simon turned to see Marbury at his elbow, his gaze fastened on the three-sided shaft with its glint of gold in the wall along with the stone tablet just visible in between the guests.

The earl entered the exhibit and gestured for Simon to accompany him.

"Brilliant, in fact," Marbury continued as he took in the map and other items Simon had used. He looked at Simon, his expression one of surprise and admiration. "You have explained his work in a way that even someone who isn't interested in what happened on Oak Island will be intrigued. You've given us all a better understanding of what David Wright saw."

The pride Simon felt at Marbury's words had him shifting uncomfortably. He wasn't used to praise and tended not to trust it. He waited for the earl to continue. To add the "but" that so often followed compliments and took them away.

Marbury only clasped his shoulder, a grin on his face, before he moved forward to join his betrothed.

"Well done," Viscount Worley said as he studied the exhibit with interest. "I'm so pleased you were the one to create this."

A wave of satisfaction settled into Simon as he watched Worley join the other guests to slowly file through the exhibit. The bits and pieces of conversation he overheard seemed to echo Marbury's sentiments. Many of the ladies reached out with tentative fingers covered in satin gloves to touch the dirt wall as if unable to resist. Several of the men lifted the pickaxe and held it in their grasp, no doubt imagining themselves digging for treasure alongside Wright.

The reaction was exactly what Simon had hoped for. He couldn't have been more pleased and hoped Norah was, as well.

He lost sight of her as she and her sisters exited out the door on the opposite side of the room. Simon trailed behind the crowd, wanting to make certain everything remained in place. He answered a few questions when asked, finding it easier to speak with people when the topic involved something he enjoyed.

Slowly, the guests returned downstairs to where the refreshments were being served, and he breathed a sigh of relief. A few wandered through the rooms of the museum while others visited with friends.

The sight of Stockton watching the guests with what looked to be displeasure on his face caused Simon to approach him.

"Is all well?" he asked.

Stockton's expression smoothed. "Of course, my lord. The evening has been an amazing success, don't you think?"

"So it seems."

"I only hope none of the exhibits were damaged with this many people walking through." His brow crinkled with worry.

Simon was puzzled by the man's concern. "I do believe the goal of the museum is to have as many visitors as possible."

"Yes, but not like this." Stockton shook his head. "It will take us a week to clean up and make certain no exhibits have been harmed."

"I hardly think so. It's not as if the guests are a bunch of unruly schoolboys."

"I'm sure you're right." His expression suggested otherwise. "The evening has gone very well."

Simon gave a single nod and then walked away before he said anything more. Stockton seemed to have changed in the past month or two. He was no longer the enthusiastic director Simon had hired. What to do about it would have to wait for another time.

As a quartet played in another of the rooms and the guests continued to mingle, Simon searched for Norah, without success. Her sisters were still in the refreshment room, speaking with acquaintances. When several minutes had passed and there was still no sign of Norah, Simon grew concerned.

He moved to the rear of the museum and took the back stairs two at a time and returned to the exhibit to see if she was there.

He drew back the velvet curtain and found her alone, staring at the display. "Norah?"

She turned to look at him, blinking back tears despite her smile. "Simon. I just wanted to look at it again."

"Is all well?"

"Yes." She released a breath—half laugh and half sob—that hinted at the well of emotion she was obviously feeling. "Don't mind me. I am caught up in memories, I suppose." She continued to look at the items as if determined to keep her gaze away from him.

He drew nearer, wanting to offer comfort but uncertain how. "I'm sure you miss him. Do you miss your life there as well?"

If he didn't know better, he would've almost thought she winced at the question.

"Parts of it." At last, she turned to meet his gaze. "I know it's terrible to say, but I miss very little of our life there. I miss my parents, of course. Terribly. So much so that at times, it's difficult to breathe." She waved a gloved hand before her face. Did she hope it might help dispel her tears?

"I understand." That was certainly something to which he could relate. Though memories of his parents had faded, he still missed them so much. Missed what he thought their relationship would be if they still lived. "It's the oddest things that bring them back. The smell of lavender. My father's cologne. The tilt of a stranger's head in the pew in front of me at church."

Norah gasped and reached for both of his hands. "Yes. Yes, that's it exactly. Grief comes when you're caught unawares and pulls you down again."

He nodded, turning his hands to hold hers. "The emptiness left behind is difficult to fill."

"Impossible." She looked down at their joined hands. "And yet…"

"Yet what?" He rubbed his thumb along her inner wrist through the glove, imagining her skin would be as soft as the satin.

She lifted her gaze to his, tears filling her eyes. "I didn't love our life there." She whispered the words as if they were a confession. "I couldn't wait to leave. I was already searching for a reason to go. Some way to forge a life of my own." Her expression suggested she was horrified to have felt that way.

"Norah." He released her hands to draw her into his arms. "I think that is normal. We are born to make our own lives. Our own choices. Don't you think? That doesn't mean you didn't love them."

She nodded against his shoulder, her breath hitching. "I just feel so guilty about it." She glanced over her shoulder as if to make certain they were still alone. "Please don't tell my sisters."

"I won't, but you should share how you feel with them. Chances are they feel the same way." He envied her having someone with whom she could discuss these feelings. He'd never had that.

Norah rested her head on his shoulder again. "Never. I can imagine how Ella would look at me. Lena, as well. I have enough guilt as it is."

He had the feeling there was more that she hadn't told him. But who was he to ask her to tell her secrets? Instead, he rubbed a hand along her back in an effort to comfort her.

The feel of her in his arms stirred the memory of her request for a kiss. That had him drawing a long, slow breath, which proved to be a mistake when the scent of gardenias filled his senses.

He clenched his jaw, trying to remember what she'd just said rather than thinking about how she might taste, with little success.

"Norah?"

She lifted her head to meet his gaze. "Yes?"

"I should very much like to kiss you." How ridiculous that he couldn't think of a way to ask without simply repeating the same phrase she'd used hours ago.

"Yes."

He blinked, wondering what she meant, his thoughts too muddled to be certain.

"Now, Simon." Then she lifted onto her toes even as she pulled his head down to meet hers.

Her mouth was soft yet firm. Sweet yet spicy. Everything he wanted and more. Damn, but he felt greedy. He wanted more. Rather than the sweet, tender kiss he'd intended, he devoured her. His tongue tested the seam of her lips, grateful beyond measure when she opened for him. The kiss deepened—part exploration, part enjoyment.

The sound of a violin caught his ear, and he tried to reconcile why he heard it in the museum. Only then did he remember the party. The guests. Her sisters. All nearby. He jerked back, his gaze sweeping her face, wondering if he should apologize.

"Oh, yes." Norah loosened her hold on his neck. "That was a kiss." Her eyes were dark with the same passion gripping him. She licked her lower lip as if she could still taste him, and it was all he could do not to kiss her again. "I suppose we should rejoin the guests," she whispered.

"I suppose." He forced himself to release her and step back. "You go first. I'll follow shortly." He needed a moment to settle his thoughts and the hardness of his body.

She smiled, causing his chest to tighten, then she was gone, with only the swinging curtain evidence that she'd been there.

Thank goodness it would be some time—if ever—before he saw her again. Odd, but the thought was anything but pleasing.

Chapter Five

NORAH PAUSED OUTSIDE her grandfather's study the following morning, pondering what to say if she ventured inside.

That she was disappointed he'd chosen to not come to the unveiling? Angry? Frustrated?

In truth, it was all of those and more. Her sisters would agree. Though she knew he had difficulty even saying her father's name, let alone viewing a display to honor his work, she had still wanted him to come. It would've meant so much to her and her sisters.

None of them had spoken of it as of yet. That didn't mean they weren't all keenly aware of his absence.

Hoping the right words would come, Norah knocked on the door and heard his muffled reply.

"Good morning," she said as she entered.

"Norah. How are you?" He barely met her gaze, suggesting he felt guilty, but perhaps she was reading things into his reaction.

"Well, thank you." She walked forward, hands clasped before her, still uncertain how to approach the situation. Though they'd grown closer, he was not an easy person with whom to speak. "I've come to provide a report on last evening."

"Last evening?" His brow furrowed, but she didn't believe his supposed confusion for a moment.

"Yes. The unveiling at the museum."

"Oh. Was that last night?"

She shook her head with a resigned smile. "No need to pretend. I can't say I'm not disappointed you weren't there."

"Hmm."

When he said nothing more, she didn't press the matter. Disagreements were not her strong suit. She need only think of the cross words she'd shared with her father to be reminded of the consequences of speaking her feelings. If the duke wasn't interested in seeing the exhibit, why attempt to change his mind?

"At any rate," she continued, "the event was a success. We raised a significant sum for the orphanage."

He smiled, meeting her gaze at last. "That is excellent news."

"It is, yes. I don't have an exact amount yet, but I do think all parties involved will be happy with the outcome." Except for Mr. Stockton. He'd worn a scowl most of the night. Norah had caught him glaring at the guests more than once, though she couldn't imagine the reason. She was beginning to wonder why Simon kept the man employed. "Hopefully, many of the guests will return to the museum and recommend it to friends."

"That should make Vanbridge happy."

The mention of Simon brought him to the forefront of her thoughts. Again. Heat filled her cheeks as her mind flooded with the memory of their kiss. What a kiss it had been—everything she'd dreamed of and more. So different than the other two she'd endured. Thinking of it sent a flutter to her stomach and warmth through her entire body.

"Norah?"

She glanced over to see her grandfather staring at her with a puzzled expression, making her realize her thoughts had gotten away from her. "I'm sorry. What did you say?"

"I asked what you thought of Vanbridge."

"Oh." It was all she could do to keep from pressing a hand to her hot face. "He seems nice enough." Handsome, shy, and incredibly thoughtful. Luckily, she managed to keep all that to herself. "He is clever and creative. Almost an artist of sorts. The exhibit allowed the guests to have a view of Father's work, unlike anything I could have dreamed." She caught herself as she realized she was getting carried away on a topic her grandfather didn't want to hear about.

She shook her head. "I know you don't care about the details. Suffice it to say that he did an excellent job. We're pleased with his efforts."

"Now you've made me curious. And it's not that I don't care."

"I know." Well, she sort of knew. He cared about her and her sisters. Just not her father. At times, it was difficult to understand the distinction. From what Ella had told her, Grandfather had admitted his own behavior had played a role in his only child eloping with David Wright. But that changed little from what Norah saw. The duke still seemed to resent their father.

"I'm sure you're relieved to have it behind you."

Norah bit back a sigh. Unfortunately, she didn't feel much relief. While she'd done all she could to honor her father's memory, her guilt had yet to lift. She feared Simon was right, and she needed to tell her sisters what had happened with her father. But how could she?

"At the very least, I'm pleased you won't have to associate with the marquess anymore. One never knows the true manner of a man who keeps to himself as much as Vanbridge does."

Norah clenched her hands at her sides as she tried to hold back the urge to defend Simon. But she couldn't. "I found him to be a most pleasant gentleman." So pleasant that she couldn't get him out of her thoughts.

"I believe that makes you one of only a handful of people who think so. At any rate, thank you for sharing your impressions of the evening." He smiled, something to which she was still becoming accustomed.

"My pleasure. I will leave you to your work." With a curtsy, she left her grandfather to his thoughts, hoping she'd shared enough to make him want to see the exhibit for himself and reconsider his opinion of Simon. Whether he'd admit to doing so remained to be seen.

She returned to her bedroom, deciding to send a message to Simon despite her grandfather's concern. It was important to see the event through to the end, which meant learning how much money had been raised for the orphanage. As she penned a note requesting a meeting for the following day, she shook her head. This was only an excuse to see him one more time.

Hopefully by then, she'd have her emotions better under control. Never mind how delighted she was at the prospect of looking into those thoughtful green eyes or witnessing that slow smile. Would there be an opportunity to share one last kiss?

SIMON TOLD HIMSELF to ignore Norah's message. To allow her to assume he'd forgotten her request to meet. Yet at two o'clock the following afternoon, he arrived at the museum just as she'd asked. What had happened to his absent-mindedness?

Norah Wright. That was what.

The entire morning, he'd watched the clock he'd had Fletcher put on his desk. Now, as he hurried up the stairs to the front door of the museum, he couldn't deny a simmering excitement at the thought of speaking with her.

It was only because he hadn't expected to do so again now that the unveiling was complete. If only he could stop thinking about their kiss.

However, given the fact that he had no intention of attending balls or other functions, it was unlikely that he'd come upon her ever again. Was it so wrong to take this one last opportunity to be with her?

He nodded at several people entering the building in addition to a few who were leaving. More people were milling about inside than he'd seen in a long while. The clerk who took the entrance fees nodded at him before returning his attention to the queue of people waiting to purchase tickets.

Simon smiled. He needed to thank Norah for the influx of visitors. Perhaps they should hold unveilings more often. He took the stairs only to pause when he reached the floor of her father's exhibit, nodding at Norah's servants, who stood outside of the entry.

The blue velvet curtain had been removed, leaving the exhibit visible. Several people were viewing it, speaking in hushed tones as museum visitors so often did.

His gaze caught on the feminine form standing just inside the wide doorway. Norah wore a green gown today with a small black hat and looked beautiful. She watched the nearly half a dozen guests who studied her father's exhibit rather than the exhibit itself, making Simon wonder at her thoughts. Then her gaze shifted to him, as if she felt the weight of his regard.

Her smile was one of such genuine pleasure that his chest clenched in response. This lady posed a serious threat to his peace of mind. The realization concerned him.

"Simon." She walked to him and curtsied. "I'm so pleased you were able to meet me."

He nodded as he bowed, deciding it best not to share how equally pleased he was to see her. As intrigued as he was by Norah, he wouldn't give her the wrong impression. He wasn't available for a future with her or any other woman. Not when he was meant to be alone. Opening himself up to more loss wasn't an option.

He'd only inherited because of a terrible accident and didn't intend to marry. He would leave the holdings in an improved financial condition than when he'd inherited. The rest was up to his younger cousin, who would take the title upon his death.

"The exhibit still seems to be working its magic," she said in a whisper with a glance over her shoulder at the visitors studying the posters.

"I'm pleased to see that." He drank in her loveliness for a moment before forcing himself to look away and move on to the purpose of the meeting. "What is it that you wanted to review?"

"I was hoping you might have a final accounting of the amount raised for the orphanage at the unveiling."

"I think Stockton has it." Simon gestured toward the stairs. "Shall we see if he's in his office?"

"Perfect." She glanced at him as they climbed to the next level, her servants following. "How is progress on the carving?"

"It's coming along, though a few of the markings remain unclear." He did his best to smother his pleasure that she'd remembered what he'd been working on. Yet the interest in her expression was difficult to ignore. Few people expressed interest in his projects.

They continued the conversation until they reached Stockton's office. As usual, the man was sitting at his desk. Simon frowned. Didn't he ever walk the corridors to see how things were progressing? To see what had caught visitors' attention? To see what needed updating?

Though aware of the paperwork involved in the position, it still seemed as if there were more than enough hours in the day to deal with it as well as keep a closer eye on the activities.

"Stockton." Simon nodded. "Do you have the final numbers from the unveiling?"

The museum director stood and bowed. "Yes, of course." He shuffled through the papers on his desk and pulled forth one to hand to Simon.

Simon skimmed the information, pleased by the numbers. He handed the sheet to Norah, who seemed surprised he'd given it to her. Did she think he wouldn't share them? What sense would that make when it was the reason for her visit?

She nodded as she read the report. "Even better than I'd hoped. When will the funds be presented to the orphanage?"

Simon raised a brow. "When would you like?"

"The sooner the better." She handed the paper back to Stockton with a smile. "I would like it done in the museum's name, of course. None of this would've been possible without its involvement." Her gaze shifted to Simon. "Without your help."

"We'll mention your father's name as well, if that's acceptable," Simon suggested.

The pleasure on her face warmed him. "I appreciate that, as will my sisters." She glanced around as if uncertain of what else to say. "I should be going. I don't want to take up too much of your time."

"Allow me to walk you downstairs." Simon gestured toward the stairs, then looked at Stockton. "I will return shortly."

The man nodded.

An awkward silence descended, the air heavy, as if both of them had unspoken thoughts they kept to themselves.

Norah paused when they reached the floor of her father's exhibit. "Do you mind if I look one more time? I was watching the other visitors earlier rather than looking at the exhibit."

"Of course." He was touched that she wanted to. He suddenly missed the curtain that might've given them a bit of privacy— or at least the semblance of it.

She stepped into the room, and he followed, annoyed to see one of the lanterns missing. The light wasn't as warm without it, nor was it as easy to read the posters. He frowned as he glanced around to see what else had changed since he'd last looked closely at it.

Then his breath caught as he noted the empty spot in the locked display case, shock spreading its cold fingers along his spine. *The coin was missing.* A coin that was irreplaceable as far as he was concerned. His thoughts raced. Where could it be?

"Is the coin being cleaned?" Norah asked as she joined him. She turned to Simon, eyes widening as she took in his alarm. "Simon?"

"I certainly hope so." Yet somehow, he knew it wasn't.

NORAH PACED SIMON'S office as she waited for his return. They'd hurried back up the stairs to ask Stockton about the missing coin only to be met with a puzzled look from the museum director.

"You must be mistaken." He rose from his desk with a shake of his head.

Norah had felt Simon's outrage at the man, especially since it matched her own. At times, the director's attitude bordered on insolence. Simon had calmly asked Norah to wait in his office while he and Stockton returned to the exhibit.

There was no mistake. That much, Norah knew for certain. How could someone have taken it? It had been in a locked display case. There hadn't been any sign of damage to the case. Besides, the coin had only a moderate value as it was copper rather than gold and just one coin.

But it was precious to Norah and her sisters.

Though she had worried each time she left the artifacts in the possession of museums in the past, she had been less worried here than at any other place.

She wished she'd looked closer earlier when she had stopped at the exhibit, but the visitors had caught her attention rather than the exhibit itself.

The sound of voices echoed in the corridor, and she strode to the doorway to see Simon and Stockton returning. It took only one look at Simon's face to know the coin was indeed missing.

A lump formed in her throat. The chances of getting it back were slim to none. She knew that from personal experience. The previous year, their father's journal had been stolen. It had taken weeks of effort to get it back, not to mention the danger they'd encountered.

A coin was different. Far more difficult to trace and far too easy for someone to hide.

"No clues?" she forced herself to ask as she joined them.

"None as of yet." Simon's lips tightened, and she could see the muscle flex in his jaw as he glanced at Stockton.

"I will interview the other staff members and see if anyone

noticed anything unusual," the director advised. Then, with a dip of his head, he hurried down the stairs, the strands of his hair that were supposed to cover his bald head flapping in his wake.

Simon glanced at Norah's servants, then gestured toward his office. "May I have a word?"

"Of course." She followed him inside but left the door ajar.

"Norah." He turned to face her only to briefly close his eyes. "Please accept my apologies for the missing coin." His distraught expression made it clear just how upset he was. "I promise that I will do everything in my power to get to the bottom of this."

There was no denying his sincerity. Nor could she deny how much she wanted to believe him.

He shook his head. "Nothing like this has ever happened before. The coin was in a locked case."

"Nothing else is missing?"

"Only a lantern. There is no damage to the exhibit. Not even to the case. It's still locked."

"Why would someone take that but not the other items?" she asked. "And how could they remove it while the case remains locked?"

"I don't know." He ran a hand through his hair. "Stockton is going to take inventory of the other exhibits, but, at a glance, nothing else seems to be missing." He stilled, his eyes narrowing as he stared into the distance.

"What is it?"

"I noticed something missing earlier in the month but forgot to mention it to Stockton." His scowl spoke of his displeasure. "Curse my absentmindedness."

"Forgive me, but it seems as if it's Stockton's job to notice such things since he's here more often than you."

"I am the one who hired him. The blame is mine."

Norah bit back a reply. She appreciated that Simon was taking responsibility since it was his museum, even if she felt Stockton was at least partially to blame.

What truly mattered was finding the coin as quickly as possible. How would she admit to her sisters another failure with regard to their father when she hadn't told them about the first one?

Chapter Six

NORAH KNOCKED ON Ella's bedroom door later that afternoon, her stomach in knots. She'd hoped to tell both Lena and Ella the terrible news at the same time, but Lena was out riding. Norah couldn't stand to wait until her return.

"Yes?" Ella said.

Norah opened the door, now more sympathetic to when Ella had told her and Lena their father's journal had been stolen a year ago. That had been a dark day, and several more followed. Would that hold true this time as well?

"Do you have a moment, Ella?" she asked upon seeing her sister sitting at her desk.

"Of course." Ella set down her pen. "I've been writing a few overdue letters." Her breath caught as she looked at Norah, and she rose to cross to her. "What is it? What's happened?" She grasped Norah's hands in hers, her obvious concern bringing a well of emotion bubbling up in Norah.

"I fear I have bad news." Norah held tight to her sister's hands, taking comfort in her support and hoping it would continue after she shared what had happened. "Father's coin has been stolen from the museum."

"What? Oh, no! How could this have happened?"

In the past, Norah had felt as if Ella could find a solution to any problem set before her. But much like the argument she'd had with her father, Norah knew her older sister couldn't solve this.

"I met with Simon at the museum to review the results of the unveiling and see how much was raised for the orphanage." She paused as her stomach clenched again. "We stopped by the exhibit on the way out and noticed the coin was missing."

"Simon?" Ella asked with a look of surprise. "Are you on such familiar terms with him?"

Norah realized her mistake too late. "I mean Vanbridge, of course."

"Oh, dear." Ella's brow furrowed. "We will return to the issue of just how close you are to the marquess at a later time. The coin was in a locked case, was it not?"

"Yes. The odd thing is that the case wasn't damaged. Nor was anything else missing except for one of the lanterns."

"That is strange. Does the marquess have any idea who did it?"

"Not as of yet." Norah released Ella's hand to rub her brow where a headache brewed. "Perhaps I shouldn't have suggested the exhibit, let alone the unveiling. Then we'd still have the coin."

"Nonsense. This isn't your fault." Ella's lips tightened. "If anything, it is Vanbridge who should've taken more care."

The urge to defend him caught Norah by surprise. But she couldn't allow Ella to think he was at fault. "He took every possible precaution. He even used replicas of several items and locked up the others."

"I suppose that's true." Yet her sister's expression suggested she wasn't completely convinced. "We will see what Leo has to say."

"He's the one who recommended I speak with Vanbridge," Norah felt compelled to point out.

"True. Still, Leo might have a suggestion as to what action we can take." Ella shook her head. "I can't believe this is happening again. How terrible."

"Will you send him a message? He was so helpful the last

time we faced this situation." Norah's thoughts held on Ella's remark. Should she have questioned Simon? Should he be at the top of the list of suspects? "Do you truly think we should consider that Vanbridge could be involved?"

Ella lifted one shoulder in a shrug. "We don't really know him, do we? I mean, he's a recluse, a bit of an oddity. What if he's behind this?"

"I have difficulty believing that." The idea caused Norah to shiver. Could she be so wrong about him?

"Well, after what happened with Father's journal, don't you think we should suspect everyone until we know beyond a doubt they're innocent?"

Norah sighed. She understood Ella's point. The identity of the person who'd taken the journal had surprised them all.

Though she hated to admit it, Norah tended to trust everyone. Did that make her naïve? Yes. Yet, how could it be wrong to believe the best in others? Then again, she liked to think she'd be the first to act if someone took advantage of her or her sisters.

"I will be anxious to hear what Marbury suggests," Norah said. If he thought they had any reason to think Simon could be behind this, Norah wouldn't hesitate to speak her mind to the marquess. Never mind their stirring kiss.

THE FOLLOWING MORNING, Simon tossed aside the report Stockton had provided on his interviews with the staff and the state of the other exhibits in the museum. The dry statements weren't helpful in the least. Supposedly, nobody knew anything, and nothing else was missing other than the clay pot, the coin, and the lantern. Stockton hadn't noted the clay pot.

What Simon truly wanted to know was who the hell had taken the coin. Of all the exhibits, why did something of Norah's have to be missing?

He blew out a frustrated breath, then paced the length of his study as he considered what his next step should be.

According to Stockton's report, not one member on the museum staff of over a dozen could provide any clues. That couldn't possibly be true. Someone had to know something. It was only a matter of convincing that person to come forward. The lack of damage to the display case meant either a key had been used or someone had picked the lock. Either option suggested someone associated with the museum had to be involved.

But who? And how could Simon uncover the culprit?

Simon had the keys, and another set was kept at the museum. Stockton was the first possibility that crossed his mind, as he had access to the keys, but he wasn't the only one who did. Though tempted to fire the man on the spot, proof was required first. That Simon wasn't satisfied with the director's work of late was a separate issue.

However, the man had provided an account of his whereabouts without Simon even asking. There seemed to have been little opportunity for him to have taken the coin unless he'd done so while the museum was open. If he'd attempted that, surely one of the other employees would've seen him and come forward.

Yet, if it wasn't Stockton, who else could it be? Until he knew for certain, Simon intended to keep an eye on the director. The best way to do that was to keep him employed at the museum.

Finding the damn coin was all that mattered. How he hated to let down Norah. Especially after exceeding her expectations with the exhibit. The look of delight on her face had been replaced by dismay. Soon that would be replaced with suspicion. The thought brought a weight on his shoulders he couldn't shrug away.

"My lord?"

Simon looked to see Fletcher standing in the doorway. "Yes?"

"The Earl of Marbury is calling. Are you receiving?"

Simon nearly groaned. No doubt the lord was appalled that Simon had lost the coin. He supposed he should count himself lucky the Duke of Rothwood wasn't calling. If only he hadn't gotten involved. Yet, how could he regret doing the exhibit when it had given him the chance to become acquainted with Norah?

"Please show him in." Simon nodded, hoping to convey that Fletcher had handled the announcement perfectly.

The butler offered a single nod and then backed out to show in Marbury. His uncertainty with handling callers would've been amusing if Simon wasn't so upset.

Marbury strode in, his expression causing Simon to stiffen. It was obvious the earl wasn't pleased. That made two of them.

Rather than wait for the earl's disdain, Simon went on the offensive. "Marbury. Are you here to aid or berate?"

"It depends." Marbury leveled him a look, but he couldn't possibly make Simon feel worse than he already did. "Do you have any word on the coin?"

"Not as of yet."

"Then both. What the hell happened?"

"I don't know." Simon lifted a hand only to drop it. To have one of the few men he considered a friend glare at him as if he'd kicked a puppy made him feel physically ill. "It was in a locked case. There is no sign of damage. All the employees have been questioned but without results. At this point, we know nothing."

"Unbelievable." Marbury rubbed a hand over his face, then glanced about the room as if perplexed. "You have no chairs for visitors?"

"I rarely have any." Never, in fact. At least, not until the past month. It seemed he was being pried from his reclusive lair regardless of his unwillingness to socialize.

The earl frowned. "You need two just in case."

"Hmm." Simon was less than convinced. He didn't want to make a habit of visitors, despite the recent influx. To his surprise, Marbury carried the chair from in front of the fireplace and set it before Simon's desk then sat down.

"Tell me what you know."

"As I said, it's very little." Simon sank into his own chair as he shared the few details he had. "If you have any suggestions, I'd be pleased to hear them."

"I can't believe this is happening again." Marbury shook his head, his expression taut.

"Again?"

"David Wright's journal was stolen soon after Ella and her sisters arrived in London. I believe I mentioned there was a story behind the article I wrote about Wright's work on Oak Island."

"Yes, you did."

"The reason I wrote the first article sharing the reasons why I thought Wright was digging in the wrong place was because someone stole his journal. I hoped that by discrediting his work, the person who had taken the journal wouldn't be able to sell it. We offered a reward instead."

"Who took it? Could they be behind this?" Hope speared through him only to falter at Marbury's dour expression.

"No. The man is in prison for theft as well as murder. Not only did he steal the journal, but he also killed someone who wasn't cooperating in his scheme."

"Murder." Simon drew a breath, his thoughts racing. The seriousness of the situation struck even harder.

"We'll hope this situation doesn't come to that. I'm sorry to think the Wright sisters have to deal with yet another problem regarding their father's treasured items."

"As do I." The weight of the problem settled even heavier on Simon's shoulders. "Especially under my watch."

"There are no suspects?"

"Not as of yet."

"Have you contacted the police?"

"Yes, but they were of little assistance." Simon had held the faint hope of handing the matter over to them up until he'd spoken with the constable, who clearly had no experience with stolen artifacts. The man's lack of interest in the case had been disappointing.

"How unfortunate. Still, their involvement can't hurt.

There's always the chance that whoever took it is taking other things as well."

"Two other items are missing, based on the inventory we took. Only one could be considered expensive but then only to a collector. The other item is the lantern from the exhibit. It seems odd that it was taken rather than something of value."

Marbury scowled. "According to my research, the coin, while interesting, isn't particularly valuable."

"That is my understanding as well. Which makes me wonder if the theft is personal, considering the theft of the journal last year." Personal to whom was the question.

"It is difficult to believe they are related." Marbury's gaze focused on the view out the window for a moment before returning to Simon. "Perhaps it's somehow personal to you."

Simon shifted in his chair, unnerved that Marbury had the same thought. Somehow, that made the possibility more likely.

"Is there anyone who has expressed anger over your work? Or something the museum has done?"

"Not that I recall." Simon didn't have contact with many people, and it wasn't as if his work was especially controversial.

"I would encourage you to consider it closely. Think back over the past few months. Perhaps write down the various projects you've worked on, as well as the people you have encountered to see if any conclusions can be drawn."

"A bit like a scientific experiment, eh?" Simon almost smiled at the thought. Somehow, it made the task feel more possible.

"Exactly. I only hope this one results in a successful outcome. When I was trying to find the stolen journal and had no clues, I resorted to speaking with those I knew who might be interested in it to see if they'd heard anything."

Simon nodded. "That might have merit in this case as well." He didn't bother to mention how uncomfortable the idea of seeking out various acquaintances made him. But if that was what it took to find the coin, he'd do it. Anything to get it back.

"Can you think of anyone who would like to see the museum

discredited? Or even closed?"

Simon considered the question. "Perhaps." His cousin, Anna, the Countess of Mendenhall, for one. She had been appalled when she'd learned of his plan to turn her family home into a museum and made no secret of it. "Though it seems odd that someone would act now after all these years."

"One never knows what is going through another's mind."

"True." He certainly couldn't begin to guess. Human nature, including his own, never failed to surprise him. Take his recent fascination with Norah Wright, for example. He never would have guessed he'd experience an almost chemical reaction to her.

His attraction to the lady only made him more determined to find the stolen coin and reveal whoever had taken it. Marbury was right. This was beginning to feel personal.

"Do you think we should request the exhibit be taken down?" Lena asked as she, Norah, Ella, and their grandfather reviewed the situation in the drawing room the following morning.

Norah's heart pinched at the suggestion, as it made her feel guiltier for having insisted on the display to begin with. While she truly did want people to know more about her father's work, she had also wanted to assuage her guilt. Would she have pressed so hard for the exhibit if not for that?

She wasn't viewing the situation with a clear mind, so held back from offering an opinion on the question. Instead, she waited for Ella's response.

"I don't think so," Ella said, though her eyes were narrowed as if she seriously considered the idea. "If whoever took the coin wanted the other artifacts, they would've already taken them."

"True." Lena shook her head. "I simply can't believe this is happening again." She stood and walked over to the window, clearly unable to contain her upset.

Norah shifted her attention to their grandfather. She'd reluctantly shared the news with him the previous day, half-expecting he would blame her. That one of them would, no matter if her worry was illogical. How could they not when she blamed herself?

"What do you think, Grandfather?" Ella asked, much to Norah's relief as it saved her from asking.

"The situation is indeed unfortunate." He tapped a finger on his lip, a gesture he and Ella shared. "I see no purpose in closing the exhibit. As you said, apparently the only item the thief wanted, he took." He looked at Norah. "No further word from Vanbridge?"

"Nothing as of yet." Norah understood even better why Ella had felt compelled to take action when their father's journal had been taken. It was impossible to think of anything else. Not when she felt so guilty. "What can we do to help find it?"

Ella's smile of understanding eased the tightness in Norah's chest. "Would it help if we once again spread word of the theft?" Ella asked.

Lena frowned. "That depends. Would it involve visiting more antique shops again? I confess doing so lost its appeal soon after we walked through the second one." She glanced at Norah with a worried expression. "Not that I don't want to help. You know I'll do anything necessary."

The three sisters had walked through far too many antiquity shops after the loss of the journal to see if any had been approached to buy it.

"Perhaps we should first share the news with those who attended the unveiling," Norah suggested.

Their grandfather stood. "Excellent idea. Someone might have seen something the night of the unveiling. Meanwhile, I will have a word with Vanbridge to see what he's doing and how we can aid him."

Though Norah knew the two men were acquainted and were both members of the Royal Geological Society, her stomach tightened at the thought of them speaking. It wasn't as if Simon would tell her grandfather about their kiss. Far from it.

Yet as the duke promised to advise them of anything he learned and took his leave, she couldn't set aside her nervousness.

Determined to push it from her mind, she considered what more she could do. There had to be something else. Action felt better than worrying. "Why don't we review the evening of the unveiling? Did you notice anyone taking particular interest in the coin or the exhibit?"

As she and her sisters shared their impressions of the evening, the matter felt even more hopeless. Norah could hardly stand to think she had once again failed so miserably.

Chapter Seven

SIMON RELUCTANTLY ENTERED the Royal Geological Society offices on Saville Row later that morning, at the behest of the Duke of Rothwood. While he'd expected the duke to request a meeting, Simon was still apprehensive. The fact that Rothwood's granddaughters' coin had been stolen surely didn't sit well with His Grace. Angering a powerful lord, let alone Norah's grandfather, was nothing Simon welcomed.

The duke was already seated in the small room where they'd arranged to meet. "Good morning, Your Grace," Simon said with a stiff bow. "I hope I didn't keep you waiting."

"Not at all." He gestured toward a chair at the table, his expression unreadable. "Marbury will be joining us as well."

"I'm pleased to hear that," Simon said as he took a seat, a tight band around his chest keeping him from drawing a true breath. Yet he was determined to take responsibility as well as any action he could think of to repair the loss. That meant starting with an apology. "Allow me to offer my apologies for the theft of the coin. Please know I don't take the matter lightly."

"I would hope not." The duke's bushy grey brows lowered over his eyes, lending him a fierce appearance. "In addition to upsetting my granddaughters, this could damage your museum's reputation."

"I realize that." Simon shifted in his chair, uncertain if the duke pointed that out in order to prod Simon into doing more or if it was a threat. "Marbury suggested the reason for the theft could be to force me to close the museum." Simon had pondered the possibility at length without a result.

Before he could say anything more, Marbury entered the room and bowed. "Good morning."

"Vanbridge was just telling me of your idea that the theft could be part of a plan to put an end to the museum." Rothwood glanced between the two men, clearly expecting answers.

Simon wished he had one to offer.

"Yes," Marbury said as he took a seat. "It seems that if whoever took the coin hoped for money, they would've taken additional artifacts. That means there must be another reason." His gaze settled on Simon. "Have you given the matter further thought?"

"I have, though there's no one I'd seriously consider."

"Do I hear hesitation in your tone?" Rothwood asked.

"The possibility of this person being involved seems highly unlikely." Simon would be appalled if word of his suspicion spread. He didn't want Anna to have a reason to detest him more than she already did.

"Let us all agree to keep everything in confidence that is said," Rothwood advised. "We should speak freely to share any and all ideas."

"My cousin, the Countess of Medenhall, was unhappy with my plan to use her family home for a museum. However, I can't believe she could be behind the theft. Why would she have waited this long to cause problems when the museum opened five years ago?"

"That does seem unlikely," Rothwood agreed. "Is there anyone else you can think of?"

"Perhaps there's someone who had other plans for the museum's location," Marbury suggested. "Or someone who hoped to get an artifact that you acquired instead."

"Not that I know of. Nor has anyone expressed unhappiness

with my work."

"That you know of." Marbury raised a brow.

Simon nodded. "The chances of me hearing about a problem are lessened by the fact that I rarely attend social functions."

"Or at all," Marbury suggested with a teasing glint in his eye.

"I find my time is better spent elsewhere." Simon refused to feel embarrassed about his reclusive tendencies. He'd put aside any hurt long ago at people's opinions of him. Such worries had ended with his school days. At least, that was what he preferred to believe.

"I didn't notice anyone especially interested in the coin the night of the unveiling," Simon continued. "But I confess my attention wasn't fully on the exhibit." He'd watched the reaction of Norah and her sisters along with a few other guests, but he'd also been involved in making certain all went smoothly. He did his best to smother the thought of how distracted he'd been by Norah. His attention had been thoroughly caught watching her most of the night.

"Several fellow members of the Society were there. It might be worth asking if they noted anything unusual." Marbury listed those he remembered seeing, and Simon was surprised how many had been in attendance. Then again, he hadn't paid close attention. "Would you like assistance in speaking with them?" Marbury asked.

"I would appreciate that," Simon agreed with no small measure of relief. The idea of speaking to so many was overwhelming, but he would do nearly anything to find Norah's coin. "Some of them I have yet to meet."

"Have you considered involving your granddaughters in this?" Marbury asked the duke.

"They already intend to speak with those who attended the unveiling to see if they noted anything unusual." Rothwood frowned. "However, I will not have them placed in any danger."

Simon watched with interest as Marbury cleared his throat, suddenly looking uncomfortable.

"Let us hope that what happened last time doesn't occur again." The earl studied the table as if it required his undivided attention.

Curious as to what Marbury was talking about, Simon intended to ask at the first opportunity.

"Vanbridge, are you certain you're prepared for the questions you'll face because of this?" the duke continued.

"The only thing that matters is the return of the coin." If visitors at the museum slowed because of this, so be it. The concern was secondary. He detested knowing the theft was causing Norah and her sisters distress. "In my opinion, the more people who know, the better, much like the situation with the stolen journal."

"That's true," Marbury agreed. Then he looked between Simon and the duke. "Shall we see who happens to be here this morning? We could begin our questions now."

"No time like the present," Simon agreed, doing his best to ignore how uncomfortable he felt. The sooner the thief was uncovered and the coin returned, the better. Then he could return to his home and his work, where he belonged.

"Miss Norah?"

"Yes?" Norah looked up to see Davies in the drawing room doorway, where she worked on her embroidery. It seemed a silly thing to do when it felt as if she should be out searching for the coin. But where?

"The Marquess of Vanbridge is calling."

Surprise flooded her. "Please show him in." Her entire being tingled at the thought of Simon here. Did it mean he had news? She set aside her embroidery and rose. Though she doubted he'd discovered anything this quickly, she couldn't help the hope that bloomed within her.

Ella and Lena were out shopping, but Norah hadn't felt like joining them. It was difficult to enjoy anything at the moment. The coin consumed her thoughts, and her upset was made worse because there was so little she could do about it.

While not truly appropriate for her to receive a male caller with no one to chaperone, she knew Davies would take care. Besides, if Simon had news of the coin, she wanted to hear it. Surely her sisters would agree.

Simon strode into the room, and she drank in his presence. His tousled dark hair suggested he'd recently run his hand through it, and his green eyes were troubled.

Still, her heart lifted at the sight of him, though she couldn't say why. Not when it was obvious from his expression the coin had not been found.

"Good afternoon." Norah curtsied, unsurprised when Dorothy, her maid, came to stand in the doorway. Davies must've sent for her.

"Miss Wright." Simon bowed. "Thank you for seeing me."

"Of course. Has any new information come to light?"

"Unfortunately, no. I understand from your grandfather that you and your sisters are planning to speak with some of the other guests who were in attendance that evening."

"Yes, though we have yet to attend any functions to do so." She gestured toward the couch and they both sat. "I am happy to mention the theft to others and ask if they noticed anything out of the ordinary."

Concern darkened his eyes, and his lips were pressed tight. He looked tired, making her wonder if he'd been sleeping as poorly as she had.

"Thank you. I appreciate that. Marbury and I have started the same process with some of the members of the Society whom we've encountered as well."

"None of the museum staff were helpful?" she asked.

"Nothing they're willing to say."

"Not even Mr. Stockton?"

"No." He frowned. "To be honest, he was a primary suspect as far as I was concerned, though I can't imagine what his motivation would be if he took the coin. However, he has already told me where he was during the time we think it was stolen."

"I'm relieved I'm not the only one who wondered about him," Norah admitted with a smile.

"I have only been concerned of late. He used to be much more reliable and effective." He shook his head, suggesting he was puzzled by the change. "At any rate, I would appreciate you advising me if you learn anything."

"Of course. Will you be attending any functions?"

He stilled as if appalled by the idea, his gaze holding on her in disbelief.

"It's only that it could be awkward if you don't," Norah said gently. "People will surely want to know how you're dealing with the problem. I don't want them to avoid the museum because of this."

"The museum will survive."

"But will your reputation as an expert?"

"It's kind of you to worry over that, given the circumstances." His jaw clenched, a muscle bulging along its length. "I have endured worse."

"I don't want you to endure any of it." She reached out to touch his arm, wishing she could comfort him. He looked so alone in this moment. So distant. He seemed to be holding himself apart with the hope doing so would offer protection. "If you joined us, we could show our support and faith in you."

He raised a brow. "It's hard to believe you don't have some doubt as to my abilities given recent events."

"Not at all. My sisters and I have discussed it and have nothing but respect and admiration for you." Perhaps she was overstating her sisters' opinions, but that was how she felt.

He blinked in surprise as his gaze held on her. "But you don't know me."

"I like to think I do." Her cheeks heated, much to her dismay, as she thought of their kiss. "I very much admire your museum. Since you're the one behind it, there's much to admire about you as well." She forced a polite smile even as she wondered what on earth she was saying. It was just that she didn't want him to think she had designs on him. Talking about the museum was easier. Less unsettling. "I also think we came to know each other a little over the past two weeks."

Why couldn't she stop talking? The more she explained, the hotter her face became. More tingles ran over her skin. If only he weren't so attractive. All that quiet reserve was maddening. Why couldn't he be arrogant and annoying like so many of the gentlemen she'd met since her arrival in London?

He watched her for a moment as if he were processing what she'd said. Then his slow smile arrived, starting with a light in his eyes, then moving to curve his lips. Did he have any idea how alluring that was?

"I like to think so." He placed his hand over the top of hers, which still rested on his arm. The warmth of his skin against hers caught her breath, even as it seeped slowly into her, like wine soaking into a tablecloth. Then his gaze fell to her lips. Perhaps he was thinking about their kiss, too.

Norah risked a glance at Dorothy, who still stood in the doorway, but realized the maid's view of their touch was blocked by Simon's back. Knowing their contact was illicit somehow made it even more appealing, much like their kiss behind the curtain at the museum. Surely, it was the fact that this interaction was forbidden that made it so pleasing.

Something in the pit of her stomach suggested that wasn't quite true. There was a connection between her and Simon she couldn't easily dismiss, no matter how much she wanted to.

She didn't want to be attracted to him or any man. Not when she had so many things she wanted to experience before she strapped herself down with marriage. The thought had her jerking her hand from his arm. If only she could break the tether that bound them as easily.

Dorothy frowned, suggesting Norah's behavior concerned her.

Norah managed a smile, hoping to put the maid at ease, well aware she had overreacted. Chances were Simon didn't feel any of the complex emotions running through her.

He watched her, the warmth in his eyes cooling.

"Now then, the Underwood Ball is tomorrow evening," Norah began in an effort to bring their attention back to the topic. "Many of the guests from the unveiling will more than likely be there. I'm certain we can arrange for you to be sent an invitation. Can you attend?"

⟫⟫⟫⟫⟫⟪⟪⟪⟪

Simon tugged at his silk tie as he stared into the mirror, feeling as if it were strangling him.

"My lord, we don't have another to spare," Miles said in a dry tone. "You've already ruined two."

"It doesn't seem as if it should be cutting off my air supply," Simon retorted even as he forced himself to drop his hands. "Are you sure this is right?"

"Without a doubt." Miles brushed the shoulder of the new black wool suit coat. "It fits you perfectly."

Simon moved his arms back and forth. "Then why does it feel so tight?"

"You're not going to be boxing in it. Just dancing."

"I'm not dancing this evening." The very idea had Simon's breath hitching as panic threatened.

"It's a ball, my lord. While I have never attended one, I do believe dancing is expected." Miles met his gaze in the mirror. "Surely you were taught how."

"That was a long time ago."

"There are some things we never forget how to do. I am certain the steps will come to you when you hear the music."

Simon's stomach pitched once again. Still, he studied his reflection in the mirror, wanting to be certain he would fit in with the other gentlemen in attendance. Would his appearance please Norah? "I should've had my hair clipped."

"I believe I mentioned that several days ago."

"I should listen to you more often, Miles."

"May I remind you of that when needed?" The valet's smirk had Simon smiling in return.

"No, you may not." Simon turned away from the mirror, realizing he would never be satisfied with his appearance. In his mind, he remained the small boy with a too-thin frame and grief-stricken eyes. He shrugged his shoulders in an attempt to dispel the memory. He wasn't that child anymore.

"You look as you should, my lord," Miles said as he eyed him critically one last time. "Very much the marquess."

The valet seemed to have become aware of several of Simon's insecurities, including the fact that he didn't feel as if he should've inherited.

"Thank you." Simon appreciated the compliment and the man's support. He frowned as he pondered his dancing abilities, only to shove aside the concern. Regardless of what Miles said, the point of attending the ball was to discuss the stolen coin with others. He needn't worry about dancing. Never mind how appealing the idea of holding Norah in his arms was.

With a deep breath to steady his nerves, he strode toward the door, hoping the evening passed quickly and that someone could shed light on the missing coin.

Chapter Eight

NORAH TAPPED HER toe in time to the music at the Underwood Ball where she waited near the ballroom entrance with the hope of seeing Simon's arrival. Or should she say if? She was beginning to wonder if he'd come. Given his reluctant agreement to her suggestion of attending, she wouldn't be surprised if he didn't.

But she would be disappointed.

"Why are you hovering near the entrance?" Lena asked as she joined her. "I thought you were looking forward to dancing this evening."

"I was. Or rather, I am." Yet the idea of dancing with anyone other than Simon was less than appealing. Silly when she didn't even know if he would dance with her. Norah attempted to shove her unsettled feelings aside as she looked at her sister. "You look particularly lovely this evening."

Lena's gown was a deep pink silk with a tight-fitting bodice that reached the top of her thighs, making her look slender and even taller. The long overskirt with white lace trim was drawn into a bustle in the back and draped in layers that showed the white ruffled underskirt. Several of her blonde strands were braided and twisted with long curls left to trail onto her back.

"Why, thank you. I do believe this is my new favorite."

Norah glanced down at her green gown with its ecru lace,

wondering if she should've worn something fancier. However, it was too late now to worry about such things.

"I expected Vanbridge to arrive by now." Norah heaved a disappointed sigh. The ball had lost its appeal.

"Wasn't the purpose of this evening to spread news of the stolen coin? If so, we don't need him to do that." Lena glanced around. "You standing here by yourself certainly doesn't help share the news."

"I wanted to wait to do so until the marquess arrived," Norah said in her own defense. "As you know, he rarely attends balls. I intended to lend my support."

Lena watched her more closely. "Is it my imagination or are you becoming rather smitten with the marquess?"

"Good heavens, no." Norah shook her head, doing her best to hide her feelings from her intuitive sister. Lena was far too adept at sensing such things. "Nothing of the sort. My focus is on finding the coin. Not on Vanbridge." Thank goodness there was no sign of Simon or she might've been caught in the lie.

"Hmm." Lena appeared unconvinced but didn't press the matter. She reached out to squeeze Norah's arm. "We were able to locate the journal, and we will do the same with the coin."

Norah studied her expression, deciding Lena was thinking positively rather than sharing a feeling she had. Still, Norah appreciated her confidence. "I hope so." She glanced once more toward the entrance, then turned away, resigned to proceeding without him. "I suppose if he's not coming, we should begin with our plan."

"We may have spoken too soon." Lena nudged Norah, her gaze fastened on something just past Norah's shoulder. "Doesn't he look handsome this evening?"

Norah turned to see for herself, even as the now familiar tingling sensation swept along her skin. Her breath caught at the sight of Simon standing in the doorway, surveying the ballroom with a decidedly undecided expression. Would he stay?

His black evening attire fit him well, revealing his lean

strength. His green eyes were enhanced by the dark attire, and his brown, wavy hair brushed to one side.

Norah's heart skipped a beat at his handsome appearance, only to stop completely when his gaze met hers. The relief in the depths of his eyes melted her heart and made her pleased she'd waited for him.

He ignored others who stared in surprise at his appearance and walked directly toward her. Norah was grateful for Lena's presence at her side or the gossip would begin with his single-mindedness so apparent.

"Good evening, my lord," Norah said as she curtsied.

He bowed, his body stiff. "And to you." Only then did he seem to realize Lena stood beside her. "Miss Wright."

Lena curtsied, an amused smile playing about her lips. "Good evening, Vanbridge."

Simon bowed, then glanced around, obviously uncomfortable. "My apologies for my tardiness. Have you already started speaking with some of the guests?"

"Yes, a few," Norah said, holding back the urge to take his arm to lend him further support. He was a grown man and didn't require her assistance. "I thought it best to wait until you arrived."

He took a deep breath, seeming to brace himself. "Who do you suggest we speak with first?"

"Why don't we make our way around the perimeter and see who we come across first?" Lena suggested.

"Very well," Simon agreed despite a frown. "Please lead the way."

"Of course." Lena glanced at Norah and then started forward. "I see Lady Stewart. Shall we begin with her?"

"Excellent idea." Norah did her best to push aside the delight Simon's presence brought and focus on the task at hand.

The trio slowly made their way around the ballroom, conversing with those they'd seen at the unveiling, along with a few others they considered friends. Simon was quiet for the most part.

Those who recognized him were obviously surprised by his presence.

Norah felt the questioning looks from some of those they spoke with. No doubt they thought it odd that Norah and Lena weren't upset with Simon over the theft of the coin since it had been taken while in his care. Those looks made her pleased Simon was there.

She mentioned the coin had been in a locked case numerous times with the hope to make it clear that Simon had not been careless. He received more than a few questions about whether anything else had been taken.

Simon responded politely, though he didn't expand on the topic. Yet the more people they spoke with, the more apparent was his upset.

"I say, Vanbridge, perhaps you need better locks if the coin was so easily taken," Lord Burton said. He was an older gentleman and a member of the Royal Geological Society.

"We are certainly looking into that." Simon's nostrils flared in response, and soon a muscle twitched along his jaw.

Within the hour, Norah was having difficulty holding back her anger as well. "No one is helpful in the least. Why do they think we want their advice?"

Simon smiled, the first in some time. "I find it frustrating, too."

Lena sighed. "I am ready to think of something else, if only for a few minutes." She glanced over the crowd, her gaze catching on someone in the distance. "I see a friend near the refreshment table. If the two of you will excuse me." Then she paused to look between Simon and Norah. "Why don't the two of you relax and enjoy yourselves for a few minutes? Perhaps a dance is in order."

She turned and walked away, leaving Norah with her mouth dry at the thought of dancing with Simon.

Would he ask her?

➤➤➤✦◄◄◄

Simon scowled, wishing Norah's sister hadn't suggested a dance. He had to believe it wouldn't go well given his lack of practice. What could he do but ask Norah?

He turned to her, surprised to see a lovely blush tinting her cheeks. "May I have the honor of this dance?"

"I should like that very much."

Perhaps this wouldn't be so terrible, he thought, as he offered his elbow and they started toward the dance floor.

"I must warn you that it's been some time since I danced," he murmured. "I can't promise not to step on your toes."

She smiled with genuine warmth, and the nerves beginning to stir inside him calmed slightly. "Duly noted, though I can't imagine needing to worry about it."

"Trust me. You should." He faced her as they took their positions for a waltz.

Norah met his gaze, her smile still in place. "I do trust you."

His breath caught as his chest expanded in an alarming manner. Those simple words meant so much. Too much, perhaps. It was just that in his solitary existence, he rarely heard compliments of any sort.

Then the music began, and there was no time to ponder his reaction. Not when his entire focus was needed to take the proper steps. He counted silently and watched his feet, certain they wouldn't move where they were supposed to.

"Simon."

He looked up, fearing she would tell him he'd already taken a misstep.

"You have nothing to worry about." Her grey-blue eyes glittered with confidence. Confidence in him. "Just listen to the music."

Only then did he realize he hadn't been. Once he did, he was surprised by how much it helped. But looking at Norah was what truly aided him. In the deep recesses of his memory, the movements were imprinted. Shifting his attention to the beautiful woman in his arms, along with the music drifting through the air, caused his worries to ease as his feet kept moving.

How had he never realized how enjoyable dancing could be? At least, it was with Norah. The waltz gave him an excuse to not only hold her but to look at her as well.

She was even more graceful than he'd realized. Her posture was impeccable, her steps fluid. She followed his lead, fitting perfectly in his arms. As he was contemplating whether he should attend another ball soon just so he could dance with her again, he was bumped from behind.

"Vanbridge, is that you?"

Simon turned to see Viscount Ludham, a man he'd never cared for, staring at him with a frown. "Ludham." He bit back the urge to apologize. He didn't think it had been his fault, or had it been? He didn't remember taking a misstep.

"What has you emerging from your dusty old museum to attend a ball?" Before Simon could answer, Ludham's gaze took in Norah. "Pursuing one of the Wright sisters?" Ludham chuckled. "Surely you don't think they'd be interested in the likes of you."

Norah stiffened beside him. In an instant, Simon was transported back to his school days, when younger versions of people like Ludham had teased him as if somehow sensing his vulnerability. He'd hated it then and hated it now.

Yet his mind was blank. No quick retort that would set the viscount in his place came to mind, much like in his youth.

Ludham's partner, a dark-haired lady with an unfortunate nose, looked back and forth between them as if uncertain what to make of the situation. She wasn't the only one. Other people slowed their dancing, partly because the four of them stood in their way and partly from curiosity, based on their watchful gazes.

Simon felt a familiar, prickly heat on the back of his neck. The urge to take Norah by the hand and lead her away from this spectacle nearly overwhelmed him. Instead of taking any action, he just stood there, glaring at Ludham.

Then he felt a hand on his arm—Norah, offering her support. To his relief, she didn't say a word, as if realizing that would only make the situation worse.

"The lady is capable of making her own decisions," Simon managed. "And the museum is not dusty." With that, he turned and led Norah off the dance floor.

"Ludham is ridiculous," Norah whispered as they walked away.

Simon couldn't respond. Not when he realized what he'd said. *And the museum is not dusty.* Truly? Of all the ways he could've responded, that was what his brain had settled upon? He nearly groaned at the idiocy of the remark. Simon was surprised he couldn't hear Ludham laughing from across the room.

"Ignore him," she added as they reached the refreshment room. As if reading Simon's mind, she collected two flutes of champagne from a liveried footman and handed one to Simon. "I have never liked him, and his ridiculous behavior confirmed it."

Simon tossed back the drink, wishing it was something stronger. Never mind that he didn't really like the taste of spirits. "My apologies for subjecting you to that unpleasant encounter."

"There is no need for you to apologize. I do believe he bumped into us on purpose."

Simon took a small measure of satisfaction in that. Still, the encounter left him out of sorts. It served as a reminder of the reason he never came to events like this. He was not suited for clever retorts or stimulating conversation.

"Vanbridge."

Simon turned to see Marbury and Ella standing before him.

"Causing a stir at your first ball of the Season?" the earl asked with a teasing smile.

A hot wave of embarrassment washed through Simon. If only he could brush off Ludham's comments.

"Ignore the viscount," Ella advised with a sympathetic glance. "He is only jealous because he wasn't the one dancing with Norah."

"True," Marbury confirmed as he shared a look with his betrothed. "He's been sniffing after the three of you since I had the unfortunate experience of introducing you over a year ago."

Norah gave a mock shudder. "The man is insufferable." She tightened her hold on Simon's elbow. "Now then, let us return to the topic at hand—the stolen coin."

Simon's spirits had risen at the feel of her hand on his arm only to plummet at her words, which served as an unwelcome reminder of his ineptitude. He was only there because of the damned coin. Because it had been taken while in his care. This world was not for him, and the evening made that clear.

"We have spoken to several who attended the unveiling, but none have been of any help." Ella shook her head. "I suppose it's to be expected since the theft didn't happen while the guests were there."

"True," Marbury said. "We can continue with this course." He turned to Simon. "Unless you have any suggestions on how else to proceed."

None, Simon wanted to reply. Because it was the truth. He knew nothing about tracking down stolen artifacts. Yet, with Norah and Ella watching him with hopeful expressions, he wracked his mind for some suggestion, no matter how small.

"I intend to visit with all of the museum employees again tomorrow." He nearly grimaced at how ineffective the idea sounded.

"That certainly can't hurt. Has there been any word from the police?" Marbury asked.

"They've advised they will watch for the stolen items but suggested they might be difficult to find." Simon had hoped for more.

Norah's lips tightened into a thin line. "As Lena said, if we managed to find the journal, we will find the coin. It's only a matter of persistence and determination."

"Not to mention a little luck," Ella added with a smile as if attempting to lighten the mood.

Simon had no experience with luck. Good fortune had turned its back on him more times than he could count. He wouldn't allow himself to rely on it now. "It seems we have done all we can here tonight. Thank you all for your assistance. I will keep you apprised of any developments." He quickly said his goodbyes and started toward the door, more than ready to put the evening behind him.

He couldn't help but pause in the entrance to search for Norah one last time. She visited with Marbury and Ella. He feared the conversation would involve him and his incompetence. With a sigh, he turned away and made his way to the front door to await his carriage.

He had enjoyed the dance with Norah, despite the interruption. The chances of having another with her were nil, as he didn't intend to go to any additional balls in the future. Not when this one had gone so poorly.

Chapter Nine

TWO DAYS LATER, Norah rose from a chair at an outdoor concert with a sigh. She waited, along with her sisters, for the other guests to file out. The afternoon was a fine one with only a few clouds drifting in the blue sky and a mild temperature.

Despite the enjoyable music and setting, Norah's mood was shadowed by the lack of information they'd uncovered about the stolen coin. A mix of impatience and frustration filled her and wouldn't let go.

She could think of little else except the missing coin with one exception—Simon. He had seemed so upset over Ludham's annoying remarks at the ball. The fact that he hadn't been in touch since then concerned her.

"That was wonderful, though I do think Lena is better at playing the harp," Ella whispered as she leaned close.

"I am of the same opinion," Norah agreed with a smile.

Lena shook her head but smiled in return. "Playing in our private music room is completely different than performing at an event like this. My nerves would overcome me."

Lady Havenby and the Countess of Marbury rose from their seats as well. "What are the three of you whispering about?" Lady Havenby asked, always wanting to be a part of what was said.

"They are being ill-mannered, my lady." Lena sent a teasing look at Norah and Ella. "Ignore them, please."

"Leo has remarked several times about how talented the three of you are," Lady Marbury said as she drew closer. "I hope someday I have the pleasure of hearing you perform."

"He is being too kind," Ella replied. "We enjoy playing, but I think we all agree that we wouldn't be comfortable performing for an audience like this."

"Surely you wouldn't mind playing for me since we will soon be family." The countess raised a brow as if daring Ella to disagree. "I shall invite all of you to dinner soon and request that you play afterward."

Norah watched as Ella's cheeks turned pink, well aware of how much Ella wanted her soon-to-be mother-in-law to like her. Ella held Norah's gaze with concern in her eyes. How could they refuse the countess?

"We would be honored to play." Norah looked at Lena for support.

"Absolutely." Lena nodded. "Performing for family and friends is truly a pleasure."

From Ella's tight expression, Norah knew her sister was less than pleased. But Norah didn't see how they could escape the request.

"Perfect. I look forward to it." Lady Marbury led the way toward the aisle with Lady Havenby directly behind her.

"Norah, why would you agree to playing for her?" Ella asked in a hushed tone once the older ladies were out of hearing.

"What else would you have had me say?" Norah asked.

"The countess is well known for her fondness of music," Ella whispered. "I have no doubt I will fall short of her expectations."

"Nonsense." Norah didn't understand what had gotten into Ella. "You are excellent on the piano."

Lena's frown made it clear she agreed with Norah. Ella was being ridiculous.

"Not compared to what she's used to hearing," Ella argued. "I don't need another reason for her not to like me."

Norah lifted her gaze to the sky as she tried to gather her

patience. While the countess had little reason to like them since the lady had married the late earl after he'd been jilted by their mother, Lady Bethany, the countess seemed to have moved past that. She had shown her support on numerous occasions in public and private. What more did Ella need to see that the countess did, indeed, like her?

Norah followed the older ladies, leaving Lena and Ella to continue the whispered conversation without her. Concerns like this were another reason Norah wasn't in a rush to marry. She didn't want to worry herself with complicated family issues any more than the ones she already had. Marrying a man meant marrying his family, as well. In her experience, family relationships were complicated and often fraught with emotions from the past.

"Norah, has there been any word on the stolen coin?" Lady Marbury asked when she joined them in the aisle.

"Unfortunately, no." Norah frowned as she considered what she should do about the lack of information. "I intend to visit with Vanbridge again soon to see if he's received any news."

"So terrible," the countess said. "First the journal and now the coin. What are the odds?"

It didn't escape Norah's notice that the lady avoided any mention of David Wright and Lady Bethany. She might have released her resentment of the Wright sisters, but that didn't mean she was willing to speak of their parents. Perhaps Ella was right to still hold concern and tread carefully around the countess.

According to Leo, his father had married but remained in love with Lady Bethany rather than his own wife. His lovesick behavior had made the lives of both his wife and child miserable from what Leo had told Ella.

During her childhood, Norah had been an unwilling witness to more than one of her parents' arguments about remaining on Oak Island. After her mother's passing, their father had at times been focused solely on his daughters and, other times, focused solely on digging for treasure. Rarely had it been a happy balance.

Norah was ashamed to admit that she'd resented both extremes. Then had come the final day when her frustration had erupted, and she stated her feelings to her father. She'd said terrible things when he'd denied her request to spend time with a friend and her family in Montreal. The memory of those moments cast a hot, sick feeling of remorse and regret throughout her entire being. If only she'd held her thoughts to herself.

Norah was weary of those sorts of complications. She wanted to enjoy her time rather than take on a new battle. Somehow, when it came to family relationships, it was always a battle.

Yet it would be impossible to relax and throw herself into the social season until they'd found the coin.

With determination, she turned back to Ella and Lena as they continued to slowly exit the seating area. "I'm going to visit the museum after this and see if there's any news."

Ella frowned. "Norah, you cannot continue going there without people talking. Someone will notice. Then there's the danger to consider."

"I hardly think I need to worry about running into a thief," Norah protested.

"Isn't it doubtful that Vanbridge will be there?" Lena asked.

Norah drew a breath to hold her patience. Both of her sisters had valid points. "Very well. I shall send him a message instead."

Lady Milner, a friend of Lady Havenby's, joined them, and they visited for several minutes, much to Norah's dismay. She wanted to return home to send a message to Simon.

"Did I see you dancing with the Marquess of Vanbridge the other evening?" Lady Milner asked Norah with a bemused expression.

"Yes, you did." Norah waited to see what the woman had to say, as something seemed to be on her mind based on the way her attention held on Norah.

"I was surprised to see him there. Why, it's been years since he attended a social event." She glanced at Lady Marbury as if for confirmation.

"He is rather reclusive," the countess agreed.

"Do be careful," Lady Milner warned, leaning close as if sharing a secret. "He is an odd, eccentric sort of gentleman. Do not get your hopes up for him as a possible suitor. You'll only be disappointed."

Norah blinked, uncertain of what to say, torn between wanting to defend Simon and insisting she didn't consider him—or any man—husband material. "I don't know him well, but he seems kind and considerate."

"You are being too gracious. Especially after the incident on the dance floor." Lady Milner waved her hand to dismiss Norah's remark. "Imagine him deliberately bumping into Ludham like that." She shook her head.

"It was Ludham who bumped into Vanbridge." Norah had given it considerable thought. She'd been focused on the dance and Simon, but she was certain they hadn't taken any missteps.

"Of course, you'd say that." Lady Milner smiled. "At any rate, take care with Vanbridge. You know what they say, still waters run deep. His seem to run too deep."

The conversation turned to other matters before Norah could form a reply. Whatever had the lady meant?

SIMON ENTERED BROOKS'S late that afternoon to meet Marbury. Though he would've preferred to meet at the Society offices, Marbury had suggested the club. It was another place Simon rarely visited. He had little in common with the members. Why come to a place when he didn't enjoy being there?

However, he wanted to speak with Marbury to see if he had any suggestions regarding the search for the coin that Simon hadn't already tried. His lack of success was wearing on him. Especially when he wanted to return to his other projects.

Though he told himself it was the stolen coin rather than

Norah who caused his distraction, he wasn't completely sure that was true. In fact, he was certain of it. Her stormy blue eyes and sweet curves, not to mention her fierce determination, filled his mind. He'd been certain a day or two away from her would ease his interest, but thus far, it had proven quite the opposite.

To his relief, Marbury was settled at a table with a drink before him. Simon hadn't relished the idea of sitting alone waiting for him. With his luck, Ludham would've shown up and continued his barbs from the other evening.

"Vanbridge." Marbury nodded as Simon joined him. "Good to see you."

"Thank you for meeting me."

"Would you care for a drink?" Marbury glanced around and caught the eye of a waiter who came over directly.

Simon requested coffee.

"You don't have a fondness for alcohol, do you?" Marbury asked.

"Not especially. I prefer my thoughts to remain clear." That was one more area where he was different from other men.

"I hope you don't mind, but I requested Viscount Worley to join us," Marbury said.

"I saw him at the unveiling but only spoke with him briefly." Simon had always liked Worley, though he couldn't claim to know him well.

"He was helpful in the search for the stolen journal," Marbury continued. "I thought, perhaps, he might have some ideas to aid in the search for the coin."

"At this point, I will take all the help I can get. That's precisely why I requested this meeting." Simon nodded at the waiter who brought his coffee.

They spoke of news from the Society offices until Worley arrived a few minutes later. After exchanging pleasantries, Worley sat and then rubbed his hands together as if in anticipation. "I understand we have another case to solve."

Marbury chuckled, then glanced at Simon. "Forgive his excitement. He is overdue to go on another exploration trip. Too much time in England makes him restless."

Worley shifted in his chair. "Perhaps that is true. I am certainly ready for something more than social engagements to take my interest. Have you discovered anything?"

Simon shared his progress, or lack thereof. "If only a clue had been uncovered, I would feel more confident as to what the next step should be."

"Frustrating." Worley twirled the tip of his impressive mustache. "Why would someone take just the three items? The clay pot might be valuable, but the lantern certainly wasn't. Was the coin the only thing of value in the case?"

"Yes and no," Simon replied, having wondered the same thing. He thought the lantern had been taken to upset him or to make sure someone noted the missing coin. "It depends on what you consider valuable, I suppose."

"Such was the case with the journal," Marbury said. "David Wright's notes were of interest to some people but certainly not everyone. So often, value is in the eye of the beholder."

The discussion continued, each man sharing their thoughts and potential paths to continue the investigation.

"Assuming the coin was taken after hours, who has keys to the museum and the cases?" Worley asked.

"The director and I are the only ones." Simon frowned, realizing he hadn't verified that with Stockton. He hoped the man hadn't provided keys to anyone else without consulting Simon first. "However, several employees have access to them."

"How well do you know this Stockton fellow? Do you trust him?" Worley took a sip of the whiskey that now sat before him.

"I did, though a few matters of late have caused me to question that trust." Simon scowled, aware he was part of the problem. It wasn't Stockton's fault that Simon was absentminded. No matter how often he told himself he needed to remember certain things, he simply didn't.

"It might not hurt to look further into his background," Marbury suggested. "Perhaps see what he does in his spare time." He raised a brow at Simon as if to garner his opinion.

"I will see what I can discover." While Simon agreed that it would be a good idea, spying on the director would be awkward, especially if he were caught.

"No offense, Vanbridge," Worley began, "but perhaps it would be better if someone else did this. Stockton is unlikely to recognize Marbury or me."

"I can't ask either of you to spend time doing that."

"We'd be happy to," Marbury assured him. "Tell us what you know about him."

As Simon did so, he realized how little he knew about the man. "While you're researching him, I will look into the other employees more closely. Stockton recently hired a man I'd like to know more about."

No matter how often Simon tried to remember Stockton telling him of hiring Emerson, he couldn't. It worried him, in all honesty. What else might have he forgotten? That sort of behavior wasn't acceptable, given that he was a marquess with responsibilities. If he weren't careful, he could easily make a mistake that could hurt those who depended on him for their livelihoods.

The concern was enough to have him glaring into his coffee, wishing, not for the first time, that he hadn't inherited. He wasn't fit for the title.

"Something amiss?" Marbury asked.

"Not at all. I appreciate you both helping more than I can say." Simon clamped his lips tight before he said anything further. He well knew that sharing his concerns was a sign of weakness and something others pounced upon.

"But?" Worley asked.

Simon hesitated, taking the measure of both men. He truly didn't know them well. Yet, if he didn't share his concerns with them, then who? Still, he couldn't bring himself to do it. "Nothing."

"I hope we all have something to share in the coming days," Marbury said.

Simon thanked the two men and took his leave, pleased that he didn't have to speak with anyone else on his way out. His social interactions had become too numerous of late.

He decided to stop by the museum on the way home to discover where Emerson lived. A glance at his pocket watch showed the hour was later than he'd thought. It was nearly time for the museum to close. Perfect, he decided. He would follow Emerson home.

Simon waited until the carriage neared the museum before tapping on the roof.

"Yes, my lord?" Jarvis asked after he'd opened the small door.

"Drop me before we reach the museum. I'll walk from there."

"Very well," was the driver's muffled reply, but his surly tone made his opinion of Simon's request apparent.

Simon sighed. Jarvis always took it personally if he requested to walk. Why it mattered, Simon didn't know.

Soon the carriage rolled to a halt, and Simon hopped out. "I'll see you at home, Jarvis."

"You're certain you don't want me to wait, my lord?" he asked hopefully.

"No, thank you." Simon waited for him to pull away before considering his options.

Emerson would obviously recognize him if he saw him, so it was important to find a place where he was hidden yet close enough that he wouldn't lose the man. Simon settled on waiting beside a tree across the street. Chances were the man wouldn't look in this direction, especially since the street was rather busy at this time of day.

At one minute after six o'clock, the door to the museum opened and the remaining visitors who'd been inside filed out. A few minutes later, several employees departed as well. Soon Emerson emerged, wearing the same brown suit he'd worn nearly every time Simon had seen him. He paused at the top of the steps to glance about.

Simon eased behind the tree. He breathed a sigh of relief as the man descended the stairs and headed north to walk at a leisurely pace, in no hurry to return home. Did that mean there was no Mrs. Emerson awaiting him?

Maintaining a fair distance between them, Simon followed. He tried to keep his gaze on the ground so that if Emerson looked back, he'd be unlikely to recognize him. They walked for nearly half an hour before entering a residential area. Simon glanced around with interest, wondering if they were close to Emerson's home.

Fewer people were nearby, so Simon slowed his pace, keeping Emerson just in sight. At last, the man approached a modest two-story Tudor-style home and inserted a key in the door.

Simon walked slowly past but could see little in the windows. He crossed the street and walked by the home again and this time was rewarded with movement visible inside. An older man and woman who looked as if they could be his parents were speaking with Emerson. Did he live with them?

Well aware he couldn't linger outside their house for long without drawing notice, Simon glanced around, hoping a neighbor might be willing to share a few details with a nosy stranger. Sure enough, an older gentleman approached with the aid of a cane.

Simon forced a smile. "Good evening, sir."

"And to you." Wrinkles creased his eyes and white mutton-chops lined his jaw. He looked friendly enough.

"A fine day it has been," Simon said, wishing he was better at exchanging pleasantries.

"Indeed." The man paused and glanced up at the sky. "Though my bones suggest it might rain tomorrow."

"I shall keep that in mind. Do you live in the neighborhood?"

"Indeed, I do." He pointed at a house two doors down from where they stood.

"I don't suppose you know John Emerson?" Simon gestured toward the house he'd been watching, hoping Emerson didn't choose to emerge and see him.

"Why, of course. Known him since he was no more than ten years of age. His parents have lived there since before I came to live in the neighborhood."

"He seems like a nice chap, eh?"

"Indeed. He visits his parents every evening. I don't know why he doesn't continue to live with them, given how often he visits. His father is in poor health, so it's good that he does."

"How kind of him." Simon waited, hoping the man might share more.

"I heard he found a position at a museum recently. He's always been fond of books and the like, so I suppose he must enjoy it."

"I'm sure." Simon hesitated, wondering how much more he dared to ask. "Pardon my curiosity, but you don't happen to know if the family is experiencing financial woes, do you?" At the alarmed expression the man gave him, Simon added, "I would like to help them if they are."

"Oh. I see." His expression turned thoughtful. "I don't think so. Nothing I've seen would indicate that. Otherwise, I believe John would move back home."

"That makes sense." Money wasn't the only reason someone might resort to thievery, but it was certainly the most common. "Thank you for your time. Have a pleasant evening."

The older man wished him well and continued toward his house.

Simon glanced toward the Emerson's window one last time and saw the three had settled into chairs for a visit. The scene was cozy, the flickering flames of a fire visible. The woman sat forward in her chair, her attention riveted on her son, apparently delighted with his visit. The father nodded as he listened to John.

Simon's chest tightened as a memory from long ago with his own parents drifted through his mind. He quickly shoved it away as he started the walk home, having learned not to dwell on them. They only made him long for what couldn't be. Yet the prospect of spending the evening alone didn't have the same appeal as it had in the past. There were advantages to having a family. If only the risks weren't so high.

Chapter Ten

NORAH WAITED IN uncomfortable silence with her maid and footman in Simon's entrance hall late the following morning. James and Dorothy's disapproval of the visit was obvious but couldn't be helped. Heaven forbid if Ella discovered she hadn't truly gone shopping.

She should've given Simon more time to respond to her message. However, not knowing what was happening was driving her mad. She found this new, impatient version of herself unsettling and blamed it on the reclusive marquess. If he would've replied to her request for an update, the visit wouldn't be necessary.

"This way, miss," the odd butler said when he returned from seeing if Simon was receiving callers. His gestures were rather dramatic, and she hid a smile as he motioned with a wide-sweeping hand for her to follow him to Simon's study.

He held open the door for her to pass through, then took a bow as though he'd just completed a performance on stage.

A glance at Simon showed him shaking his head at the servant. "That will be all, Fletcher."

"Of course, my lord." The man backed out of the door as if Simon were royalty.

Norah curtsied, then lifted a brow as she continued forward, drawing a deep breath as awareness filled her. She'd missed

Simon and the way he made her feel—tingles running along her skin and a knot of passion in the pit of her stomach. "He has interesting mannerisms."

"I've told him that isn't necessary to no avail. He has a background in the theatre."

"Ah. That explains it." She studied Simon as he stood behind his desk, noting he looked rather tired. She hated to think the missing coin was causing him such distress. "I hadn't received a reply to my message, so thought I'd call to see if you had news."

He rubbed a hand along the back of his neck. "I can't say that I do, though, of course, I'm continuing the search. No additional clues have arisen, which makes progress nearly impossible."

"How frustrating." Norah had suspected as much but was still disappointed. She glanced at a chair that now sat before his desk, certain it hadn't been there her previous visit.

"A recent addition to accommodate the callers I've had of late," Simon said dryly as he gestured to it. "Please, have a seat."

"Thank you." She sank into the chair, rather pleased it was there. "I have been thinking of ways to help with the search but thought it best to speak with you first."

"I would prefer you didn't do anything," he said as he sat. "It could be dangerous."

"Yes, we experienced a bit of that while trying to find my father's journal. Or rather, Ella did."

"All the more reason for you not to involve yourself in this." Simon moved a piece of paper on his desk, the motion catching Norah's gaze.

She gasped. "What on earth happened?" She rose and leaned close. "Your hands look terrible." His knuckles were cracked and bruised, the skin raw in places.

He flexed his hand with a frown, apparently annoyed by the injuries. "Nothing serious."

"They're bleeding." She tugged off her gloves and set them aside to take one of his hands in hers, examining it more closely. "That must hurt terribly."

"A bit tender, though no one's fault except my own."

She walked behind him and tugged on the bell pull, then returned to lift his hand again, gently running her fingers over the bruises. "You need to put something on this."

"It will pass. It always does."

"What causes it?" She couldn't imagine why this could be a frequent occurrence.

He gave a one-shouldered shrug as if embarrassed. "A bit of boxing."

"Boxing? With whom?" Warmth spread through her at the thought of Simon sparring, his lean body shirtless, muscles flexing, skin glistening with perspiration. She shut her eyes tight to dispel the image with little success.

"A bag."

Her eyes flew open at his answer, trying to process it. "You did this by punching a bag?"

"Yes." He pulled away his hand, then brushed at the cracks as if that would make them disappear. "Boxing is supposed to provide mental clarity and deeper concentration. It also happens to be hard on one's knuckles."

Of course, that would be the reason he would practice the sport. She should've guessed. "Perhaps you should wrap your hands or wear some gloves."

"Miles suggested bare-handed would be best for a time. Toughen up the skin."

"Miles?"

"My valet."

"Is he an expert in boxing?"

"He was in the infantry for years and is talented at many physical activities. My hands should toughen after a time, but I might have overdone it with my last session."

"Indeed, you did." Norah looked up as the butler appeared in the doorway. "We are in need of some ointment and bandages to wrap his lordship's hands, please."

"That is not necessary," Simon said, only to scowl when

Norah waved for him to remain quiet.

"Quickly, if you please," she told Fletcher. He nodded, bowed, and backed out of the door again, much to her amusement. "Does he do that if he comes all the way to your desk?"

"I've convinced him to turn around and walk out for those occasions." Simon shook his head, seemingly resigned to the man's antics.

In short order, the butler reappeared with the items she requested. "Mrs. Fletcher insists her ointment is sure to have his lordship healed by this time tomorrow."

"Excellent." Norah doubted the timeframe, based on the state of Simon's knuckles, but anything would help. "Thank you."

The butler departed, and Norah opened the tin of ointment to smell it, relieved it didn't have the terrible odor some did. "I detect a hint of rose water."

"Are you suggesting I'll smell like a girl?" Simon asked with a lopsided smile.

She much preferred his smile over the frown he'd worn earlier. "Only slightly. If someone remarks on it, be sure to tell them your injuries are from boxing. That should silence them."

He chuckled as she dabbed ointment on the cracks. The sun shone through the windows, giving her plenty of light in which to work. The quiet of the study and his faint, appealing scent settled around her. His skin was warm, and she felt her own body heat as awareness seeped into her.

The situation was highly inappropriate. She could too well imagine what Ella would have to say if she found out. But how could Norah not help with this small task? Her maid and footman weren't far, and the door to the study was ajar. Yet their presence did nothing to lessen the flutters in her middle. Holding his warm, callused hand in hers filled her with an unexpected longing. What might those fingers feel like trailing over her bare skin?

Silently berating herself for her wandering thoughts, Norah focused on the task. She released his hand to wind the linen strips over his knuckles a few times, then tucked the tail under a strip. "There. Hopefully that won't be in the way. The ointment needs to stay in place for the remainder of the day so it can do some good. Preferably overnight."

"I'm impressed by your nursing skills." He examined the bandage while she worked on his other hand. "Where did you learn such things?"

"Injuries were common in my father's line of work. Whichever one of us was available tended his wounds. We're all fairly adept at giving aid."

"Norah, your numerous talents amaze me."

She smiled as she secured the bandage on his other hand. "I hardly think this requires skill."

Then she made a terrible mistake.

She looked into those green eyes, fascinated by the gold flecks visible in their depths. His lashes were ridiculously long for a man. His brows were dark slashes, so masculine in appearance. Almost as if of its own accord, her gaze dropped to his lips, remembering all too well how they felt pressed against hers.

She desperately wanted to kiss him again. "Simon?"

"Yes?" His answer was hardly more than a whisper, as if he were gripped by the same tension as her.

She hesitated, also remembering that she'd been the one to ask him to kiss her the first time. Did that mean he hadn't enjoyed their kiss? The idea had her frowning.

Then he placed his bandaged hands on her waist and drew her closer. And closer still, until she stood against his knees. To her shock, he pulled her down onto his lap. Her breath caught in her throat as her body pulsed in rhythm with her heartbeat. His gaze held on her lips, that focus incredibly appealing.

What could she do but lean closer with the hope he'd take the hint?

Then he kissed her with enough mastery to send desire through her in a hot rush. Like he couldn't get enough of her. His lips were firm against hers and so warm. The hardness of his muscled thighs was evident through the layers that separated them. Her emotions spiraled as passion took a firm hold.

He eased back and then nibbled before his tongue pressed along the seam of her lips. She opened her mouth to allow him entrance. The invasion was both shocking and lovely, creating a whole new set of feelings coiling inside her.

His hand squeezed her waist, and her breasts tingled in response. For a man who didn't get out much, he was alarmingly good at kissing.

She vaguely wondered if he studied techniques, much like he studied carvings in rocks and the like. Or perhaps it was the boxing that had provided an additional level of focus. Whatever it was, she was grateful for it.

He pressed kisses along her jaw, then down her neck, and her entire body came alive. She tangled her fingers in the waves of his hair along his collar. It was softer than she imagined. She moved her hands to explore the breadth of his shoulders, easily able to feel the contoured muscles and appreciate his boxing practice all the more.

"Simon?" she whispered as she tilted her head to give him better access to her neck.

"Yes?"

"You are very talented at kissing."

His gaze met hers, and the slow smile that lit his eyes and then curved his lips melted her completely. What could she do but kiss him again?

She poured all her feelings into it, hoping he felt even a portion of what she did. This man was special and a threat to her plan for the coming years. However, now wasn't the time to worry about such things. This chance might not come along again. How could it be wrong to enjoy it?

"Are you here alone?" Simon asked between kisses.

"No." The reminder of Dorothy and James waiting in the entrance hall was like a splash of cold water. If she didn't emerge soon, one of them would surely come looking for her.

"Damn." His whispered response made her smile as she eased back.

"I should go." Whether she was telling him or herself, she didn't know.

"Yes, you should." He released his hold and she rose.

To her surprise, he also stood, then kissed her one more time. Her heart squeezed at his gentleness. Lady Milner might think him odd and eccentric, but Norah thought him wonderful.

Only as she departed in the carriage did she realize she hadn't shared her idea for assisting with the search. She supposed that meant she would have to meet with Simon again soon. The thought made her smile.

SIMON TIMED HIS visit to the museum the following afternoon so he arrived fifteen minutes prior to closing. That should give him long enough to visit with Emerson before he left for the day. Since following him had resulted in little information, the time had come for direct conversation. A few well-worded questions might gain Simon more insight than simple observation.

He flexed his hands, pleased with how much better they felt after Norah's tender care. His improved spirits were a direct result of her visit and their kisses. His feelings for her were growing deeper than he expected. Yet he couldn't deny the pleasure her company provided. She was a bright spot of sunshine in his cloudy life. He couldn't bring himself to turn away from that or her.

Simon nodded at the employee who sold tickets just inside the front door and proceeded upstairs. Rather than going directly to the offices, he turned and walked through several exhibits, hoping to find Emerson. Though Simon wasn't involved with the day-to-day operations, he thought Emerson gave tours and answered visitors' questions, as well as tidying the exhibits and making certain all was in order.

The realization that Simon didn't know for certain what the man's duties were only made him more aware of how distant he was from the running of the museum. Perhaps too distant.

While he'd hired Stockton so he wouldn't have to deal with those things because he preferred to spend time on his own research, he realized that at the very least, he needed better communication with those he employed.

Several people were still wandering through the displays, which made Simon smile. He had Norah to thank for the continued increase in visitors. Apparently, word of the theft hadn't spread far as of yet.

He spotted Emerson speaking with a few of the guests who stood before a replica of a Pre-Columbian Olmec colossal head and paused nearby but out of sight to hear what Emerson said.

"It may surprise you to learn that these civilizations had permanent settlements and were often engaged in agricultural activities. As evidenced by this statue, they were skilled craftsmen and many of their buildings were significant in size."

Simon nodded in approval. Too often, tour guides either delved too deeply into the artifacts and lost the attention of those who only wanted to spend a few hours looking at something interesting, or they said too little and failed to capture the visitors' curiosity.

While much of the information was noted on cards and posters so visitors could read as much or as little as they liked, hearing someone speak while looking at the exhibits often had the best results. Visitors learned something new. That had been Simon's intent when he'd started the museum. Few people had the opportunity to explore other cultures. He wanted the exhibits to be both entertaining and informative. He liked to think his father would've approved of what he'd built.

After asking a few additional questions, the visitors moved on, leaving Emerson alone.

"Good evening," Simon said as he approached.

Emerson's eyes went wide. "Good evening, my lord. I didn't see you there."

"I happened to hear some of what you shared with the visitors. Well done."

"Thank you." Emerson's pleased smile made Simon glad he'd complimented the younger man. "I enjoy sharing history with visitors, especially about the pre-Columbian exhibit."

Simon studied the large stone head replica, which stood as tall as he was. "That must've been an intriguing time period in which to live." Though he'd had a chance to buy an actual statue, he thought it important for most items to remain with the country of origin. In fact, he'd had copies created of some of his uncle's pieces and returned the originals to museums closer to where the artifacts had been found.

Emerson's face lit up in a familiar way. "So many were, don't you think?"

Simon felt much the same and was pleased the museum employed someone whose enthusiasm nearly matched his own. "Agreed. Every historical era has something fascinating to offer."

Emerson moved around the exhibit to walk closer, wearing his customary brown suit. "May I ask if you have a favorite?"

"I tend to think whatever artifact I'm studying at the moment comes from my favorite civilization," he admitted with a chuckle. "Stone carvings of any sort are a puzzle I can't resist. What of you?"

"Oh." Emerson's brows raised for a long moment as if he were astounded Simon had asked. "I'm most impressed with the Incas, I think. An odd mix of sophistication and brutality. The lack of crime during their reign is a testament to the harshness of their laws."

"Do you think we should increase our punishments to better match theirs?" Simon asked, genuinely curious.

"No. From what I've read, they didn't allow people to have a second chance. We don't all get it right the first time." Emerson stared into the distance. "I should very much like to visit Peru someday."

"I hope you have the opportunity to do so. Studying cultures is wonderful but traveling to see them up close gives one a completely different perspective." Simon cleared his throat, reminding himself to focus on his purpose—to find out more about Emerson's personal life, not his dreams. "Is there a Mrs. Emerson?"

"No, no." Emerson chuckled and dipped his head as if embarrassed. "No prospects on the horizon, so to speak. Not that I'm in any rush to marry." He looked up at Simon with a furrowed brow. "Of course, I'm more concerned with my career."

"Of course." Simon hid a smile. Emerson seemed to think he was supposed to say that, but perhaps it was true. "Speaking of your position, I wanted to check again with everyone to ask if anything else has come to mind regarding the missing coin. Have you thought of any information that could be helpful? Something out of the ordinary or that struck you as unusual?"

"The situation is so distressful." The younger man shook his head. "It's terrible. Just terrible. Who would take it? And what do they intend to do with it?"

"Excellent questions to which I have no answers." Simon lifted a brow. "Has anything come to mind?"

Emerson considered the question for a long moment, quickening Simon's hopes. "Perhaps out of the ordinary behavior in someone? Anything at all," Simon prompted.

With an uneasy look, Emerson glanced around as if to make certain no one would overhear them. "There is an older gentleman who has visited several times and spoke with Mr. Stockton. I only mention it because I don't know if he paid the admission fee."

Simon released the breath he hadn't realized he was holding. "That could prove helpful." Though it seemed unlikely. "Can you provide more details?"

"Certainly." He described a tall, thin man with dark hair and a receding hairline, as well as when he'd seen him. Unfortunately, the stranger didn't sound familiar, nor did his presence seem significant.

"Thank you for sharing this," Simon said. "And please know that I will hold what you said in confidence."

"Thank you, my lord. I very much enjoy my work here and wouldn't want to do anything to jeopardize it."

Simon reached to shake the younger man's hand. "I appreciate your loyalty. Let me know if you note anything else of interest."

"Of course." Emerson offered a relieved smile. "Happy to help."

Funny how often people said that but how rarely they were. Simon went upstairs to see if Stockton had discovered anything of interest, though he was beginning to lose hope of ever finding the coin.

Chapter Eleven

NORAH SMILED POLITELY at her dance partner, Viscount Salverson, wishing the dance was over. Yet the music went on and on while he gripped her hand tighter and tighter.

"You look positively stunning, Miss Wright." His smile made her uncomfortable, as did his gaze, which ran down the length of her, pausing to linger on her breasts.

"Thank you." She wracked her mind for a neutral topic of conversation, anything to take his attention from her. "The weather was certainly fine today, don't you agree?"

"Not as fine as you." He chuckled as if he'd said something terribly clever.

Norah held back a grimace. While aware that many considered the Wright sisters attractive, she much preferred to associate with those who looked beyond appearances to consider her as a person. After all, looks faded. Character mattered. It wasn't as if she had any hand in her appearance other than taking care of herself and her attire.

"I should like to call on you tomorrow," he said. "Perhaps you'd enjoy a ride in Hyde Park?"

Viscount Salverson was one of a handful of gentlemen who had expressed interest in courting her numerous times. They requested a dance at every ball and frequently paid her compliments. But none made an effort to truly come to know her. She'd

116

done her best to rebuff them and make it clear she wasn't interested. Unfortunately, those attempts were met with little success.

She didn't enjoy dancing with any of them and had no desire to consider kissing them, which confirmed her determination to not allow them to court her. The idea of marrying Salverson or one of the others nearly made her shudder. She wasn't ready to marry, but if she were, she certainly wouldn't want to marry one of *them*.

Being shackled for life to someone like Viscount Salverson was unimaginable. Thank goodness her grandfather wasn't pressuring her to find a suitable husband. If only she could get Ella to agree. Norah suspected he wasn't ready for any of them to move away when he was only just beginning to know them. That was one of the reasons Ella and Marbury had decided on such a long betrothal.

Viscount Salverson seemed incapable of understanding that she didn't appreciate his efforts to flatter her. He was handsome enough with blonde hair and even features but looks weren't everything. His blue eyes were rather pale and when his gaze swept over her, it left her chilled. From what she could discern, he wasn't interested in having a true conversation with her about anything of importance.

"How kind of you to offer, but I am otherwise engaged tomorrow." It seemed silly to continue to say she was busy when it would've been more effective to simply tell him that while she was flattered, she wasn't interested. If only he'd take the hint.

"Oh?" He frowned like he thought that impossible. "Doing what?"

Norah blinked as she tried to think of a response, though it was none of his business. "I am going to the Museum of Antiquities with my sisters."

"Vanbridge's place? Whatever for?"

That he hadn't heard about the unveiling or the stolen coin only proved he truly wasn't interested in her or what she considered important. Somehow the thought of Simon eased her distress. How different it was to spend time with him compared to someone like Viscount Salverson. Thinking of Simon gave her an idea.

"I recently read an intriguing book about the Inca Empire." If the mention of reading didn't put him off, hopefully talking about history would. "Did you know the Incas completed rituals involving sacrifices in an effort to change the weather?"

"Sacrifices?" He repeated the word as if it were foreign, the interest in his gaze fading.

"It is fascinating to learn about other cultures' beliefs, don't you think? I would be happy to lend you the book if you'd like. Also, the Museum of Antiquities has a wonderful exhibit on the Incas you might enjoy."

"I didn't realize you were so enthusiastic about history." The viscount released his hold on her as the dance ended at last.

"History is my passion," she lied as she resisted the urge to wipe her gloves on her skirt. "Someday I hope to visit Egypt to see the pyramids, as well as Greece to see the ruins. Mythology is another fascinating subject, wouldn't you agree?"

He eased back, studying her as if she'd suddenly grown a wart on her nose. "The topic is not one I particularly enjoy."

"What a shame. I find it enthralling." She turned in the direction of where Ella and Marbury stood, hoping the viscount would at least take this hint.

To her relief, he offered his arm and returned her to their side. He bid them good evening and took his leave.

Ella studied her with narrowed eyes. "Viscount Salverson's interest in you seems to have waned."

"I noticed that as well." Norah hoped her relief didn't show on her face.

"I thought him rather nice." Ella glanced at Marbury as if hoping he would confirm her opinion, but he was conversing with someone else.

"Then obviously you haven't spoken with him other than to

exchange pleasantries." Norah hesitated, wondering if this was the right time to once again attempt to explain that she was in no hurry to marry. The last few times Norah had shared her feelings, Ella had said she understood, only to point out the next eligible gentleman who crossed their path.

"I realize how happy you and Marbury are," Norah began, keeping her voice low. "As I've said before, I would prefer to wait a few years to wed. There are so many things I want to see and do before then."

"Do you intend to do those things alone?" Ella shook her head, clearly puzzled. "Wouldn't you rather do them with your husband?"

How could Ella not remember the example their own parents had set and see how unlikely that was? While their mother had supported their father's dreams of digging for treasure on Oak Island, Norah knew she hadn't thought they'd spend their entire lives on the small island. Any dreams her mother held had been set aside for her husband's. He'd always been so sure the next season would lead to a discovery.

Ella and Marbury seemed to share similar interests, which was unusual from what Norah had witnessed. She wasn't willing to take the same risk her mother had.

"Be careful you don't wait too long," Ella advised with concern in her eyes. Ever the eldest sister. "The good ones will be gone, and you'll be left with little from which to choose."

Norah only smiled. That was a risk she was willing to take.

Thoughts of Simon still filled her mind.

A man like him, completely different than any others she'd met, was certainly a temptation. She believed he truly saw her, not just her appearance. And the way he made her feel was shocking—so much more than anything she'd experienced. The question was whether Simon felt the same.

IN AN EFFORT to spend more time at the museum, Simon brought a couple of papers he wanted to further study in addition to the most recent news sheet from the Royal Geological Society to review so he'd have something to do while there.

He also intended to speak with the employees again and walk through the exhibits. After all, he wasn't going to find the coin in his study.

While he wasn't comfortable around most people, he liked to think he had instincts for those he trusted and those he didn't. Stockton had done most of the hiring and only a few remained of the ones Simon had chosen when he'd first opened the museum. The time had come to better know the employees.

He climbed the stairs to his office, preferring to collect himself before he braved the public and the employees.

"Good morning, Stockton."

The man lifted his head in surprise and jerked to his feet to bow. "My lord. What brings you by so early this morning?"

"I thought I'd spend time here today." Simon glanced at the papers on the director's desk, trying to decide whether he looked guilty of something. Perhaps Simon had just startled him.

"Oh? Any particular reason?" Stockton shifted the papers on the desk but didn't attempt to hide them.

Simon realized he was being overly suspicious. "We are still pursuing the stolen coin, of course. Until we discover who is behind the thefts, I will be dropping in on a more regular basis."

"We?" Stockton adjusted his spectacles.

Simon considered whether it was wise to share more. Then again, it was unlikely Stockton knew either Marbury or Worley, despite the fact that they had been following the museum director on occasion. They had been at the unveiling, of course, but Stockton had made no effort to socialize with the guests, nor had Simon introduced him to any.

The realization made Simon wonder if he'd handled that wrong. Stockton was an important part of the museum's operations, and it certainly wasn't Simon's intent to make him feel otherwise.

"The Earl of Marbury and Viscount Worley, friends of mine, are assisting. As fellow members of the Royal Geological Society, they have numerous contacts among both treasure hunters and collectors. If there's any word of the coin, they'll be sure to hear it."

"How reassuring."

Yet Simon wondered if he felt otherwise, based on the bland expression that came over his face. "Has any additional information come to light?"

Stockton glanced at his desk again. "Unfortunately, no. I continue to make inquires, of course." He offered a one-shouldered shrug.

Simon was curious who the man had thought to ask. "What sort of inquiries? With whom?" Perhaps he should've involved Stockton more in the search all along.

"Well, the employees, as you already know." He frowned, suggesting he was trying to remember. Or perhaps to think of what he should say. "I considered sharing the issue with a friend or two who work at other museums, but I decided against doing so."

"Oh?" Simon was acquainted with several other museum owners but was abashed to realize he hadn't thought of mentioning it to them.

"Obviously, I wouldn't want to do anything to harm the museum's reputation. We have had enough problems getting visitors to come. Suggesting there is an issue with security surely won't help."

"While the museum's reputation is important, the best way to maintain it is to find the coin. If you think speaking to any of your acquaintances could help, please do so."

"Are you certain?" Stockton shook his head. "The last thing we need is for other museums to know about the problem. What if they start telling their visitors in an effort to discourage them from coming here?"

"Perhaps the public will come here just to learn more about the theft." As he knew from personal experience, nothing spread faster than bad news. With that, he moved to his door, reaching into his trouser pocket for the key. Though it seemed ridiculous to bother locking his door when he didn't keep anything inside, he had always done so, especially after hiring Stockton. He'd had the sneaking suspicion that otherwise he'd arrive at the museum one day to find Stockton sitting in his office.

Simon settled behind his desk, pushing aside the thought of how much he preferred his study with the cheerfully burning fire and his books. Then again, he'd found it impossible to concentrate on work there the previous day. Not when images of Norah in his lap filled his mind. Thinking of her now was enough to have him drawing a deep breath.

He glanced at his hands, which were healing nicely. He'd removed the bandages, not wanting to draw attention to his hands while at the museum. She had been right. Putting the ointment on with the bandages had quickened the healing. Never mind how Miles had shaken his head at the sight and asked how he'd ever toughen his hands if he tended them in that manner.

That was all right. He'd take Norah's tender ministrations over toughened hands any day. Perhaps it was time to wear some sort of gloves when he boxed from now on. He didn't want to announce his new hobby just by the state of his hands.

He'd been so upset after the encounter with Ludham, in addition to his lack of success with the investigation, that he'd taken his displeasure out on the boxing bag. Though the bout had indeed left him calmer and better able to focus, his hands had been sore. Thank goodness Norah had called.

Only then did he realize he couldn't bring to mind even one of the ladies who'd been at the ball. He'd only had eyes for Norah.

With concerted effort, he put aside his thoughts of her to pull out a sheet of paper and ready his pen in case he wanted to jot notes while studying the articles he'd brought.

Time passed slowly as he worked his way through his reading material. Deciding he needed a respite, he rose and stretched. A glance out his open office door showed Stockton still at his desk. What on earth did the man have to do that involved so much paperwork?

Simon exited his office, wondering if it might be worth looking through the man's desk after he left for the day. He didn't want to question him about the issue now. It would no doubt cause him to hide anything that might be helpful.

"I'm going to walk a bit." Simon locked the door, deciding he didn't want Stockton snooping through his notes, even if he intended to do the same thing to him later.

"Very well." Stockton dipped his head.

Simon went down to the entrance hall and approached Mr. Johnson, the man who greeted visitors and helped them with tickets and information. A few questions provided Simon with what he wanted to know. The museum was still seeing an increase in visitors despite the loss of the coin. Few people asked about it. Most were interested in the location of the Oak Island exhibit along with the Inca one. The Egyptian display was third at the moment.

Mr. Johnson seemed delighted by the increase in guests as it made his job more enjoyable. He was reserved in his response to Simon's question about Stockton. Though he'd said nothing that suggested a problem, neither did he offer a glowing endorsement of the director.

Simon walked through the exhibits on the lower floor, pausing to listen to visitors' comments as they viewed various displays. He wanted to make a few updates on some and made mental notes about them. Nothing needed to be done immediately, but he didn't want to let it go overlong.

The more he walked through the museum, the more he realized needed to be done. Cobwebs had taken over a corner of the Egyptian area. Several small statues were laying on their sides in a locked display case in the Incan exhibit. Why weren't those issues being noted and addressed?

Emerson was at his post, sharing information with visitors. He nodded at Simon with a smile. If Emerson and the other employees didn't have time to tidy the exhibits, someone should be hired to do so.

Two employees were on each floor to assist visitors. Only one was free, so Simon spoke with him at length. The man said he made certain to walk through the exhibits on his side of the floor as often as possible but hadn't seen anything amiss.

"Except for the clay pot, of course," the man added.

"Clay pot?"

"It's been missing for at least a week now. I mentioned it to Mr. Stockton, but he said it was being cleaned."

"I see. Thank you." Simon cursed as he walked away. He didn't think for a moment that the pot was being cleaned. Were things slowly disappearing from the museum? Why hadn't Stockton mentioned the clay pot when he'd provided the recent inventory?

He returned to his office, annoyed to find Stockton absent. Just when he'd intended to have a few words with the man, he disappeared. Simon reached in his pocket for the key to his office, only to have the door open beneath his hand. He blinked in surprise, certain he'd locked it when he'd left. Hadn't he? While he remembered thinking of doing it, he couldn't say for sure if he had.

He slowly pushed open the door, half expecting to find Stockton searching his desk. But the room stood empty. Once again, Simon wondered if he was becoming so forgetful that he couldn't be trusted with the simplest task. The thought was very unsettling.

"FLOWERS FOR YOU, Miss Norah," Davies, the butler, announced the following morning as he entered the drawing room where Norah and Lena were doing some needlework.

"How lovely," Lena said as she looked up from the intricate pattern she was stitching for a pillowtop. "Those look like spring."

The sight of the bouquet of roses and lilies caused Norah's stomach to fall. Flowers meant a gentleman had sent them. The only person whose name she'd be excited to see on the card was Simon's. The thought of him thinking to do something such as that was almost laughable.

"Aren't they pretty?" Lena frowned at Norah when she didn't respond.

"Yes. Very much so." With a sigh, Norah rose and gestured for Davies to set the vase on a nearby table. She couldn't resist leaning close to draw in their fragrance. She should be more appreciative of them, but they were a sign of complications as far as she was concerned. With no small measure of trepidation, she lifted the card to read it, dismayed to see they were from Viscount Ludham of all people. "How annoying."

"What is it?" Lena asked.

"Ludham sent them with an apology for interrupting my dance the other night."

"That's odd. Why send them now? If he felt that way, he should've sent them the following day."

"Exactly. But why send them at all?"

"He must want to stay in your good graces," Lena suggested.

"It's too late." She shared a look with her sister. "He was never in them."

"Nor mine. He was sorely disappointed when Marbury and Ella announced their betrothal. I fear he's still determined to marry one of us."

Norah sank into her chair once again, glaring at the flowers. "How annoying that he thinks any of us will do. Is it because we are the duke's granddaughters? Or because we look similar?"

"I don't think we'll ever know the answer. I would venture to guess he doesn't know it either." She smoothed the stitches she'd made, then lifted the needle once again. "I certainly don't intend to consider him as a suitor, do you?"

"No. Definitely not."

"Then who?" Lena raised her brows up and down suggestively. "Vanbridge?"

"Please." Norah waved a hand in dismal but could feel her cheeks heating. Part of her wished that was possible. Though she tried to smother the feeling, it refused to budge. "He is far too interested in the past to consider the future."

"You're interested in the past, too."

"Not to the extent he is. I also appreciate the present."

"As do I." Lena gave a wry smile. "Which makes me feel incredibly guilty."

"How do you mean?" Norah stared at Lena in surprise.

Lena hesitated. "Life is different here. Certainly more entertaining. Is it terrible of me to say that?"

The worry in her gaze had Norah rising to take her hands in hers. "Not at all. Enjoying this life doesn't mean we don't miss Mother and Father."

Relief filled Lena's expression, as did remorse. "Then why do I feel so guilty?"

"Don't," Norah ordered, realizing she was telling herself that as well. "Our parents' choices weren't ours. We shouldn't feel guilty for enjoying the life we've found here."

Lena lifted her chin even if doubt remained in her eyes. "You're right. We shouldn't. Thank you for saying that."

Norah only wished she felt it as well. Guilt remained despite what she'd told Lena. Would she ever be able to set it aside?

❧ ❧ ❧

Chapter Twelve

NORAH READ SIMON'S response to her latest message requesting an update with no small measure of frustration. It said little and therefore made it impossible to interpret what he was thinking. Since he'd responded, she wasn't able to call on him when she couldn't justify the risk of doing so.

Had his intent been to keep her at arm's length?

She rose from the desk to pace her bedroom. One thing was clear—she wanted to find the coin. The best way to do that was to help Simon, regardless of whether he wanted assistance. Perhaps the time had come to do what the sisters had done when their father's journal had been stolen—start a search of their own.

Why would anyone take the coin except to sell it? Money was the most obvious motivation. It might be helpful to compile a list of shops that specialized in collectable coins. They could advise the shops to be on the watch for the coin, thereby making it difficult for someone to sell it.

She had to take action of some sort. Waiting and worrying was driving her mad. Each day that passed made her more sympathetic with Ella and the steps her sister had taken to find their father's stolen journal. The same persistence Ella had shown would work favorably in this situation as well.

How did one find shops that bought and sold coins? Perhaps they would advertise in the news sheet. She hurried down the stairs toward the drawing room where Davies placed the news sheet after her grandfather read it at breakfast. She and her sisters usually left him in peace for the first meal of the day but often shared dinner with him.

Norah smiled as she remembered the first few weeks after their arrival in London. It had taken persistence to convince their grandfather to allow them into his life. Finding the coin was no different. She lifted her chin, even more determined to act as she entered the drawing room and found Ella sitting by a window with her needlework.

"Good morning," Norah greeted her as she walked closer. "What are you working on?"

Ella smiled. "I am embroidering a few handkerchiefs for Leo as a wedding gift." She showed the fine white linen to Norah. "What do you think?"

"Monogrammed with his initials? How perfect." Norah squeezed her sister's arm. "I am so excited for you, but I can't imagine you not being with us every day." The idea put a lump in her throat.

Some of her emotion must've shown on her face because Ella quickly stood to hug her. "You won't have a chance to miss me. I will be here more often than you think."

"I hope so." Norah returned her embrace. "We need you."

Ella leaned back and studied Norah. "I'm not so sure that's true. You and Lena are managing quite well on your own. I couldn't be prouder of the exhibit you and Vanbridge did for Father."

Norah grimaced. "I was as well, until the coin was stolen."

"Do not worry. We will find it."

"Speaking of which…" Norah hesitated to share what she had in mind, fairly certain her sister would discourage her.

"What are you thinking?"

Norah told her the idea of finding coin dealers.

"While I applaud the making of a list, please don't do any-thing on your own."

"I won't. I remember what happened to you all too clearly." The memory of Ella being struck on the head in an antique shop was still vivid. "That is nothing I want to repeat."

"We could share your list with Leo and Vanbridge and ask what they think."

Norah's heart gave a leap at the mention of Simon's name, making her realize just how enamored she had become with him. "I thought to begin my search by checking the news sheet for advertisements."

"Excellent idea. A few of the magazines have them, as well. Would you like some assistance?"

"I wouldn't want to keep you from your project." Norah smiled as she glanced at the handkerchief. If only her sister knew what she and Lena had been working on in secret. "I shall keep you apprised of my progress."

The sisters each settled into their work. The peaceful quiet of the drawing room with the company of her sister was poignant since Ella would soon be gone. These were the moments Norah would miss.

Change was part of life. Both good and bad. Sweet and tragic. Not so different than the fabric her sister stitched—all the threads woven together to create a pattern often unclear until one stepped back. She understood why Simon and her father appreciated history so much. How she wished she'd had more respect for her father's interest when he'd still been alive. Reviewing the past could help make sense of the present and give a hint of what the future held.

If only it also hinted at who had taken her father's coin.

An hour later, Norah studied the short list she had. There were surely more than the ones she'd found thus far. "I wonder if Lady Havenby might know of some coin collectors among the *ton.*"

"Private ones?" Ella asked. At Norah's nod, she added, "I know Leo has been making inquiries among the members of the Royal Geological Society, but not all collectors are members. I think asking her is an excellent idea. She knows so much about everyone. Why don't you invite her for tea this afternoon?"

SIMON'S BREATH CAUGHT at the unexpected sight of Norah in the open doorway of his office in the museum. He'd done his best to stay away from her, as he was becoming far too accustomed to having her in his life. Her presence was temporary, and it wouldn't do to become dependent on her.

Yet seeing her now when he was caught unawares was like a refreshing sea breeze. A bright spot of sunshine on a rainy day. Good heavens. He was waxing poetic. How unlike him.

"Miss Wright." He stood and drank in her loveliness, his heart hammering in response.

"Good afternoon, my lord." She wore a bright pink gown with brown trim and a matching hat. While blue was his favorite color on her, this one might be a close second. It brought a hint of the same rosy hue to her cheeks.

But it was her warm smile that tugged at him. He'd missed her and the vitality she brought.

He'd spent much of the past three days at the museum, speaking with all the employees several times. None had any helpful information to share. Nor had any acted suspiciously.

Much to his surprise, he'd been distracted by conversations with visitors. While he didn't think he enjoyed talking to people, the experience was much different when discussing artifacts and history.

He'd spoken to Stockton, who claimed the clay pot had been broken by a visitor. The director hadn't told Simon because he thought Simon had enough to worry about. Somehow knowing the pot had been broken rather than stolen was a relief. Yet Simon thought it odd none of the employees had known the pot had been damaged beyond repair. Stockton should've told him earlier.

Simon had also met with Marbury and Worley, but they hadn't discovered anything interesting either. They'd followed Stockton several times without finding anything helpful. Though the three had discussed a possible motivation for the thefts, they hadn't come to any conclusions.

"I hope the day finds you well," Norah said as she stepped into his office.

"It does now." The reply escaped before he could stop it, though her answering smile made him pleased it had.

His feelings for Norah seemed to have grown in the brief time they'd been apart. And he had no idea what to do about that.

"Did you receive my reply to your message?" he asked. He was coming to realize that if he didn't respond immediately, she would appear.

"Yes, thank you."

He gestured to the chair before his desk, and they both sat. "I wish I had more to tell you."

"As it happens, I have two things to share with you." She pulled a sheet of paper from her reticule and handed it to him. "I took the liberty of making a list of shops that deal in collectible coins with the hope it could help."

He studied the names, appreciating the same precise and feminine script he recognized from her messages. "Excellent. I will share it with Marbury and Worley. Surely between the three of us, we can make quick work of it."

"I would be happy to visit a few with my sisters." Her hopeful tone nearly made him smile.

"Thank you, but I think it best to avoid that based on past events."

Her lips twisted in disappointment, which made him long to kiss her again.

"I have also learned that Lord Stanwick has an impressive coin collection. He's not a member of the Society, but it might be worth speaking with him. As it happens, he and his wife are hosting a ball tomorrow evening. If you attend, I'm certain it would be possible to speak with him about it."

"Another ball?" Simon frowned as he considered the disaster of the last one. "Is that truly necessary?"

"Attending might provide the opportunity for him to introduce you to any of his friends who also collect coins." Norah's enthusiasm was impossible to ignore. Not that he could ignore anything about her presence.

How could he focus on the reasons he wanted to refuse when her appearance was so distracting?

"Wouldn't it be best if we simply called on him at another time? He'll be busy with guests at the ball."

"Perhaps, but we could also speak with other guests about the stolen coin. While we've spoken with most of those who attended the unveiling, that hasn't helped. It's time to expand our efforts."

He couldn't disagree. Not when he had nothing to show for his own inquiries. Still, he dreaded attending when his skills in dealing with people weren't good enough to navigate the nuances of conversations at such events.

But when he looked at Norah, there was only one answer he could offer. "Very well."

Her delighted smile eased the reluctance that swept through him and elevated his spirits. He feared he'd grant her anything if pressed.

"Perfect. We will meet there and decide who are our primary targets."

"Primary targets?" She made the evening sound like a military operation rather than a social event.

"Of course." She gave a single nod. "Some people are more helpful than others, wouldn't you agree?"

"True." Even he, who spent so little time with people, understood her point.

"We shall start with Lord Stanwick. No doubt he can offer

the names of additional collectors." She raised a brow. "Will you keep me apprised of anything interesting that comes from my list?"

"Certainly, but it will take time to visit them all." He would do anything to find the coin, no matter how long it took.

"Which is why my sisters and I would be happy to assist with the process." She smiled as if she'd shared excellent news.

"No, thank you."

Her crestfallen expression nearly had him changing his answer. He pressed his lips tight to keep from doing so.

"We will take the utmost care. There would be all three of us plus a maid. Nothing will happen."

"So, you admit the mission is dangerous." He clasped his hands on his desk and leaned forward. "Very dangerous. Thieves are unscrupulous characters."

"I am aware of that. That is the reason we would take precautions."

"The answer is still no."

"But—"

He held up a hand. "I can't believe Marbury would agree that it's a good idea."

She hesitated, which confirmed his thoughts. "I only—"

"Norah." He held her gaze, wanting her to truly understand. "While I appreciate your assistance in creating the list, I cannot abide the thought of anything happening to you or your sisters."

"That seems unlikely when there would be four of us visiting the shops."

"I know for a fact not all are fine establishments. Some are in the rougher areas of the city. While you're relatively new to London, I cannot believe you aren't aware of that."

She sat back in her chair with a huff. "I only want to help."

"You already have." Yet he could see that wasn't enough. "I'm certain there are more coin dealers than the ones you provided. I wonder how we could find them."

Norah latched onto his remark like a fish biting a baited hook.

"I am happy to continue my research to locate any others."

"That would save me considerable time. Thank you." She still looked rather disgruntled, so he added, "I know progress is slow, but Marbury and Worley are aiding us, too."

The thought brought a wash of emotion that tightened his chest. He'd never had this sort of support. Not since his parents had died. Though he told himself this was only temporary, part of him wished otherwise.

"I appreciate your efforts. Truly." Norah lowered her gaze. "I didn't expect immediate results, but it's still difficult to wait. Especially when I can imagine the coin moving farther away. Possibly forever out of reach."

"I think it's more likely that whoever took it is holding it until talk dies down. If we don't allow that to happen for some time, perhaps the thief will grow impatient and do something reckless."

Norah met his gaze once again, slowly nodding. "That makes sense." She straightened. "It also means that you attending the ball is all the more important."

Only too late, he realized he'd justified her request that he attend the ball. Then again, he would agree with nearly any of her suggestions. "Yes, I suppose it does."

"Excellent." She rose, her reticule in hand. "I look forward to seeing you tomorrow evening." With a sparkle in her eyes, she leaned close. "If time permits, I should very much like another dance."

He studied her in surprise as he stood. "Truly?" He would've thought she would rather avoid dancing with him after their last experience.

"Absolutely." She walked around the corner of his desk to stand before him.

His entire body shifted into high alert. He told himself to keep his hands at his sides. The two servants who accompanied her everywhere were right outside the open door, even if he couldn't see them. Now was not the time to indulge himself.

Then her skirts brushed his legs as she took another step

nearer. His skin prickled, much like if she'd reached out and touched him.

"I can't remember enjoying a dance more." Her whispered words had his gaze dropping to her lips.

"I enjoyed it as well." At least until Ludham had ruined it. That could easily happen again, but how could he worry over that when Norah stood before him now? She was a bright promise of all the good in the world. Was it so wrong that he wanted to reach out and hold her?

As if of their own accord, his hands cupped her elbows. The contact anchored him in an unexpected way. The brown plume in her clever hat trembled slightly. Perhaps she was just as affected as him. That made her even more appealing. Irresistible, in fact.

He took her mouth with his, absorbing the wave of desire that washed over him and sent his heart thundering. Then he eased back. "I look forward to our dance."

"As do I." With a smile, she dipped into a brief curtsy and left, taking all the air in the room with her.

Tomorrow evening couldn't come soon enough.

Chapter Thirteen

NORAH TOLD HERSELF not to watch the ballroom entrance this time. Simon hadn't indicated when he'd arrive and staring at the doorway wouldn't make him appear. Yet there she stood barely able to pull away her gaze.

"Looking for Vanbridge?" Lena asked as she joined her. Lady Havenby was nearby, visiting with several friends. Ella and Marbury were on the opposite side of the room, having just finished a dance.

"Not at all."

Lena raised a brow, bringing heat to Norah's cheeks and making it obvious she didn't believe her. There was no purpose in trying to deceive Lena. Her sister seemed to have an additional sense at times that allowed her to see more than others. She hid it when possible, knowing she was different. Different was rarely welcome. She tended to guard her reaction carefully, sometimes even with her sisters.

"I admit that I expect him soon," Norah relented. "Remember, we plan on speaking with Lord Stanwick about his coin collection." Hopefully, that would be enough to keep Lena from pressing her about her feelings for Simon.

"I was surprised when Lady Havenby told us he had one, since he's reputed to have an impressive painting collection."

Norah followed Lena's gaze to where the lord stood with a

few other guests. "We're hoping he knows of other collectors as well," Norah added.

"Do you think one of them actually has the coin?" Lena's brow furrowed and sent Norah's spirits sinking. She was already anxious about Simon's late arrival, and Lena's doubt didn't help.

"No, but we are continuing to spread the word to keep whoever has it from selling it. If one of them is approached about buying the coin, they'll advise us."

"It seems as if everyone should already know," Lena said. "The news has been the topic of nearly every conversation I've overheard."

"I agree." She glanced at the large clock that stood in the corner. She almost wished the ballroom didn't have one. It was impossible not to watch the minutes tick away with no sign of Simon.

"Perhaps he changed his mind and isn't coming," Lena suggested as she tugged at the fingertips of her gloves. "He was certainly uncomfortable the last time he attended a ball."

"I don't think that's the case. He thought it a wise notion to speak with the lord." She met her sister's gaze, unable to deny a nagging worry that refused to subside. "And we agreed to dance again."

As if realizing just how concerned she was, Lena reached for her hand. "Then no doubt he'll be here soon."

Norah nodded as she squeezed Lena's hand in return. "Will you tell me if you…feel anything about Simon?" She hated to ask because there were times when Lena dearly wanted that knowing feeling to come to her, but it didn't. The gift was limited and couldn't be ordered on command, especially when she'd spent most of her life denying its existence.

"Of course. Always." Lena's gaze dropped along with her hand. "I wish I could be of more assistance."

Norah's heart pinched. She knew how distressing Lena's gift was to her at times. Lena became frustrated when she felt a knowing only to receive it too late to do any good. The worst of which was the day their father had died.

Lena had been so restless that day, but much of it had passed before she'd known beyond a doubt that something was wrong. Too late to attempt a rescue. Too late to save him.

Norah and Ella had both told her she expected too much of herself and her gift. Lena had declared it a curse and asked what purpose it served when she couldn't help those she loved.

Unfortunately, neither Norah nor Ella had an answer. Since that difficult day, Lena preferred to pretend she didn't have the sense. Norah understood but thought denying part of herself wouldn't give her sister peace. She hoped Lena just needed more time to come to grips with her intuitiveness and better understand its limits. The ability truly was a gift, even if it wasn't always dependable. With time, Norah hoped she would see that.

"Thank you." Norah looped her arm through Lena's and turned in the opposite direction of the clock. Staring at it or the entrance wouldn't help anything.

They visited with Lady Havenby along with other friends who stood nearby and soon were asked to dance. But with each quarter of an hour that passed without Simon's arrival, Norah's nerves tightened. Where could he be? What might've happened to keep him from coming?

❧⟫⟫⟩⟨⟨⟨❧

SIMON EXITED THE carriage in front of the museum. "I'll only be a few minutes, Jarvis."

"Very well, my lord."

Evening had come in full, and he was late to the ball. As per usual, he'd lost track of time while working and had been startled by Miles knocking on his door to remind him it was time to dress.

Simon had left his notes on the research he'd done regarding several similar coins to the one found on Oak Island in his desk at the museum. He couldn't remember all the details he'd jotted down and thought it prudent to retrieve the information before he and Norah spoke with Lord Stanwick.

He hoped to earn the older lord's respect by sharing what he knew of the coin and therefore gain any assistance he was willing to offer. Stanwick might prove to be a helpful ally in their search, and Simon wanted to be prepared.

After retrieving his keys from his pocket, Simon unlocked the door and stepped inside, pausing a moment to gain his bearings. The moon was only half full and provided little light. How odd that the darkness seemed to make everything unfamiliar.

He shook his head at the fanciful thought, reminding himself that he knew the museum like the back of his hand. He'd lived in this house for a time before converting it to a museum of his own design. Still, he moved to the podium where the ticket seller normally stood to get the lantern and matches kept there for emergencies.

He felt around the shelf, annoyed when he realized nothing was there. Someone must've moved the blasted thing. He turned back toward the stairs, his eyes already adjusting to the darkness. Thoughts of Norah waiting for him had him taking the stairs two at a time.

Smiling that he was barely out of breath when he reached the upmost floor, he slowed since the darkness was more complete on this floor with its smaller windows.

Within a few minutes, he retrieved his notes from a drawer, folding them to put them in his pocket. He locked the door behind him, then descended the stairs, his thoughts on waltzing with Norah. The pleasant reverie was interrupted by a thump that echoed through the house.

Simon paused, listening closely to determine where the noise had come from. Had it been from inside or outside? Or had he heard it at all?

He moved down the stairs as quietly as possible. Another sound filled the air that brought to mind a crate being slid along the floor. Anger filled him at the thought of someone being here who shouldn't.

But the way sounds echoed in the quiet of the museum, it was difficult to determine exactly where they'd come from. No matter. If he had to search each floor to find whoever was here, he would.

Simon paused at the floor with David Wright's exhibit. Another sliding sound drifted to him, coming from one of the rear rooms they used for storage. He neared the closed door and saw a faint light and shadow moving beneath it. Unease shivered along his spine. Something was amiss. Anger propelled him forward, and he reached for the knob just as the scuff of a shoe sounded behind him.

He started to turn only to have pain erupt in his skull. Then all went black.

⟫⟪

NORAH CURTSIED AFTER finishing a dance with Viscount Worley, one of her favorite partners on the rare occasion she could convince him to dance. His black evening attire was accented with a gold and black striped waistcoat, his dark hair neatly parted in the center.

"Thank you, my lord."

His brown eyes sparkled with warmth. He bowed and offered his elbow to escort her from the dance floor. "The pleasure is mine. Before I return you to Lady Havenby's side, why don't you tell me what's wrong?"

"I don't know what you mean," Norah protested, though it sounded weak even to her ears.

"Come now. Surely, we're friends of the sort who don't need to pretend with one another." Worley turned them, making it clear he intended to take a circuitous route back to Lady Havenby to give them ample time to visit.

"I was expecting Vanbridge, but he has yet to arrive." Even

now, Norah glanced at the entrance to the ballroom, something she'd done more times than she could count.

"Vanbridge at another ball? Surely that's as unlikely as the moon descending to the earth."

"True," she agreed with a laugh. "But we spoke of it just yesterday, and he liked the idea of asking Lord Stanwick about his coin collection."

"That is a fine idea."

"Vanbridge thought so, too, yet he isn't here." Norah didn't mention the dance they'd planned, even if that was one of the reasons she worried at his absence. Simon had acted as if he were looking forward to it as much as she was.

"Odd. While the marquess tends to be reclusive, he is a man of his word."

Worley's words only made her more concerned.

Norah caught movement out of the corner of her eyes to see Lena approach. "Something's wrong," her sister whispered, her eyes dark with concern.

"What is it?" Worley asked, his brown gaze darting between the sisters.

"Lena agrees that Simon should've been here by now." Norah didn't want to reveal the true reason. "I'm going to take the carriage to see if—"

Worley shook his head. "You jest. If you feel that strongly, Marbury and I will venture to his home and see if anything is amiss." He skimmed the crowd to look for his friend and moved Norah in that direction with Lena at her side. "Though you do realize chances are he lost track of the time."

"Possibly." But a glance at Lena's face was all it took for Norah to think otherwise. "I do appreciate you checking."

"I'm happy to. We shall return within the hour. No doubt we'll have Vanbridge with us, as well."

"Excellent," Norah said, relieved that Worley had offered.

He left them with Lady Havenby and, after a few quick words with Marbury, the pair left.

"How concerning to think something could've happened to Vanbridge," Ella said as she joined them. "Do you truly believe that?"

"He said he'd be here but isn't." Norah knew that for certain, regardless of whether Lena sensed anything. Added to that was the tight ball of worry in her chest. While she knew he often lost track of time, surely his servants would've reminded him. "I don't think he's home."

"Then where?" Ella asked.

Norah glanced at Lena. "The museum," they both said at the same time.

"But it's been closed for hours," Ella reminded them.

"Yes, but it would be more likely for him to have forgotten the time while working there," Norah said. "I'll see if I can catch Worley and Marbury."

"I'll advise Lady Havenby that you're not feeling well and we're returning home." Ella hurried away.

Norah made her way through the crowded ballroom as quickly as possible, aware Lena was directly behind her. They rushed outside and hurried down the steps, only to see a carriage pulling out of the drive.

"I do believe that was Marbury's," Lena said.

"Then we shall take our carriage to the museum." Norah hurried toward a waiting footman to request theirs be brought around.

"I'll gather our things and tell Ella to hurry." Lena rushed back inside.

Within a few minutes, their carriage pulled up to the front. Norah explained to Samuel, the driver, where they wanted to go as Ella and Lena joined them.

"Please hurry. This is an urgent matter," Ella told Samuel before he could protest. He wouldn't dare contradict her.

"Very well, miss." After handing them up, James, the footman, hopped onto his post at the back, and they were off at a fast pace through the dark streets.

"I have to think Leo and Worley will come to the museum once they find Vanbridge isn't home." Ella glanced out the window before turning to look at Norah and Lena, her determined expression visible in the dim carriage light. "But until they arrive, what is our plan?"

Norah had already considered the possibilities—either he was still working or had forgotten something there. "We'll check his office first."

"Will we be able to get inside?" Ella asked.

"Excellent question." Norah hated to think they couldn't find a way in. "We'll soon find out. I would think his carriage and driver would be waiting for him if he's there."

"True. We'll have additional assistance then."

"I'm so pleased you're both with me," Norah said. "Thank you."

"Of course." Ella managed a smile. "We shall get through the situation together like we have done countless times before."

Norah reached for both their hands, appreciating her sisters more than ever. "Together," she agreed. She only hoped Simon was well.

The remainder of the brief trip was completed in silence. Norah imagined Simon looking up from his desk, startled at the sight of the three of them in their ball gowns as they invaded his office. Yet, somehow, she was certain that wasn't what would happen.

"Remember what Mother always told us," Ella said with a firm look in Norah's direction. "Don't borrow trouble."

Norah nodded. "There's no purpose in thinking the worst."

"Exactly," Lena murmured. Her lack of conviction had Norah glancing out the window again to see how much farther they had to go, though it was difficult to tell even with the gaslit streets.

Soon the carriage slowed to a halt before the museum. The footman lowered the step and opened the door before Norah had scooted to the edge of the seat to alight.

She stepped out to see Simon's carriage just ahead and hurried toward it. Though the horses' reins were tied off, the driver was nowhere to be seen. Her stomach tightened as she hurried up the steps to the museum. "The driver must be inside with Simon."

James followed them up the stairs and reached the door first. "Allow me, please."

Norah nodded, grateful he'd thought to bring one of the carriage lights along.

As she'd suspected, the front door was unlocked. James stepped inside, then held the door for them. "The place is quiet as a tomb."

Norah tightened her lips, not appreciating his choice of words. She considered calling out, but the silence kept her from doing so. Where were Simon and his driver?

"I don't remember the museum being this eerie, do you?" Lena asked in a whisper as she looked about.

"Definitely not. Although we've never been here in the dark." Ella gestured toward the stairs. "We'll follow you, Norah."

Norah led the way with James directly behind her, holding the light aloft. The swinging glow was welcome yet made their surroundings even more unsettling as the shadows danced around them.

They reached the first floor of exhibits and Norah paused briefly. "Simon?" For some reason, she couldn't bring herself to call for him too loudly. Whether a part of her feared someone was in the building who wished them ill or fear of finding something was truly wrong with Simon, she couldn't say. Neither option was appealing.

After a moment of listening, she continued up the next flight of stairs to where their father's exhibit was. Again, she paused. "Simon?"

An odd sound reached her, almost animal-like. Goose pimples ran over her flesh as she looked at her sisters. Their startled expressions confirmed the noise hadn't been her imagination.

Though she couldn't think of what might make the sound,

there was only one way to find out. With James at her side and hands clenched, she moved toward their father's exhibit, dread and hope filling her in equal measure.

Chapter Fourteen

"SIMON?"

Simon frowned, uncertain if he'd heard a voice. Not with the pounding in his head making it impossible to think, let alone focus. A gentle hand settled on his shoulder as he laid on his side, the touch somehow helping to ease the hammering inside his skull.

"What happened?"

The feminine tone was familiar, but he had difficulty understanding the words. They sounded muffled, as if they came from another room. Then a hand gently touched his cheek and anchored him. He wasn't alone. Relief seeped into him as his thoughts slowly cleared.

"Where are you hurt?" Those hands roamed along his back before skimming his temple and cheek. He couldn't help but moan as her fingers grazed the painful spot on the back of his head.

"There," he managed to say.

"Bring the light closer."

He kept his eyes closed but could sense the light.

"Oh, goodness," she said as she examined the injury, causing him to wince. "That is a terrible lump. It's bleeding."

Simon forced his eyes open with the hope of making sense of the situation. Norah shouldn't be here. Worry flooded him, and he lifted to his elbow, only to have his head ache all the more, the room swinging alarmingly around him.

"Don't move, Simon. Not until you feel well enough."

He studied Norah, who knelt beside him, then glanced about to see he was in the museum. His memory of the moments leading up to the blow slowly returned.

"Do you know what happened?"

"Someone hit me." He lifted a hand to test the tender spot but immediately regretted it. Even the slight touch hurt like hell. Still, he managed to sit upright. He drew a slow breath, then another. The pain in his head made him nauseated.

"Did you see who it was?"

The lantern shifted. Norah's two sisters and her footman became visible.

"No." He placed his elbows on his upright knees, willing his brain to start functioning again.

"Are you injured anywhere else?" Norah asked.

"I don't think so." He was careful not to shake his head. "I wanted my notes and realized I'd left them at the museum." He frowned at Norah. "How did you come to be here?"

"When you didn't arrive at the ball, I started to worry."

"You thought to look here?"

"Marbury and Worley went to your home to see if you were there," she explained. "We thought this might be more likely."

"Jarvis, my driver, was waiting for me." Alarm filled him at the thought of the older servant.

"Your carriage is out front, but we didn't see any sign of him."

Simon shifted to rise, only to hiss when his head felt like it would split open.

Norah placed her hand on his arm, her expression pinched with concern. "Don't move yet. You need more time."

Ella leaned forward. "Norah, why don't we leave you to watch over Simon? James, Lena, and I will look for the driver."

"Excellent idea." Norah glanced at Simon before looking back at Ella. "Call out if you find him."

"Be careful." Simon directed the order to the servant, hating how weak his voice sounded, but his aching skull made him feel positively ill. "Whoever struck me could still be in the museum." He was relieved the sisters had their footman with them.

"We shall take care, my lord," the footman said with a bow. The man lit a nearby wall sconce, then followed Ella, holding the lantern aloft.

Soon he could hear her calling for Jarvis, her voice echoing through the quiet of the museum.

"Oh, Simon." Norah scooted closer and ran a finger along his brow, her cool touch incredibly soothing. "I'm so sorry this happened. Why would someone hit you? Surely the museum was closed."

"Yes. The front door was locked." He patted his pocket to make certain he still had his keys. "I left it open while I ran up to my office but thought nothing of it since Jarvis was waiting outside."

He looked over his shoulder, careful to move slowly, relieved his memory was returning. "I heard what sounded like a crate sliding along the floor and went to investigate. Then I heard footsteps behind me. As I turned to see who it was, they hit me."

"My goodness. Then there was more than one person in here. What could they have been doing?" She glanced around but little moonlight shone through the small window by the stairs.

"I don't know, but I intend to find out." Simon managed to get to his knees, grateful for Norah's arm to help balance him. "First I want to find Jarvis."

He rose to his feet, head spinning so much that he closed his eyes briefly, willing away the pain.

"Are you certain you feel well enough to walk?" Norah kept her arm wrapped tight around him. "We should call for a doctor."

"No need." Thanks to her supportive grip, he thought he could walk. He wasn't about to admit how weak he felt.

Before they took more than a few steps, voices sounded in

the hall.

"We found him!" Lena called from the first level.

"Thank goodness." Norah heaved a relieved sigh that nearly matched his own.

"I hope his head doesn't feel like mine," Simon said.

The faint glow of the lantern drew nearer, and four figures became visible. Simon's gaze latched onto Jarvis, pleased to see him upright, though Lena held his arm.

"I'm so sorry, my lord," the servant said. "When you didn't return, I came looking for you. Some bloke snuck up on me from behind." His outrage matched Simon's.

"Are you well, Jarvis?" Simon asked.

"A bit of a bump." He reached up to gingerly touch his head. "Nothing serious."

But Simon noted how his hand trembled. He was obviously more shaken than he admitted.

"I'm pleased to hear that." Simon reached to clasp the man's shoulder, already feeling better to know he wasn't badly hurt. "Did you see who hit you?"

"No, my lord. Sorry to admit that I didn't see whoever it was."

"There was more than one," Simon said. Before he could suggest they look in the area where he'd heard the crate moving, more voices echoed in the entrance below.

"Ella?" Marbury's voice was recognizable despite the rather frantic tone.

"Here." She hurried over to the stairs. "We are all up here."

The rush of footsteps reached them, followed quickly by Marbury and Worley, who also held a lantern. Marbury's fierce expression eased as his gaze found his betrothed. He took her hand, the tautness in his face softening at the contact.

The intimacy of their silent communication made Simon realize just how much they cared for one another. A pang of longing swept over him as he wondered what it might be like to share that sort of relationship with a woman. Of their own accord, his eyes sought Norah, who also watched the moment. Her smile suggested this wasn't the first time she'd seen the connection the pair had.

"What happened?" Marbury asked as he shifted his attention to Simon.

Simon explained, with Jarvis adding his version.

"I want to look around to see if we can tell what they were doing." Simon gestured in the direction of the sound he'd heard beyond Wright's exhibit.

"Shouldn't we send for a doctor to examine you both?" Norah asked. "Investigating can wait until the morning."

"That might be too late." Simon glanced at Marbury, hoping his friend understood.

"He has a point," Marbury agreed. "Worley and I can certainly look, but we might not know if anything is amiss."

"Lead the way," Worley said as he lifted the lantern.

With reluctance, Simon stepped away from Norah. The ground heaved beneath his feet at first and then settled, much to his relief. "I thought it came from over here."

He walked through the exhibit, looking around carefully for a crate and anything out of place. In truth, he wasn't certain he could concentrate well enough to know, but still, he had to try.

"Anything?" Marbury asked as he, too, searched the area.

"No."

"What's this?" Worley bent low to pick up something off the floor. "Looks like a bit of straw."

"Might be packing material from the crate I heard." Simon took it from Worley but couldn't tell what it came from. "Unfortunately, it's rather common and used to pack various items."

The straw was near the Aztec exhibit, though nothing appeared to be wrong. At least, not that he could tell in his current state.

His distress must've shown on his face, for Marbury suggested, "Now that we have a better idea of what we're looking for, why don't Worley and I search a bit more and meet the rest of you downstairs?"

Though he didn't like leaving the search to someone else, Simon couldn't do much more until he felt better. "I would appreciate that."

Simon returned to the others, his world settling as Norah took his arm once again. He covered her hand with his own, not caring if her sisters noticed. Right now, he needed her and was grateful for her presence.

"How is he?" Norah asked the moment Fletcher opened the door at Simon's residence the following afternoon.

The butler bowed and gestured for her to enter with the usual grand sweep of his arm as he held the door. "He is in his study, refusing to remain abed." The disapproval in his tone nearly made Norah smile as she shared a look with Lena, who had accompanied her, along with their maid.

"That sounds like him." Norah shook her head. "We'd like to see him if possible." At the butler's frown, she quickly added, "We won't stay long."

"Very well."

"Has he eaten?" Norah bit her lower lip, remembering how Ella's appetite had been off for a few days after she'd been hit on the head.

"Not especially well," Fletcher answered.

"Perhaps you could bring tea," Norah suggested, wishing there was more she could do to aid Simon's recovery.

Lena nodded in approval. "Smaller meals worked best for Ella, didn't they?"

"I remember that, as well," Norah agreed as they followed Fletcher down the corridor to Simon's study.

The butler knocked on the door and opened it to reveal Simon resting on the couch with his eyes closed and a brightly woven blanket over his legs. The sight of his rather pale face caught Norah's breath, bringing a wave of emotion over her.

"I'll speak to Mrs. Fletcher about tea," the butler said in a quiet voice before departing.

"I forgot to mention something to Dorothy," Lena advised in a whisper. "I'll return directly."

Norah frowned, unable to think what that might be. Then Lena winked, making it clear she was giving Norah a moment to greet Simon in private. She could've hugged Lena for her thoughtfulness.

She turned back to Simon as Lena stepped out, reluctant to wake him when he was resting. Ella had taken frequent naps while recovering from her injury, so Norah had to think it was normal, even if she didn't care for how pale he looked.

She walked slowly forward, the rustle of her gown audible in the quiet study. A fire burned cheerfully in the hearth. Her breath caught when she saw Simon watching her.

He smiled. "Norah."

That was all it took for her to hurry to his side. She sat on the edge of the couch, taking his hand in hers. "How are you?"

"How is it that you keep appearing in the most unexpected places?"

"I had to see how you were." She tugged off a glove to run a hand along his forehead. The fact that he hadn't sat up was enough for her to know he still didn't feel particularly well.

"Fine."

She shook her head. "I don't believe you. How are you truly?"

"My head aches."

Norah waited, certain there was more.

"And I feel slightly nauseated."

She raised a brow.

"Tired as well."

"As expected." She nodded. "Ella felt much the same way

when she received a blow to the head."

"What happened to her?"

Unable to resist, she ran her fingers over his brow, hoping to ease the ache. "She entered an antique shop by herself when she thought she saw someone we knew. The owner didn't care for her questions and thought to frighten her, resulting in a shelf falling on top of her."

"Good heavens." His brow furrowed. "That's terrible."

"Yes, it was. Something heavy struck her. Speaking of which, can I see how your injury looks?"

"Yes, but Miles already looked at it and declared I will live."

"Your valet?" she asked as she rose and bent close to locate the lump. He might not be feeling his best, but he was still so appealing. His scent begged her to breathe it in to better enjoy it. His hair was soft beneath her fingers as she moved it aside to look.

"I believe I mentioned that he was in the military for many years. He tended more than his share of injuries."

The lump was large, but the cut wasn't overly deep. "Are you certain you don't want a doctor to have a look to be sure?"

"Quite sure," he said dryly.

"Very well, though I'd feel better if you did." She returned to her seat at his side. "What of Jarvis?"

"Much the same as me. I ordered him back to bed."

"I'm surprised he listened, since you are up and about."

"As you can see, I didn't go far. I hoped to get some work done, but reading is not pleasurable at the moment."

She gave him a sympathetic look. "I would guess not. Surely you can take a day or two away from your work without it causing problems."

"I suppose."

She had to laugh when he sounded more like a young lad denied a sweet treat rather than a man denied his work.

He smiled as his gaze held on her face. "If I felt better, I would kiss you."

The flutters in her middle immediately came to life as if in full agreement. She leaned close, her hand cupping his cheek. "Since you can't, I will." Her eyes closed as she pressed her lips to his, the contact causing her body to pulse.

"Lovely," he whispered when she drew back.

"Yes, it was."

"I meant you." Then he reached a hand along her neck to draw her close for another kiss.

Her heart filled with a tenderness that frightened her. Or was it something more? The description seemed inadequate for what flowed through her. His hand that held her elbow was warm, the one behind her neck gentle, giving her the option to pull back if she wanted.

The problem was that she didn't. If anything, she wanted to settle along his length and continue this.

A throat clearing just outside the door had her jerking back to stare into Simon's green eyes. "Lena is with me."

He blinked as if it took a moment for her words to register. "Good."

Good? At the moment, Norah thought it terrible. She straightened but decided against moving away from him. She didn't want to. A glance behind her showed Lena peeking around the door.

"Good afternoon." She stepped into the room, glancing about with curiosity before her gaze settled on Simon. "How is the patient today?"

"In pain," Norah supplied, unable to resist running another hand over his brow.

Lena nodded, her expression sympathetic. "Head injuries are so painful."

"Are there any injuries that aren't?" Norah asked, still irritated that their kisses had been interrupted.

"I am certain some are worse than others." Lena came closer, ignoring Norah's poor mood. "Did you have any revelations about the evening's events?"

"Unfortunately, no." Simon's lips tightened. "Some dirt and more straw were discovered but not enough to provide a true clue. I sent word to the museum director to take inventory of the exhibits to make certain nothing is missing and to have the locks changed again, though I'm not sure that will solve the problem. The police came by earlier to speak with me as well."

"I'm just relieved your injury wasn't worse." Norah couldn't imagine what she would've done if they'd discovered a lifeless Simon on the floor, something she'd considered numerous times during the night. The thought made her shudder.

"As am I," Simon agreed as he sat upright and put his feet on the floor. "But I still intend to find out who was behind it."

"Do you think it's related to our father's missing coin?" Lena asked.

"Yes, I do."

Before Norah could suggest they worry about that once he was feeling better, Fletcher entered with a tea tray. Norah rose to move out of his way, and he set it on the low table in front of the couch, another new addition to the room.

"We thought you might enjoy some tea and a little something to eat," Norah said.

"Mrs. Fletcher included your favorite cake, my lord." Fletcher gestured toward the tray as if their attention wasn't already focused on the piles of biscuits, small sandwiches, and thin slices of frosted cake.

"Please thank her for me," Simon said with a smile.

Fletcher carried a chair close for Lena, and Norah settled onto the couch, careful to keep a respectable distance between her and Simon.

They passed a pleasant half-hour visiting as they had tea. Norah was pleased to see Simon eat several of the selections while he shared the history behind some of the more interesting exhibits in the museum.

Norah watched him closely, noting when his cheeks once again lost their color. She leaned close to touch his arm. "I do believe we should take our leave and allow you to rest."

"No need."

She rose anyway. "I am certain with a good night's sleep, you'll feel better tomorrow."

Soon she and Lena were settled in the carriage. "Thank you for coming with me," Norah said. Though she knew that having her younger, unmarried sister along hadn't provided a proper chaperone, she liked to think these were extenuating circumstances.

"Of course. The pleasure was mine." She held Norah's gaze for a long moment. "I like Vanbridge."

Norah smiled. "So do I." Then she turned her attention to the passing scenery before her sister could ask her just how much she liked him. That was a question to which she didn't have an answer. But she feared it was too much.

Chapter Fifteen

THE FOLLOWING MORNING, Simon gritted his teeth, willing away the pounding of his head as he walked up the front steps to the museum. He was dismayed by how much he still hurt but couldn't wait any longer to speak with Stockton and the other employees.

With each hour that passed, his chances of finding the persons who'd struck him and Jarvis lessened. At least, that was how he felt. Then there was David Wright's missing coin to consider, not to mention the other items. He had no time to feel ill. If only his head would cooperate.

Norah's visit the previous day had been a pleasant surprise. He'd truly enjoyed having tea with her and Lena. They were wonderful company and had taken his thoughts away from his pain and frustration. The interlude had done more to improve his well-being than he could've guessed.

Mrs. Fletcher had been overjoyed to prepare a "proper tea," as she called it, and had been certain to tell him after the ladies departed. No doubt she hoped to encourage similar events in the future. He didn't have the heart to tell her that was unlikely.

After the sisters left, he had plenty of time to think about what had happened the previous evening. Whoever was taking the artifacts had made the effort to injure both him and Jarvis when they could have just as easily hid or left.

The situation had become very personal.

Stockton had sent word that he'd completed the inventory Simon requested, but nothing else was missing, which was puzzling. What had those people been doing if not taking artifacts? Or had Simon and Jarvis interrupted them before they could steal what they wanted? A bit of straw on the floor was hardly enough of a clue to follow.

He was more determined than ever to uncover the identity and motivation of the person behind this. If they'd hit Simon to scare him off, they were in for a rude awakening.

He nodded at Mr. Johnson, who stood near the front door, only to pause as the employee hurried forward.

"My lord," he said with a bow. "I am terribly sorry to hear of the events that unfolded the other evening. I hope you are recovering."

"I am. Thank you for your concern."

"I'm pleased to hear that." Johnson nervously glanced about. "Do you feel we should be concerned for our safety?"

"I sincerely hope not." Yet the question made Simon worry all the more. Perhaps they should be. "The police are working with us to uncover the thieves."

The man nodded, his expression relieved. "Excellent. So happy to hear that. Please know that if I see or hear anything unusual, I will be certain to report it."

"Thank you." Simon continued up the stairs and entered the exhibit area, unsurprised when the next employee with whom he spoke said something similar.

By the time he spoke with Emerson on the next floor, he was beginning to think they all had met and decided what to say to him. He detested thinking any employee was concerned for his personal well-being. The blame for that fell squarely on Simon's shoulders.

He stalked up the stairs to Stockton's office, his mood black. Of course, where else would the man be except sitting at his desk?

"Stockton."

"My lord." The director stood to bow with a smile. For some reason, the smile irritated Simon to no end. "Good to see you up and about so soon. Are you sure you feel well enough to be here?"

"I'm fine." It was even more annoying to realize Stockton might be right. The nausea was returning, along with a worsening headache. If he turned his head too quickly, the room tilted. He wouldn't be able to stay long if he wanted to walk out of the museum on his own two feet. That made him doubly glad he'd ordered Jarvis to remain home to rest.

"Thank goodness." Stockton shook his head. "How terrible to think someone was in the museum at night."

But not that he and Jarvis had been struck? Simon didn't think he'd ever understand the director. "Did you change the locks as I requested?"

"Of course." He reached into a drawer and pulled forth a set of keys. "I took the liberty of having your office door lock changed as well. Here are the new ones."

"Thank you. Who else has these?"

"Only you and I. Given recent events, I will be personally locking the building each evening as well as unlocking it in the morning."

Simon frowned, surprised the director wasn't already taking that precaution. The museum hours weren't so long that he couldn't. What else did Simon not know about the man's routine? That, too, was Simon's fault. "I'm pleased to hear that. Any further updates on the inventory?"

"Each exhibit has been accounted for. We didn't find anything more missing."

"What of the storage room? Have any crates been moved?" He was still certain that was what he'd heard the night he'd been struck.

"Not that we could tell." Stockton frowned, his bushy brows drawing near the edge of his spectacles. "As I mentioned before, a bit of dust and straw on the floor, but that's all. I can't imagine who it was or what they were attempting. It seems your appearance prevented them from taking anything. They must've fled afterward."

Simon watched the man closely but couldn't tell if he was lying. Stockton met Simon's gaze without hesitation. Still, a sense of unease crawled along Simon's skin, suggesting something was amiss.

Simon released the breath he hadn't realized he'd been holding. "Yes, that must've been it." If he accused the director of anything now, Stockton would only deny it.

Simon needed to follow up with Marbury and Worley to see if they'd discovered anything more about Stockton. Perhaps allowing him to think Simon trusted him was the best way to proceed. If he was guilty and thought he was tricking Simon, he might take a misstep.

Or perhaps it was just the pounding of Simon's head that convinced him to leave the man to his duties. He turned toward his office, briefly closing his eyes with the hope he could manage another half hour before he had to give into the pain and return home to rest. The realization only made him angrier at whoever had struck him.

⇢⟫⟪⇠

Norah studied Simon for a long moment as she joined him before Stanwick House the following day, along with her maid. He still looked pale, and the shadows beneath his eyes suggested he was either tired or in pain. Both, more than likely.

"Are you certain you want to do this now?" she asked.

Since Simon hadn't been able to attend the ball, he'd sent a message to Lord Stanwick asking if they could have a few minutes of his time to discuss his coin collection. From what Simon had shared, Stanwick had been happy to agree.

"Of course." He raised the gleaming brass pineapple knocker

and tapped it three times. "Why do you ask?"

"Simon." She waited until he met her gaze. "Surely, you're still hurting. It wouldn't matter if we waited another day or two to speak with him."

He managed a smile, which helped calm her worry, if only slightly. "In all honesty, my head hurts whether I am doing something or resting. At least I'm no longer sick to my stomach."

"I shall take that as a sign of improvement." She frowned, hating that he hurt. "I still wonder if you should consult a doctor. Perhaps the injury was more serious than we realized."

"Mrs. Fletcher has provided tea from meadowsweet flowers to ease the pain, which I've been drinking before bed. It seems to help."

Before Norah could respond, the door swung open to reveal an elderly butler. After taking Simon's card, he showed them to Lord Stanwick's study, where the older man rose from behind his desk to greet them.

"Good afternoon." In his fifth decade, Lord Stanwick was a tall man with grey hair and a commanding presence. Horses were his passion. He rode most mornings and enjoyed the races as well. Marbury had shared that Stanwick won an unusual coin when he'd bet on a race and that had started his collection.

"Thank you for seeing us." Simon shook his hand and Norah curtsied.

"My pleasure." Stanwick nodded as he gestured for them to take a seat, while Dorothy remained by the door. "I understand you had an unfortunate encounter the night of our ball."

"Indeed." Simon skimmed over the details of what happened.

"Struck from behind. That's a cowardly act." Stanwick seemed rather fascinated by Simon's brush with danger, since he asked several more questions.

"We have to believe David Wright's missing coin is connected to the situation," Simon added.

"I was saddened to learn of your father's passing," Stanwick said as he cast a sympathetic look at Norah. "I had the pleasure of meeting him before he married your mother."

"Oh?" Norah was surprised. Few people she'd met had known him.

"His enthusiasm for treasure hunting was unparalleled. I wasn't able to attend the unveiling," Stanwick continued, "but I did have the chance to visit the exhibit last week. I found it provided a vivid taste of what it would be like to dig for treasure."

"Miss Wright experienced treasure hunting firsthand." Simon glanced at Norah.

"Indeed," she said. "My father was intrigued by what he might find if he dug just a little deeper."

"Collecting coins is a bit like digging for treasure in that it can easily become an obsession," Stanwick mused.

"That is why we wanted to visit with you," Simon explained. "As a collector, we thought there might be a chance someone could approach you to buy it. We're speaking with as many people as possible just in case."

"Yes," Norah added. "One never knows who might have helpful information."

"I haven't been offered the coin but will certainly let you know if I am." Stanwick kept his gaze on Simon. "Can you share a few details?"

Simon tipped his head to Norah. "No one knows more about it than Miss Wright."

After Norah described it, Stanwick said, "Sounds rather unusual. I will mention it to my fellow collectors, as well." He asked a few questions about Oak Island but directed them to Simon, much to Norah's frustration.

Again, Simon shifted the questions to Norah to answer. She appreciated him involving her in the conversation rather than talking around her, though she had the feeling Lord Stanwick would've preferred Simon be the one to speak, based on the dubious looks the lord gave her.

However, she was pleased to think Simon's work had created interest and made a difference in helping to ensure that her father and his work be remembered. She shared additional information about the island and why her father had thought treasure was buried there, beyond what had been displayed in the exhibit.

"So, you see, as long ago as 1795, searchers have been digging on the island," Norah said. "But it is not an easy place to dig. My father and his partner brought a large steam boiler and pumps to the site when I was young to attempt to remove the water that often floods the shafts. Unfortunately, that wasn't successful."

By the time she finished, Stanwick leaned forward, appearing to be riveted. "Fascinating," he said. "I appreciate learning more about the history of the island."

"What particular type of coins interest you?" Simon asked the lord, seeming anxious to return to the purpose of their visit.

Lord Stanwick was more than happy to share details about his collection and showed them several he kept in his desk. The excitement in his tone and glittering passion in his eyes as he showed them a gold Roman coin was unsettling. The lord spoke of the value of the coins more than their history.

In Norah's opinion, the worth of such objects was in the story behind them. That was why she enjoyed Simon's museum so much. He took the time to share the accounts of the objects as well as those who had found them and their journey. Not so much information that it was boring, but enough to make one wonder.

"What of you, Miss Wright?"

Norah's eyes widened at Lord Stanwick's question, dismayed to realize she'd lost track of the conversation.

"Why do coins catch your interest?" Simon asked her, much to her relief.

"The markings," she answered. "Looking into what is stamped on a coin not only tells us where they came from but helps explain what was important to the people who made them."

"I suppose I never thought of it like that," Stanwick said, looking at Norah with what she dared to think was respect in his eyes.

Norah hoped she'd given the older gentleman something to consider—something beyond the monetary value of his coins.

"What did you think?" Simon asked as they descended the front steps to return to their carriages with Dorothy following behind.

"It was interesting to speak with him but not particularly helpful." Norah glanced at Simon, waiting for him to share his opinion.

"I would agree. Unfortunately, I'm not certain if we could truly count on him to contact us if he's given the chance to purchase the coin."

Norah halted mid-step. "Truly?"

"I would hazard a guess that Lord Stanwick has already moved from collecting to obsession. While intrigued by your suggestion to consider the history of the ones he has, I have to think the importance for him is in owning them."

"You sound as if you speak from experience."

"My uncle, the late marquess. He was obsessed with owning as much as he could."

"Is that why you chose to turn his home into a museum?" she asked as they approached her carriage and stopped.

"In part," Simon answered. "My father loved history and spent much of his time reading about it. He had a few items he'd collected over the years, but the thrill for him was first learning the history and then sharing his knowledge with others. To help them find the enjoyment he did. Much different than my uncle."

Norah watched him closely. "How old were you when you lost your parents?"

Grief tightened his features. "Seven."

Her heart squeezed, and she reached out to touch his arm, all too aware of the maid standing nearby. "Old enough to remember and miss them terribly. I'm so sorry."

"It was difficult." He gave a one-shouldered shrug. "Others have experienced worse."

"May I ask what happened?"

"They were killed in a carriage accident."

Norah wished she could hug him to better express her sympathy but, given the fact that they were standing outside of Lord Stanwick's home, that was impossible. She had lost both her parents as well, but they had died five years apart. Losing both in an instant must've been devastating. Plus, she'd had her sisters to lean on. As an only child, Simon hadn't had anyone.

She pressed a hand to her heart. "I can't imagine."

Simon's gaze held on something in the distance, though she wondered if his thoughts were on those dark days of his youth. "It was difficult."

Difficult? That was an understatement. Her heart hurt for the young boy he'd been. She'd been old enough to understand when her mother died, as opposed to being a child who only wanted his parents to come home.

"I was grateful for my aunt and uncle, my mother's older brother and his wife, who took me in. Taking care of a boy couldn't have been easy, but they did their best."

The way he said it made her think they had failed to fill even a portion of the emptiness inside him. Was it any wonder he'd become reclusive as an adult? Or that his social interactions were awkward at times? Yet those qualities also made him who he was. And that she very much appreciated.

She bit her lip, uncertain what to say or how to comfort him but compelled to try. "You are an amazing man, Simon."

His gaze met hers, his expression puzzled.

"To have come as far as you have given your difficult childhood is a testament to your drive. I think your father would be proud of you for the museum and your research. I know I am."

Simon blinked, suggesting her words surprised him. "Thank you," he said at last.

"You are welcome." Obviously, no one told him that often. If she had the chance, she'd be sure to tell him so again, since he obviously needed to hear it.

Chapter Sixteen

THE SOUND OF voices in the entrance hall interrupted Simon's work the next afternoon. He had been pleased—and relieved—when he woke that morning to only a mild headache. After settling at his desk, he'd written out the facts as well as his questions about both the stolen items and the night of his injury. No surprise that he'd written down more questions than facts.

He, Marbury, and Worley had divided the list of coin dealers Norah had supplied and were steadily working their way through it. He'd also reluctantly agreed, with Marbury's approval, to accept Norah's offer for her and her sisters to visit other museums to advise them of the items missing from his museum.

While he pondered what other steps could be taken to further the investigation, he returned to deciphering the stone carving. Often, clearing his mind by focusing on such a task allowed room for the answers he sought to come forth. The same proved true with boxing. However, he wasn't feeling up to returning to that practice yet. The thought of punching the bag made his head hurt.

A decidedly feminine tone reached his ears from the corridor. His heartbeat sped at the thought of seeing Norah again so soon. He rose to his feet in anticipation, only to have his hopes dashed as his cousin, Anna Clarke, the Countess of Mendenhall, strode into his study with an unhappy Fletcher behind her.

"My apologies, my lord," the butler said with a frown at Anna's back. "Lady Mendenhall declined to wait to see if you were receiving."

"It's all right." Simon didn't bother to greet his cousin. Based on her displeased expression, this wasn't a social call.

Fletcher backed out of the room with one last glower at Anna. Simon noted he didn't offer to serve tea. The servant was quickly learning who was a welcome guest and who wasn't.

"Simon, this situation is ridiculous." Anna gripped her reticule tightly as she glared at him from the opposite side of his desk. As always, she was dressed in the height of fashion. Her pale blue gown trimmed in cream lace set off her dark hair. Her small hat in a darker blue was embellished with a narrow veil that was decorative rather than practical. The sharp lines of her face fit her rather shrewish personality, in his opinion.

She hadn't been especially kind when he'd come to live with her and her family and had taunted him for his somberness. The fact that they'd both lost their mothers hadn't bonded them in any way. Her husband was a pompous ass as far as Simon was concerned, more focused on appearance than character.

Simon had often wondered if Anna was happy in her marriage and with her two young children but knew better than to ask. She'd only view him with scorn as she so often did, much like her late brother had.

"To what are you referring?" While he was feeling better, he wasn't well enough to deal with her demands.

"The museum." Her angry tone and expression made him sigh.

The topic was one on which they'd never agree. He had tried to be respectful of her feelings while moving forward with his plans to open the museum. He'd explained his goal of sharing her father's collection with others. But those efforts had been fruitless.

He gestured for her to sit. "What about the museum?"

She scowled at the chair as if it might be tainted and remained standing. "Your…incident." She waved a gloved hand in his direction.

"My injury?" He was surprised she'd heard of it. But he wasn't surprised that she failed to ask how he was feeling.

"Yes. It is causing too much talk. This is one more reason why you should close the place immediately."

"Because someone hit my driver and me on the head?" Simon wasn't following her logic. Then again, logic was rarely a priority for Anna.

"Your driver?" Her mouth gaped open for a moment. Then she released an exasperated sigh, suggesting that was somehow all his fault. "The story grows worse by the moment. This is outrageous."

"Why don't we proceed to the purpose of your visit?" He sank into his chair, suddenly tired.

"I already stated it—close the museum." Her dark eyes glinted with temper and determination.

"No."

"The least you could do is listen to reason."

"You have yet to share a logical argument to convince me to close it." Simon folded his hands over his stomach, hoping his relaxed pose would add to her anger and cause her to walk out, leaving him in peace.

"I think it's obvious. It was a travesty for you to open our family home to the public to begin with. Now, it's apparently become a dangerous place where people should fear for their personal safety."

"There is no danger to the public. And as I explained before I opened it, the best way to honor your father's memory and his collection is to allow other people to enjoy the items he gathered. You took some of the furnishings and stated you didn't want any of the artifacts."

"Those things wouldn't go well with my décor." Anna lifted her nose as if to ward off guilt for choosing her interior furnishings based on her tastes rather than her father's memory.

"Of course." Simon well knew she'd never liked any of the items her father had collected. Then again, Simon hadn't wanted to live amidst the collection either, hence the reason he'd thought of a museum.

The late marquess had gone too far with his assortment of artifacts, even in Simon's view. He had been more interested in his collection than his children, and Simon would venture to say Anna had become demanding as a child in order to gain his attention. She lived in a world where everything was black and white—either her way or none at all.

"My friends often remark about how upset I must be to have the public walking through my childhood home," she said, adding a sniff for good measure. "Then there are the comments about how, as a child, could I sleep at night, knowing there were mummies in the house. I don't want Father's odd antiquities to become fodder for gossip any more than they already have."

Simon sighed. The argument was one they'd already covered numerous times. "I'm sorry you feel that way. But I am not going to close it." When Anna started to protest, he lifted a hand to silence her. "Again, there is no danger. Not to anyone but me." That much seemed clear. He was the connection, though he couldn't say why he was sure of that. "It will soon pass, and all will return to normal."

He was determined to get to the bottom of it. Then not only the museum but his *life* would return to normal. He brushed aside the realization that returning to his regular routine wasn't as pleasing as it should've been because his quiet existence hadn't included Norah. Once he discovered who was behind the thefts, he wouldn't have an excuse to see her anymore.

The thought had him scowling. While he told himself he would soon readjust to life without her, it wouldn't be the same. He rubbed his chest at the tightness there. "I'm not going to close the museum," he repeated.

Anna stiffened. "Mark my words. This is a mistake, Simon. The blame for any further issues will be on your shoulders." Then she spun away, her gown flaring as she made a dramatic exit.

Simon straightened in his chair. Could Anna have anything to do with the stolen items? Had she hired some unscrupulous characters to break into the museum and steal a few things? Maybe Simon had interrupted them the other night when they'd returned to take something else.

While the suspicion seemed ridiculous on the surface since she hadn't taken any action in the years since he'd opened the museum, he wrote the possibility on his list.

Perhaps he had more enemies than he realized. Who else would benefit from the museum closing?

⊱※⊰

NORAH, LENA, AND Ella entered the Museum of Forgotten Treasures that afternoon, along with Dorothy. The maid took one look at the cluttered interior and sank into a chair near the door with a beleaguered sigh.

"We won't be overly long." Norah attempted to reassure the maid while Ella spoke with the man who sold tickets and requested an audience with the director.

Lena leaned close to her sisters as they waited in the first room of exhibits. "Do you think Sally and Dorothy flipped a coin to see who had to accompany us?"

Ella laughed. "They have both had more than their fair share of visits to shops and museums, haven't they?"

"I would think they might appreciate the opportunity to step out of the house for a time." Norah shook her head. "How can they not enjoy looking at something different?"

Lena frowned as she glanced around. "Even I have to admit that some of the places we've visited have been less than enjoyable."

"True." Ella's gaze followed Lena's. "This one, in particular, is in need of a thorough cleaning."

Norah agreed. But the look on Simon's face the previous day had prompted her to find a way to help. Ella had reluctantly agreed, along with Marbury and Simon, that the three of them could visit a few museums to look around and speak with the directors to share news of the stolen items. Several restrictions had been placed on them to help ensure their safety, including their promise to only go together and only to the museums with which Simon was familiar.

Norah was relieved to take action, even if it meant looking through some of the less popular museums. While the coin and other things were unlikely to be displayed in a place like this, one never knew what might come of a conversation.

"This museum makes me appreciate Vanbridge's all the more," Ella murmured as she studied the nearby artifacts.

She was right, Norah decided. Simon's was a step above all of the ones they had viewed since their arrival in London. Then again, she thought he was a step above as well. The feelings she'd developed for him were concerning. He was forever in her mind from the moment she woke to when she closed her eyes at night. Then there were her dreams. He had appeared in more than one, and they were very unsettling, filled with heated kisses and warm caresses.

Her numerous thoughts of him were shocking. After all, she'd met a fair number of men since arriving in London without giving them a second thought. Was it only because she felt sorry for him? As much as she wished that were the case, she knew it wasn't true. She liked spending time with him. Their conversations were always interesting. He was intelligent and clever, not to mention creative. His concern for his servants and employees was admirable, too.

The man was nearly perfect. The thought made her want to stomp her foot in protest. He was upsetting her carefully laid plans by tugging at her heart.

"What is it?" Lena asked.

Though tempted to brush off the question, Norah knew that

rarely worked with Lena. "I was thinking of Simon and hoping he feels better today."

Lena's expression eased. "As do I." She lifted her chin as she glanced about the room cluttered with items. "Which makes me more determined to help in any way I can."

Norah smiled. "Exactly. Let us look through this room while we're waiting for the director."

"Anything we can do to help," Ella agreed.

After searching so many shops and museums the previous year when they were looking for their father's journal, they worked together like a well-oiled machine. They spread out around the room but stayed within sight of each other. They bent to view the lower shelves and poked into every corner. Lena sorted through a box of items while Ella examined a display case.

When the director joined them nearly a quarter of an hour later, Norah told him about the thefts and described the items.

"We haven't received any new artifacts this month, but I'll be sure to keep watch for anything like you described," the stout man said. "Perhaps the museum should change its locks."

Norah forced a smile and told him that measures had already been taken to prevent further thefts. "If you would send word to the Marquess of Vanbridge if you come across any helpful information, we would appreciate it."

"Of course."

They moved on to the next museum and repeated the process, looking about while they waited for the director. The Seafaring Museum held numerous items, but she wouldn't call them artifacts. Just because something was old didn't mean it was an artifact or an antique.

"I think I shall put together a museum guidebook after we find the coin," Lena said as they stepped out of the museum and breathed some fresh air—as fresh as London air could be. "I shall rate the museums on three factors."

"What might those be?" Ella asked as she brushed away the dust on her gown.

"Organization, cleanliness, and atmosphere." Lena narrowed her blue eyes as she considered the idea. "Some of the lesser-known ones we've visited were quite interesting. But some seem more like a deceased relative's home was cleaned out and someone decided to open a museum with its contents."

"That's how Vanbridge's museum started," Norah confessed.

"I'd forgotten that," Ella said as they settled in the carriage with the relieved maid.

"His uncle was an obsessed collector. Rather than moving out all the items, Simon moved out instead."

Lena smiled. "Clever man."

"Isn't he, though?" Norah asked. Only too late did she realize both her sisters were staring at her with interest. Too much interest. "I admire his intelligence and creativity," she admitted. "I'm sure both of you do as well."

She wasn't willing to admit more when she had yet to sort out her feelings.

Much to her relief, Ella and Lena shared a look, but neither pressed her for details. She needed to take care in the future to avoid revealing how attracted she was to him. If only her heart would listen.

"Oh, my. Who is that delicious looking gentleman?"

Norah turned to follow Lady Clara's gaze at the Fitzbright Ball the following evening, puzzled as to whom she referred when Lady Clara seemed to have analyzed and catalogued every eligible man in sight. This was the lady's fourth season, and she seemed rather desperate for a proposal.

The ballroom was crowded. Lena was dancing, and Lady Havenby stood nearby. Ella visited with Marbury somewhere, though Norah had lost sight of them, making her wonder if they'd found a secluded place to share a private moment.

Norah's breath caught as she watched Simon peruse the crowd from the doorway. It had been three days since she'd last seen him, which felt like an eternity. She had become addicted to his presence in her life. Her mouth was dry, her breathing uneven, her heartbeat rapid. She halted the already concerning mental list. Adding more to it would only increase her worry about how much she was coming to care for him.

Then his gaze found hers, and her entire being hummed, much like she was a harp and he'd plucked one of her strings. She was in serious trouble.

Only too late did she realize she was moving in his direction even as he walked toward her.

"Miss Wright?" Lady Clara called from behind her.

Norah ignored her as her feet continued toward him, aided by her reluctance to be forced to introduce Lady Clara to Simon. This selfish side of her was unwelcome but not a surprise.

She wanted Simon all to herself. There was no denying it. Perhaps seeing him so unexpectedly was what brought forth the truth. She longed to take his hand and lead him to a hidden alcove where they could share a heated kiss. Or more.

Definitely more. Her body trembled at the thought.

Then Simon was standing before her, his deep green eyes holding her gaze. A smile lit their depths before slowly tilting his lips. "Good evening, Norah."

She was truly in serious trouble.

"Simon. I didn't expect to see you here." Only too late did she realize she forgot to curtsy, and she quickly rectified it. However, she didn't think that was the reason the people around them were staring.

He bowed, that delicious smile still in place. "Marbury insisted I come."

I'm pleased he did. She bit back the words, unwilling to say them. Not when admitting how she felt might put another hole in her already crumbling defenses. "Oh?"

"There are a few gentlemen he thinks we should visit with

who will be here this evening."

"I see." She licked her suddenly dry lips, only to notice Simon watching her. Desire pulsed through her, and she nearly waved a hand before her warm face.

Absence truly did make the heart grow fonder.

"Would you care to help me find Marbury?" Simon asked.

She'd rather dance but being in his company was enough for now. "Of course." She took his offered arm and nodded at Lady Havenby, who smiled in return as they passed.

If Norah wasn't careful, the lady would be offering her another warning about Simon and how she shouldn't expect anything from him.

She put the thoughts behind her, reminding herself that the priority was finding the missing items. That was the only reason Simon was here. Not because of her.

"I saw Marbury and Ella in this direction earlier," she said as they started around the perimeter of the room.

Simon's chuckle had her looking at him before following his gaze to where Marbury and Ella entered from the terrace. The satisfied look on Marbury's face and her sister's pink cheeks suggested they had been doing more than simply enjoying a breath of fresh air. Given that their wedding was only a week away, few guests paid them any mind.

When Norah married, she wanted it to be with a happy heart and much excitement for the future, just like Ella. Perhaps Norah, too, would be lucky enough to find a man who wanted at least a few of the same things she did.

The thought had her glancing at Simon from under her lashes. What sort of husband would he be? Given his preference to remain locked in his study, she supposed his wife would be forced to remain home much of the time as well. Though the idea wasn't as terrible as it might've been a month ago now that she'd spent time with him, it still wasn't how she'd envisioned her future. Marriage should be a give and take, in her opinion. Would he agree?

"Vanbridge," Marbury exclaimed as they approached. "Glad to see you made it."

"Needed some air, eh?" Simon asked with a raised brow.

Marbury only grinned while Ella's cheeks grew even more pink.

"Yes. Quite stuffy in here." He cast a warm look in Ella's direction.

The two men visited while Norah studied Ella. She never would've guessed her sister would fall in love. She'd always insisted that seeing Norah and Lena settled was her priority. Norah had been happy to have her sister's attention shifted.

"Do take care, dear sister," Norah said with a smile. "I have to think more people than Simon and I noticed your flushed face after your time on the terrace."

Ella's eyes closed briefly, and she sighed before an exasperated look came over her expression. "I told Leo that. However, I can hardly remember my name after one kiss."

Norah laughed. In truth, it was a relief to think her sister experienced the same problem as Norah did after a kiss with Simon. How nice to know she wasn't the only one who found herself overcome with passion.

"If you ladies will excuse us briefly, we're going to see if Lord Mortenson is in the card room," Marbury said.

"Of course." Ella waved a hand before her face as the men moved away. "I need a moment to compose myself or Lady Havenby will be asking if I'm running a fever."

Norah's spirits sank as she watched Simon depart. Would he bother to find her before he left? Knowing him, he would escape the ball as quickly as possible, which meant a dance was out of the question.

"Let us find ourselves something to drink," Ella suggested. "It is terribly warm in here, isn't it?"

"Not really." Norah couldn't resist teasing her sister. "I find the temperature quite reasonable."

Ella grinned as she looped her arm through Norah's. "You

would be warm if you'd had a moment on the terrace with Vanbridge. Admit it."

Norah only smiled as they made their way to the refreshment room. "I don't know of what you're speaking."

"You can't fool me," Ella whispered. "You look at him with more than admiration in your eyes."

Her comment caused Norah a small measure of panic. Were her feelings so obvious? What if Simon noted how she felt? She lifted her eyes to the ceiling at the ridiculous question. They'd shared more than one passionate kiss. He already knew some of how she felt. That didn't mean he knew of the depth of her attraction. She couldn't claim to know how he regarded her other than enjoying a kiss or two. Or three.

Her face heated as she counted how many kisses they'd shared. How was that done? Did each press of their lips count as one? If so—

"Norah."

Her gaze jerked to Ella, who raised a brow with an amused expression. "I asked when Vanbridge arrived."

"Oh. Only a few minutes ago."

"So, you haven't yet danced?"

"No. But I hope we do."

Ella squeezed her arm. "I like him, in case it matters."

"I like him, too." Norah smiled at her sister. "And it matters."

What to do about it was another matter entirely.

Chapter Seventeen

THE HOUR WAS still relatively early when Simon's carriage rumbled through the streets, but he knew Robert Thompson would be in his office, as he was each and every morning. He couldn't believe he hadn't thought to reach out to the older man sooner. The museum owner had served as a mentor to Simon while he'd gone through the numerous steps required to open his own establishment.

Mr. Thompson was one of the few people whose company Simon had always enjoyed. Remorse filled him as he realized how long it had been since he'd last called on him.

Marbury and Worley were continuing efforts to visit the coin collectors on Norah's list, which Simon appreciated. However, he wasn't convinced that was the best use of his own time. The previous evening at the ball had been more enjoyable than he'd expected but hadn't left him feeling as if he'd accomplished anything.

Well, that wasn't completely true.

Simon smiled as his thoughts drifted to his dance with Norah. Time with her was something to treasure.

He never would've thought dancing could be so pleasurable. The reason was solely because of his partner. Norah was delightful even if he knew his time with her was nothing more than a brief interlude. A flash in his life that would soon be gone.

She'd move on to a man both she and her grandfather considered a suitable match. The thought made his chest ache and threatened to ruin his good humor, so he quickly shoved it aside.

Simon was relieved to feel much like his normal self today. He'd even done some light boxing earlier, pleased his headache was gone. That had lifted his spirits, but Norah was mostly to thank for his improved disposition.

The realization caused him to sigh. He was becoming dependent on seeing her. The thrill that ran through him each time they were together was concerning. The sooner he found the missing items, the better. Perhaps today would bring the answers he sought. Or at least point him in the proper direction.

The carriage drew to a halt, and Simon hopped out to stare at the Museum of Olden Days. Several years had passed since he'd last been inside, but it looked much the same from the outside—a two-story brownstone with a neat and tidy exterior. Mr. Thompson focused on smaller artifacts important to the daily lives of civilizations. His collection included clothing and uniforms, weapons, cooking vessels and utensils, and the like.

Simon had thoroughly enjoyed visiting the place in his younger days.

After a brief conversation with the young man who watched the front entrance, Simon was shown to Thompson's office in the rear of the building.

"Simon." Thompson's broad smile as he strode around his desk to shake Simon's hand made him feel all the guiltier for not having visited sooner. "Good to see you." He studied Simon for a long moment, making Simon wonder what he saw.

Thompson had aged in the past few years. His hair was nearly all white and lines bracketed his eyes. A bushy white mustache hid much of his mouth. But the kindness in his eyes was a constant.

"And you, sir."

Thompson bowed. "Forgive me, my lord. I too often forget that you inherited."

Simon bit back the reply that he wished he could, too. "Think nothing of it." Such things didn't bother him. Besides, he'd known Thompson long before he'd become a marquess.

"What brings you by this morning?" Thompson asked as he gestured toward the chair before his desk.

"I wish it were simply to visit with an old friend. However, three items have gone missing from my museum." He explained the situation, including the injury to himself and Jarvis.

"That's terrible." Thompson appeared stunned by the news. "Why would anyone do such a thing?"

"I have yet to determine the reason. It's been a challenge to uncover who is behind it."

"Why take items that are unrelated?" Thompson ran a hand over his mustache as he pondered his own question.

"That is part of the puzzle. I am starting to believe the reason is personal."

"I would think so as well if I were in your shoes." Thompson shook his head. "I know you met with some resistance from your family when you converted the late marquess's home into a museum, but surely none of them would go to this extent to close it."

Anna's angry visit to his house came to mind, but he had to agree. "Nor does it seem as if they would wait this long to cause problems."

"Who else?" Thompson's brow furrowed. "Could it be a competitor? Museums can be nearly as cutthroat as treasure hunters. Have you gained any artifacts recently that someone else wanted?"

"That possibility crossed my mind as well. The coin and lantern were part of our latest exhibit, but I didn't think anyone else was eager to display the items, based on what the owner of them said."

"Hmm. You've interviewed your staff, I assume."

The discussion continued and, though they didn't arrive at any obvious answers, it helped to settle Simon's thoughts and was reassuring to confirm that the inquires he'd made were logical.

"Are there any museums you know of that are struggling financially?" Simon asked. That could be a reason someone was stealing from him.

"An easier question would be whether any aren't." Thompson chuckled as he glanced away, leaving Simon to wonder if his museum was in trouble.

"People seem more enamored with the latest inventions than studying the past," Simon said, watching him closely to see if he would say anything more.

"These are interesting times." Thompson shook his head. "The disparity between the rich and poor seems to widen with each year that passes."

"True. It is shocking to drive along some of our city's streets. More needs to be done and while I like to think I'm doing my part, it's not enough."

Simon was also worried about museums such as Thompson's, which served an important purpose as an education tool—one that should be affordable to the public. More visitors meant ticket prices could be kept low.

"I am considering putting together a list of museums in London for the public. Adverts would be placed in news sheets and magazines, and I'd create a brochure to offer in our museums as well. A mutual benefit of sorts. I would like to include your museum if you're interested."

Thompson smiled. "Indeed I am. I'd be happy to do my part to promote it." He lifted a brow. "I assume you're being selective in which museums are included?"

"I am. They would have to be upkept with interesting exhibits and agree to participate in actively promoting the others on the list. We all benefit by sharing."

"Clever idea. And much appreciated." Thompson's face tightened with worry. "Keeping visitors coming in the doors seems to be a never-ending challenge."

"It is for us, too." Simon didn't want Thompson to think he

was alone. "I think updating exhibits as well as reminding the public that we are here helps. I also want to share the list with Eton and other schools to encourage younger visitors."

"Ah. Excellent notion. Developing an appreciation of history in our youth is critical."

"I think so as well," Simon agreed as he rose to take his leave.

Thompson nodded in approval, then stood. "That is one of the reasons I've always liked and respected you, Simon. You think beyond yourself and beyond today. If only more people did the same."

The praise touched him. "Thank you, sir."

"You restore my hope in your peers, Vanbridge." Thompson bowed, his smile genuine.

"I'm pleased to hear that." With that, Simon bid him good-bye.

"Where to next, my lord?" Jarvis asked when Simon returned to the carriage. The driver seemed to be feeling more like himself, as well, much to Simon's relief.

Simon considered the question for a long moment. The temptation to return home was strong, but he wouldn't find the coin there. He gave Jarvis the name of another museum.

At the very least, he could continue to spread the idea of the list of museums in addition to the stolen items. That could gain a reaction.

Though he might not be able to tell if any of those with whom he spoke were the guilty party, perhaps his visit would make them nervous. Nervous people made mistakes. That was the best he could do until a better idea came to mind.

NORAH STUDIED THE flower she was embroidering, pleased she and Lena were nearly done with the fine linen nightrail for Ella. Norah was embroidering small pink flowers along the neckline while Lena was doing larger ones along the hem. Ella was going to be thrilled when they gave it to her as one of her wedding gifts.

It was a challenge to find time to work on it when Ella wasn't nearby. She was currently shopping with Lena and would soon return home, which meant Norah needed to work as quickly as possible.

"Miss Norah?"

She looked up to see Davies in the doorway of the drawing room. "Yes?"

"Lady Mendenhall is calling."

Norah stilled in surprise. She couldn't comprehend why the countess would call on her. Because of Simon, obviously. But to what purpose? Curiosity had her setting aside the needlework. "Please show her in."

Too late, she glanced down at her gown, wishing she had worn a different one. Without a doubt, she knew the countess would be finely dressed in the latest fashion, as she always was. Lady Havenby had warned her there would be days like this, and she should always be prepared for unexpected visitors. Norah should've listened. Yet it was difficult to worry over such things when they received so few callers.

Norah lifted her chin. She would act like the duke's grand-daughter. What she wore didn't change who she was.

"The Countess of Mendenhall," Davies announced a few minutes later.

As Norah had expected, the countess was dressed beautifully in a striped silk gown in shades of blue and brown with brown braid trim. The overskirt was drawn back into a bustle to reveal a cream lace underskirt. Her dark hair was pulled into an elaborate chignon with three long, perfect curls draped over one shoulder. She'd obviously taken a long time with her appearance.

The sight did not improve Norah's mood. Not for a moment did she believe this was truly a social call. She hadn't cared for the lady before this and had the feeling she would like her even less afterward. Still, she dropped into a curtsy and offered a smile.

"Good afternoon, my lady."

Lady Mendenhall's gaze swept over Norah, her lip curling in displeasure before she glanced about the room. She gave the barest of nods. "Isn't it?"

Assuming the question was rhetorical, Norah moved on to the true question. "To what do I owe the honor of your visit?"

The lady walked forward slowly. "It has come to my attention that you've become acquainted with my cousin."

Norah lifted a brow. Based on the woman's cool tone, she wouldn't have anything good to say about Simon. Norah had no intention of encouraging her to speak poorly of him.

"Vanbridge tends not to keep friends for long." Lady Mendenhall shook her head as if resigned. "He is not exactly an interesting conversationalist."

"I disagree. My talks with him have been fascinating." Norah couldn't have halted the urge to defend him if her life depended on it. "He was kind enough to arrange for an exhibit of my father's findings on Oak Island at his museum, which was met with great success."

The lady's brown eyes narrowed. "You mean except for the stolen coin. I would've thought that alone would have been cause for concern. I hate to think his lack of attention caused something of yours to disappear."

"The fact that the coin was stolen while in a locked display case is hardly his fault."

"Of course, it is. I have requested that he close the museum on numerous occasions, to no avail."

"I think it would be a shame to close it. The museum, which I understand includes numerous pieces of your father's collection, is a gift to the public. One of the best museums in the city. It invites those viewing the exhibits to step back in time. It's an educational resource to be treasured."

"If one likes dusty relics." Lady Mendenhall's disgust was obvious.

Yet Norah couldn't help but try to change her opinion. "It

seems your father certainly did. Many gentlemen are collectors, but it is those who share their treasures with others who should truly be admired."

"Yes, well, it's not your private family home where you were raised as a child and holds special memories that the public is traipsing through."

"I'm sure that must be difficult, but the memories are yours, and no one can take those away," Norah said in a gentle tone.

To her shock, the countess laughed, but the shrill tone wasn't a pleasant sound. "Oh, dear. I can see that you have…feelings for Vanbridge." She shook her head, looking at Norah with pity. "That is unfortunate. You see, he is not truly fit for polite society. He was awkward as a boy and is even more so as an adult."

Surprise kept Norah silent for a moment before anger took hold. "Show me a child who lost their parents so young who isn't awkward and in need of compassion."

"That was years ago. Besides, we all lose our parents. You lost yours, as did I. Yet we don't hide away in our study with only books for company."

Norah didn't think this was just about the museum or how Simon preferred to spend his time. There was more to the lady's emotions. "Why do you hate him so?"

"I don't know what you mean. He isn't worth that sort of passion." She raised a brow, practically daring Norah to argue.

That was a false statement. Simon was worth that and more. But Norah didn't want to waste her energy on Lady Mendenhall or her poor opinion of Simon, as wrong as it was. She had better things to do with her time.

"I'm sorry you feel that way," Norah said. "Family is precious. Even when we disagree." That much she'd learned after she and her sisters had reconciled with their grandfather. Her mother and the duke had both lost so much by letting their choices stand between them. "I hope you don't wait until it's too late with Simon."

"Too late for what?" The lady shook her head. "I have nothing in common with him."

"How sad that you believe that." Norah wasn't going to argue. Not when it would only prolong a conversation she wanted over and done.

"I thought it best if someone warned you about him. He has made it clear to the family that he has no intention of marrying. He has already stated that our younger cousin will inherit upon his death."

Norah stilled, the news nearly causing her to shiver. Not that she had expected Simon to propose. Yet she wouldn't lie to herself. She had considered—dreamed, even—what it would be like to have a future with him.

"I wouldn't want you to become entangled in a situation that could cost you dearly," the countess added.

"Is that a warning or a threat?" Could Lady Mendenhall have something to do with the items missing from Simon's museum? Would she be so vindictive as to arrange for that to happen in an attempt to force Simon to close the museum?

She smiled, a strange grim smile, her dark eyes hard. "I'll allow you to decide." With that, she turned and started toward the door, only to abruptly halt at the sight of Norah's grandfather standing there.

"Your Grace." She dipped into a deep curtsy.

Norah stared at her grandfather, realizing he'd heard the last part of their conversation. She could just see the side of the countess's face and noted the heightened color of her cheeks.

"Countess Mendenhall." He dipped his head rather than offering a true bow, his expression solemn and foreboding. "I didn't know you were acquainted with my granddaughter."

The lady glanced back at Norah, shifting so she could see them both. "We have met on more than one occasion."

Norah held her silence despite the uncomfortable look on the lady's face.

"I must ask you to clarify your answer to Norah's question. Were you threatening her?"

"Nothing of the sort." She clasped her reticule tightly. "I thought it my duty to warn her that Vanbridge can be less than reliable."

"I have dealt with him on numerous occasions and have not found that to be the case." The duke continued to glare at the countess.

"Well. That is a surprise. Perhaps my experience is different because of our shared childhood."

"Correct me if I'm wrong, but I don't believe your family chose to take him in when his parents died." He tilted his head to the side. "I wasn't the only one who thought that odd at the time. Especially since you and your brother were nearly his age. It wasn't until his aunt and uncle also died that your family had him come to live with you."

The lady's eyes widened as her cheeks flushed to a blotchy red. "I suppose my parents thought their time was already taken with their own children. Taking in an orphan can be troubling."

"Even one who is a close relative?" The duke shook his head. "Quite curious. I would think it would behoove you to set a better example now that you're an adult. That you would take the time to express your support for him since it was withheld when you were younger."

"Perhaps you're right. You've given me much to ponder, Your Grace." She glanced again at Norah, the heat in her eyes seeming to be a mix of embarrassment and anger. "And now, I must be going. My husband is expecting me."

"Of course. I look forward to speaking with him soon."

Norah's eyes widened at the veiled threat. This was a version of her grandfather she hadn't seen since her and her sisters' arrival.

"I shall tell him so. Thank you." The countess curtsied and quickly bid them goodbye, then rushed from the room as if her gown was on fire.

Her grandfather's stern expression shifted into a devilish smile. "That woman is unpleasant at best and a scheming busybody at worst. I don't want her to think she can meddle with you or your sisters without answering to me."

"Thank you." Norah lifted on her toes to kiss his cheek. "That was a much more satisfying conclusion to her visit than it would've been otherwise."

"Hmm." He looked rather uncomfortable at her display of affection. Norah liked to think he would eventually become used to it.

In some ways, he wasn't so different than Simon, living alone for so many years. He didn't trust others easily. Conversing was awkward at times. But they both had a heart of gold as far as she was concerned.

She didn't care what the Countess of Mendenhall said. She was honored to know Simon and hoped to continue this relationship with him for the foreseeable future. If he allowed it.

Chapter Eighteen

The NEXT MUSEUM Simon visited was the Museum of Archaeological Findings on Manchester Square. The three-story brown brick mansion boasted white stone that framed tall, arched windows as well as stucco cornices. The building was a pleasure to look at, even if Vincent Evans, the man who ran it, was a pompous ass.

However, it truly was one of the better museums in all of London. Simon refused to allow his personal distaste for the man to interfere with business. Or at least, he tried not to. He and Evans had become rivals of a sort over the years.

Not for the first time, he wished he hadn't allowed his research to take precedence over the time he spent at his museum after hiring Stockton as director. Simon had no one to blame but himself for the decline in visitors over the past six months. Thank goodness Norah had entered his life with her request for an exhibit. Otherwise, he might not have realized how the museum was declining until it was too late.

After alighting from the carriage and requesting Jarvis to wait, he walked through the well-maintained garden and entered the building. He decided to look around before he approached Evans, so paid for a ticket, shocked at how expensive it was. Simon had no intention of increasing his own admission price. He would prefer more people enjoy the collection rather than only those with money.

He meandered through the lower floor, noting only a few other visitors looking at the exhibits. One room displayed oil paintings, which were new to the museum. They didn't seem to fit with the theme of the place, but perhaps they'd been donated.

The next floor had actual archeological finds, which Simon found more interesting. However, the exhibits weren't particularly unique, merely groupings of items with little to no explanation of how they'd been found or what their purpose was.

"Vanbridge?" Simon turned to see Vincent Evans approaching. The tall, slender man had a receding hairline with a widow's peak made more defined by his black hair and pale skin. His prominent cheekbones lent him a gaunt look. Evans bowed, then lifted a brow. "Have you resorted to spying on the competition?"

"It's always interesting to visit your museum and see what new finds you have on display." Simon didn't add that he thought the exhibits needed to be improved.

Evans beamed as if Simon had paid him a fine compliment. "We pride ourselves on excellence."

Rather than deny the man's claim, Simon moved on to the reason for his visit. "I was hoping to have a word with you while I'm here, if you have a moment."

Evans made a show of pulling a gold pocket watch from his striped waistcoat to check the time. "I suppose I can spare a few minutes."

Simon clenched his jaw. He'd been speaking with him for less than three minutes and was already struggling to hold his patience. "Good."

Evans led the way out of the room and down a narrow, rather dark corridor with several signs noting the area was for staff only. He opened the second door on the right where a small office was brightened by two tall windows with red velvet drapes and gold sashes. Simple yet elegant furnishings were inside, including a desk, shelving, a table, and chairs.

Evans glanced around the office, seeming to make certain all was in order. Did he worry he'd left something out that Simon might see? Evans walked to the table, gestured toward the chairs, and they both sat. "What's on your mind?" Then he lifted a finger in the air to stop Simon from saying anything. "Allow me to guess. Does this have anything to do with the recent thefts at your museum?"

"In part, yes." Simon was somewhat surprised the man knew of the situation since Thompson hadn't. Though it wasn't as if museum owners gathered monthly to share such information.

"Terrible situation." Evans steepled his fingers, elbows braced on the table. "Who would do such a thing?"

Simon studied the other man, trying to determine why he had the impression that Evans was making an effort to look dismayed and sincere. "Who indeed?" Simon let the question hang in the air between them.

Evans cleared his throat as he lowered his hands. "Do you have any leads?"

"The police are narrowing down the potential suspects." In truth, Simon hadn't been in touch with the authorities for several days. Not since the morning after his injury. He didn't think they'd made any progress on the case. Evans didn't need to know that.

Simon found it interesting to note the faint widening of Evans' eyes at the news.

"You involved the police?" Evans asked.

"Of course. I'm sure you heard that I interrupted someone a few days ago and was struck on the head from behind." Again, Simon watched for his reaction.

A flash of displeasure showed on the man's face. Almost as if expressing concern was an afterthought, Evans said, "I hope the injury wasn't significant."

"Actually, it was." Simon wasn't certain why he said that. Perhaps just to see his reaction.

"I'm sorry to hear that." He shook his head. "I suppose one can only be grateful it wasn't worse."

Simon stared at Evans in disbelief. "I'm not grateful. I'm angry. Enraged, actually. I intend to find the person who did it and make them pay." The depth of his anger surprised him. Whether it was wise to allow Evans to see it was unclear.

"As you should. I would do the same in your position."

"You haven't experienced any thefts here?"

"None. Then again, I'm here every day to watch over things carefully. And I hire only the best."

The subtle dig only angered Simon more. "Good people are hard to find."

"And even harder to keep." The bland look on Evans's face suggested something, but Simon couldn't decide what.

"I would appreciate you letting me know if you hear of anything that could prove helpful in the case."

"I will certainly do that," Evans agreed, an odd gleam in his eyes.

Simon realized he should cut the meeting short before he said something he shouldn't. His personal dislike of Evans wasn't a reason to be suspicious. But he was all the same.

"On another note," Simon said, "I am putting together a list of the top museums in London that the public should consider visiting and would like to include yours." He explained his intentions and where adverts would be placed.

Evans nodded in agreement until Simon added that each museum on the list would be expected to help promote the others by offering the brochure to everyone who purchased a ticket. "I suppose I'm willing to have a stack of the brochures available in the entrance, but I hardly think I want to hand visitors a list of other museums when they've come to visit mine."

"Why not? If they've already purchased a ticket, what harm could come from telling them about others in the city?"

"Customer loyalty is something we treasure and promote. Don't you?"

"We certainly enjoy guests who tour the museum on a regular basis, but I don't believe that prohibits them from going to other museums." Simon frowned. "It makes sense to offer support for the benefit of all."

"I will consider it. But why you want to promote your competition makes little sense to me."

Simon stood, detesting the fact that Evans had the power to make him question his own judgment. Would he ever be able to release the self-doubt he'd experienced since childhood and trust himself?

"I'll be compiling the list in the coming week," Simon advised. "If you'd like to be involved, you know how to contact me."

"I suppose it's best to send a note to your home. You're not at the museum much, are you?" Evans chuckled as if he'd made a clever jest.

Simon pressed his fist against his leg with the hope of ensuring he didn't plant it in the man's face. "Best of luck to you."

He left Evan's office but didn't rush out of the museum just in case Evans watched him. The last thing he wanted was to give the man the satisfaction of knowing he'd gotten under Simon's skin. When at last he returned to the carriage, he sighed with relief.

Afternoons like this were one of the reasons he preferred to remain in his study working. People could be annoying at times, and Evans was a prime example.

He hoped the man decided not to participate in the promotion. Otherwise, Simon would be forced to speak with him again. The concern put him in a dour mood. Should he be suspicious of Evans or was it only his dislike of the man that made him so?

NORAH SAT IN the back row of chairs at the Hamptons' musical that evening, along with Ella, Lena, and Lady Havenby, keeping an eye on the entrance. She'd sent Simon a message, inviting him to attend, but didn't know if he'd received it in time to join her.

The Hampton home was elegant and boasted a large music room with blue and gold accents. Nearly thirty guests awaited the performance, visiting quietly. Norah recognized many, as they often attended the same concerts she and her sisters did.

While having a true conversation at an event like this would be difficult since it afforded little privacy, she wanted to tell him of his cousin's visit.

She wrinkled her nose at the thought since it was a partial lie. What purpose would be served in pretending she wasn't anxious to see him? She should at least be honest with herself.

"What is it?" Lena leaned close to ask.

The musical wouldn't begin for at least another ten minutes. The Hampton twins and two of their cousins would be playing this evening. Norah had high hopes for the performances. She'd heard they were accomplished musicians.

"My nose itches," Norah said, only to grimace at yet another lie.

Lena frowned, seeming to suspect her answer wasn't exactly truthful.

Norah debated whether she dared to turn around and look at the entrance again when someone took the chair next to her.

Simon. Her entire being settled at his presence. No, that wasn't quite true, for immediately after, her spirits soared as if on wings. Oh dear. She was in serious trouble.

"Good evening, my lord," she managed, hoping her voice didn't reveal the tumult of her emotions.

"Good evening." He greeted her sisters and Lady Havenby, too, then turned to study Norah, those green eyes searching her face. "You greeted me with surprise. As if you weren't expecting me."

"I wasn't." Her face heated when several of the other guests turned to stare at Simon.

"But you sent a message requesting that I attend."

Lena nudged Norah's side. "Is that true? Why didn't you tell us?"

"Because I didn't think he'd be able to on such short notice."

"I nearly didn't," Simon muttered.

Norah turned from Lena to look at Simon, certain she'd have a sore neck by the end of the evening at this rate. "I'm so pleased you did."

His slow smile was its own reward. "You managed to save me once again."

Norah's heart flipped over at his whispered admission. "I did?"

"Just when I decided never to leave my study again, you reached out and pulled me from the brink."

"The brink of what?" Lena asked, leaning forward to look at Simon, her expression curious.

Norah glared at her. "This is a private conversation." It was difficult to put the proper anger in her tone when she was whispering.

"Would you rather I pretend I can't hear? Because I'm right next to you." Lena scowled as she sat back in her chair. "Perhaps the two of you should step outside."

"That's an excellent idea," Norah agreed.

"No, it's not." Now Ella leaned forward to glare at Norah, ignoring the guests nearby who watched them closely. "The musical is about to begin."

Exasperated, Norah heaved a beleaguered sigh, giving up on the notion of privacy, at least from her sisters. The best she could do was ignore them. "What chased you into your study?"

"I visited several other museums with the hope of finding out if they knew anything about the thefts."

"Did they?"

"Difficult to say. It's surprising how adept people can be at hiding their emotions."

"Isn't it, though?" She found his words ironic, given that she was trying to do that exact thing. Did he have any idea how much she was coming to care for him?

"There is one person who raises my suspicions, but I wonder if that's because I don't like him."

"It's difficult to remove personal opinions when investigating. We encountered that while searching for our father's journal last year." Norah watched as the twins and their cousins moved to the front of the room, signaling the performance was about to begin. "Where is the line between listening to one's instincts and allowing biases to interfere?"

"Excellent question." He glanced at her with surprise. "I hadn't considered instincts."

"Perhaps you should. Your bias against this man might be there for a reason." She need only think of Lena to know how helpful listening to one's internal voice could be.

"Interesting idea. I shall give it further thought." He leaned closer as the ladies warmed up their instruments, making it more difficult to converse. The warm press of his arm against hers sent tingles along her skin. "What did you wish to speak with me about?"

Norah drew in a breath to speak, catching his subtle scent, which sent desire swirling within her. Suddenly, her mind was blank. What had she been going to say? "Your cousin called on me."

He blinked in surprise. "Cousin? Lady Mendenhall?"

"Yes."

A muscle ticked in his jaw even as his nostrils flared. "I assume it wasn't a social call. What did she say?"

"That she wanted you to close the museum." Norah frowned. "I'm not certain why she thought to mention it to me."

"She called on me a few days ago, as well, and stated the same request. Again. She suggested the talk of the stolen items is embarrassing."

"How ridiculous. I don't understand why she doesn't like you."

"I don't think she liked sharing what little attention she received from her parents with me. She hasn't forgiven me for that.

My apologies that she bothered you. I will speak with her."

"No need." Norah smiled. "My grandfather overheard part of what she said and expressed his displeasure to her."

Simon's eyes widened. "Oh?"

"She seemed embarrassed and upset when she left. I don't believe we need to concern ourselves with her for a time. I think Grandfather is coming to like you."

"I'm pleased to hear someone does."

Her heart thumped rapidly at his whispered words. "I do, too." She pressed her arm more firmly against his, hoping the contact reassured him.

To her delight, he pressed back. A subtle hug of sorts. A private moment in a somewhat public gathering. It warmed her inside and out.

"We like you, too." Lena leaned forward as did Ella, both of them smiling at Simon.

Norah couldn't help but chuckle at Simon's startled expression. The music started, saving him from having to respond.

The performance was lovely. The four ladies played very well. Norah added her applause to the rest of the guests at the conclusion.

"That was more pleasant than I expected," Simon said as they rose.

"I don't suppose you attend many musicals."

"Never."

"I enjoy music," Norah admitted. "I can't imagine life without it."

"Do you play?"

"Yes. Several instruments."

"How interesting." He frowned as if he couldn't quite imagine it.

"It calms me and clears my thoughts. Especially when I'm the one playing." She shared a smile with him. "Perhaps it's like boxing for you."

"I don't think I've ever heard boxing and playing music compared before."

They moved with the other guests toward the refreshment room where an array of small sandwiches, biscuits, and cake were offered, along with lemonade.

"Excuse me for a moment," Simon said, then walked over to speak with their host, Lord Hampton.

"I must say how surprised I am that you and Vanbridge seem to have formed a friendship of sorts," Lady Havenby said as she halted beside Norah, a glass of lemonade in hand. "Is it because of the missing coin?"

I hope not, Norah wanted to say. "In part, I suppose. Though I enjoy his company. We share several common interests."

"Based on the way you watched him cross the room, I have to wonder if it's more than that." Lady Havenby kept her gaze on Simon, her brow furrowed. "Guard your heart with that one, my dear. From what I've heard, he has no intention of marrying. A reliable source advised me that he has already started grooming a cousin to inherit."

Hearing the news from Lady Havenby in addition to Lady Mendenhall should've relieved Norah since she didn't plan on marrying soon, but it didn't. She told herself she wasn't ready for marriage. Not for several years. Yet that didn't stop the deep ache in her chest.

She wanted to offer a light-hearted reply. Something that made it clear the information didn't matter. But she couldn't force anything past the lump in her throat.

As if unaware of the upset she'd caused, Lady Havenby turned away to speak with someone else.

Before Norah had regained her composure, Simon returned. "What is it?" he asked, his brow furrowed as he looked at her.

The fact that he'd noted her distress amazed her and confirmed how close they'd become in the weeks they'd known each other. It was as if an invisible thread linked them together, much like what she'd witnessed with Ella and Marbury.

The realization caught her breath. As did the notion that she didn't want the thread to be cut. Why was it that she was starting to see what she wanted, only to learn Simon didn't want the same thing?

✦

Chapter Nineteen

SIMON ROSE FROM his desk at the museum and stretched. He'd spent several hours there each day over the past three days, taking care to vary his schedule so no one knew when to expect him. He also staggered the times he walked through the exhibits. His hope had been to find something—anything—that would provide a clue as to who was behind the thefts. However, his efforts hadn't provided any results thus far.

Whether any clues would come to light looked doubtful. Yet he had to try something. He'd visited several more museums with no results, though he now had a list of the ones interested in participating in the promotion he'd proposed.

He hadn't heard from Norah since seeing her at the musical but hadn't expected to. Her sister and Marbury were to be married come morning. No doubt the sisters were busy with whatever planning that entailed.

He missed her. More than he should. He'd thought having some distance would ease her hold on his thoughts, but that hadn't been the case. She had become an integral part of his life in the past few weeks. The plans he'd made for his future were no longer certain because she made him question them. How did he want to spend the rest of his life? Remaining home alone in his study had lost its appeal. But before he could consider his path, he needed to solve the thefts.

As quietly as possible, Simon moved to his office entrance where his door stood partially ajar and peeked out. Sure enough, Stockton was at his desk, frowning as he stared at a sheet of paper. Did the man ever step away to see what was happening in the rest of the museum? Simon could count on one hand how often he'd come upon Stockton near one of the exhibits.

Just as Simon reached to open the door fully, Emerson came into view.

"Mr. Stockton? There's a situation we would like your assistance with downstairs."

"Oh?" The obvious annoyance in the director's tone irritated Simon. Part of his job was to deal with problems. Perhaps Simon should move the man's office to the main floor so he would be encouraged to watch over operations more closely. "What is it?"

"I think it's best if you review it yourself." Emerson shifted as if impatient. That made two of them.

"Very well." Stockton shoved back his chair and stood, taking time to turn the paper he'd held face down.

Simon shifted out of view and listened closely. Within a few moments, only the faint sound of voices could be heard as they walked downstairs. Simon hurried to Stockton's desk, curious to see what he'd been reviewing with such intent focus.

The paper seemed to be a page pulled from a ledger and noted various numbers, amounts, and checkmarks, along with two circled items. It appeared to be an inventory of some kind or a shipment list. But the numbers and letters neatly listed in a column might as well have been in code, for they made no sense to Simon. Did they have anything to do with his museum? He looked over the rest of the desk but didn't open the drawers, not certain how much time he had.

The sound of footsteps on the stairs had Simon hurriedly putting the paper back in place and rushing back to his office to push the door partially closed again. He moved behind his desk but before he could take a seat, a knock sounded on his door.

"Yes?"

Stockton appeared in the entrance. "Would you care to see the latest arrivals from South America? Emerson is unpacking them now by the exhibit."

"Of course." He followed the director, deciding to return this evening to have a closer look at Stockton's desk. He'd pick the locks if he had to. The inventory list struck him as odd, and he wanted to see if he could find any other clues.

⋙⋘

"ELLA?" NORAH CALLED quietly after tapping on her door that evening. They'd had a lovely dinner with their grandfather earlier, but it had been bittersweet. Each of them had done their best to be jovial, yet a hint of melancholy had permeated the mood.

Now the hour was late, and everyone had retired for the night. But Norah couldn't sleep. She had the feeling Ella couldn't either. Not when her wedding would take place in the morning.

"Come in."

Before Norah could open the door, Lena peeked her head into the hallway. "What is it?"

Rather than explain, Norah simply waved her closer. Lena hurried forward, already in her nightgown with a matching robe and slippers, much like what Norah wore.

Norah led the way into Ella's room, relieved to see her sister seated at her desk in her nightgown with a lamp on rather than tucked in bed. They'd already presented her with the embroidered nightgown, which she'd loved.

"What are you two doing up?" Ella asked with a look of concern.

"Coming to see you," Norah replied. "How are you doing?"

Ella rose and walked forward to embrace them both, her silence speaking volumes.

The quiet minutes with the three of them simply holding

each other brought a lump to Norah's throat. It would be some time before they shared another moment like this. The thought was impossible to believe when they'd had so many in the past. It made her realize she'd taken such things for granted.

At last, Ella released them and stepped back to look at them both. "I don't know why I'm nervous," she whispered. "I've been waiting so long for this day. Now that it's here…" Her voice trailed off as if she had no words to describe how she felt.

"It certainly arrived quicker than I expected," Norah said.

"Yes, it did," Lena agreed as she took their hands in hers. "Much quicker."

Though Norah longed to ask for assurance that everything would be all right despite this major change in their lives, she held back. The moment was not about her. It was about Ella and how she felt.

"I'm so happy for you." Norah blinked back tears and managed a smile. "You and Marbury are meant to be together." That much she knew for certain. She hated feeling selfish, but she wasn't ready for her sister to leave.

"Yes, we are." Ella drew a deep breath as her bright blue eyes filled with tears. "But I am going to miss the two of you very much. I can't quite imagine not being with you every day."

Norah's tears fell, as did Lena's. "Nor can I. Thank goodness you're not moving far."

Ella released their hands to hug them again. "Not far at all," she managed, though the words were muffled. "You'll still see me nearly every day."

"After your honeymoon." Lena's quiet remark had all their tears falling faster.

"It's only two weeks. Then I'll be back. It will pass quickly."

Norah smiled, wondering if she was trying to reassure them or herself. She appreciated it all the same. "What are you most excited about for the trip?"

"Paris in the spring? What's not to be excited about? The sites. The food."

"Nights with Marbury," Lena added with a giggle.

Ella's cheeks flushed, visible even in the dim lamplight. "Yes. I do look forward to spending time with Leo."

"It will be exciting. Do not worry about us for even a moment." Norah shared a look with Lena, wanting her to agree. "We will be perfectly fine."

Lena nodded. "Yes, we will."

"I hope so. I insist nothing exciting happen while I'm gone," Ella ordered, giving them each a pretend warning look that caused them to chuckle.

"I'm sure nothing will." Norah patted her hand. "Since we'll have nothing else to occupy our time, I hope to make excellent progress on the seat cushions we're embroidering for Grandfather."

Lena groaned. "Whose idea was that? It was a terrible one. We're never going to finish them."

"Getting further on those would be wonderful," Ella agreed. "But I truly hope you manage to find Father's coin as well."

Norah scowled. "I thought we'd have found it by now. Though it's not for lack of trying."

"Vanbridge will come through," Ella said. "Of that I have no doubt. When Leo and I return, he will help as well. He's been so distracted with our wedding plans and the honeymoon that he hasn't done some of the things he planned to." Ella's brow wrinkled. "Worley might be able to help more while we're gone."

"I'll be sure to mention that to Simon." Norah thought he would appreciate additional assistance.

"I can't help but ask—how close are you and Vanbridge becoming?" Ella asked with a twinkle in her eyes, her arms folded across her stomach.

"He is a very interesting man." Norah hoped that would satisfy her sister. She wasn't prepared to discuss how she felt when her emotions were already in turmoil.

"Interesting in what way?" Ella nudged her with an elbow.

"In various ways." Norah did her best to look innocent. "His appreciation of history is admirable."

"Do not try to tell us you enjoy spending time with him because of his interest in history." Lena shook her head. "We won't believe you."

"There is much to admire about him." Norah didn't want to be more specific than that. Saying more might reveal too much, especially when her sisters knew her so well. "But I am in no rush to form an attachment to anyone." Why did she feel like it was already too late? The realization caused a hitch of panic in her throat.

Lena smiled. "Good. Because I am not ready to lose both my sisters."

"I don't think Grandfather is ready to lose more of us either," Norah said. "He seems rather forlorn about your wedding. Especially at dinner this evening."

Ella shook her head. "I don't know what more Leo and I can do to reassure him. We've promised to visit often. And we intend to invite you to dinner soon after our return."

"It will take time for all of us to adjust." Lena bit her lip as tears filled her eyes once again. "I just can't imagine you not being here if I need you."

"I'll be here," Norah reminded her. "I hope you know I will need you, as well." She and Lena had always been close. Then again, so had the three of them, despite Ella being four years older.

"I know we came to London with the hope of finding suitable matches, but I never thought I'd be the first to marry." Ella sniffed and shook her head, seemingly still puzzled by the fact.

"But you're the eldest," Lena protested.

Ella gave a wry smile. "Yes, but I intended to see both of you happily settled before I worried about my own future. I feel rather selfish for marrying before either of you."

"Nonsense." Norah drew a deep breath, hoping to reassure Ella as she wanted her sister's wedding day to be perfect. "You have set a fine example for us to follow. Though the chances of us finding someone as perfect for us as Marbury is for you seems impossible."

Ella laughed, just as Norah wanted. "He is perfect, isn't he?" She held both hands over her cheeks as if to hide the heat in them. "We are going to be very happy together."

"Yes, you are. Now then, you need a good night's sleep. Tomorrow will be a busy day." Norah gave Ella another hug. "Lena and I will join you early to help you dress."

"Thank you. I love you both so much." Ella embraced them each again. "We should all try to get some rest."

At last, Norah settled in bed. Only then did she let the tears fall. Their lives were changing so quickly, and she wasn't sure what to do about it. Then again, nothing felt like it was in her control. Telling herself to simply enjoy each day no longer felt like enough.

When she'd argued with her father that final morning not so long ago, she'd told him she wanted to experience life rather than be stuck on the island. But never had she expected so much to happen so quickly or so drastically. First his death, then their arrival in London, and now Ella marrying. She was almost worried about what might happen next.

The question brought Simon to mind, as so many of her thoughts did of late. Was there any chance of a future for them? Or should she simply try to enjoy her time with him because it would soon pass?

She had to admit that she saw marriage in a whole new light when she imagined Simon at her side. They had many interests in common, and they were both curious people who liked to learn new things. But she could also see them enjoying some activities on their own rather than doing everything together. In her mind, they could have the perfect partnership—friends and lovers.

Hope burned bright in her chest, and she turned onto her side and cradled that feeling, wondering once again what the coming weeks might bring.

"ARE YOU READY?" Simon asked Miles and Jarvis as he exited from the carriage a short distance from the front of the museum late that night.

"Yes, my lord." Miles seemed quite confident, which helped to allay Simon's worry. It seemed silly to be concerned about entering his own museum after hours, but he couldn't help it after what happened last time.

He had to think Jarvis felt the same. He turned to the driver. "Are you sure you don't want to wait with the carriage? Guarding it is also important."

"Not at all, my lord." His fierce expression was just visible in the dim light. "If I have the chance to pay back whoever hit us, I'll gladly take it."

Simon clapped him on the shoulder. "As will I, though I don't think we'll be lucky enough to come across that person this time. We shall see. Let's go."

He led the way down the street toward the entrance and retrieved the key from his pocket as they hurried up the steps. After unlocking the door and stepping inside, he paused to listen, Miles and Jarvis doing the same. The silence was complete. Then again, it had been the night they'd been injured as well.

This time, he didn't rush up the stairs. Norah wasn't waiting for him to meet her this evening. Instead, he continued to listen as he climbed the steps. The quiet made him feel ridiculous for bringing reinforcements.

Miles tried several doors on their way up and found them locked, just as they should be. They arrived at the upper level, and Simon walked directly to Stockton's desk.

Jarvis faced the stairs to watch below.

Stockton's desk had been cleared and the drawers locked. Simon withdrew the picks he'd brought, then motioned for Miles to bring the light closer. He hadn't picked many locks, and it took several minutes for him to release the drawer.

"Why don't you look through the contents while I try my hand at the next one?" Miles suggested.

Simon handed him the pick and stepped aside to page through the papers. "Nothing of interest in this one," he whispered. Perhaps this mission would prove to be a waste of time. He put the papers back in the position he'd found them and started on the next pile from the drawer Miles had already managed to open.

In this stack, he found an unsigned letter that referenced a meeting, which was curious as it didn't specify any names. He sighed in frustration. Discovering more questions did him little good. He needed something definitive that either cleared Stockton or incriminated him.

The rest of the drawers yielded nothing. Disappointed, Simon considered his options while Miles re-locked the drawers.

"Let us check the storage area before we leave," Simon suggested.

"Excellent idea," Miles agreed with a nod.

Simon led the way down to the first level, then along the corridor to the rear of the house, and took the stairs that led to the kitchen, where incoming exhibits were uncrated. The room was eerie in the dark with odd shadows that caused him to glance about warily.

Simon was surprised by the number of crates stacked in the space. Though new Incan artifacts had arrived, they had already been unpacked. "Help me look in a few of these crates," he directed Miles.

Jarvis held the light aloft while they set a crate on the floor and pried off the lid. Straw packing filled the interior, which Simon moved aside. The crate seemed to be empty. But in the very bottom corner, Simon found a small gold statue. Had someone been so careless as to leave it inside?

"Let's check another." To his dismay, an item had also been left in that crate. The next one as well. They were Egyptian, so hadn't been part of the Incan shipment. Why were they there?

"Odd." Miles studied Simon. "Is there a possible explanation?"

"Other than sloppy work?" Simon couldn't believe the staff was so inept as to not completely unpack not just one crate but two. He stared at the last crate, puzzled by the situation, only to have a stamped number on the side catch his eye. It seemed familiar. Awareness dawned as he realized it was similar to the ledger paper he'd examined earlier in the day on Stockton's desk. What was going on?

Chapter Twenty

NORAH WIPED AWAY happy tears as she and Lena, both bridesmaids, watched Ella and Marbury say their vows to each other in the church the next morning.

Ella looked positively radiant in an understated white silk gown with a train, both trimmed in lace and embellished with seed pearls. She wore a tiara of orange blossoms with a fine lace veil. She looked exactly as a bride should.

Marbury was tall and handsome with his dark hair. His elegant attire included a white waistcoat as well as a white rose secured in his lapel. They truly made the perfect couple, both in looks as well as demeanor. The pair gazed at each other with such tender regard, their love obvious. They spoke the vows with a solemn certainty that tugged at Norah's heart.

"Mother and Father would be happy, don't you think?" Lena asked while they waited for the newly married couple to sign the register after the ceremony with their grandfather looking on.

The question was one they had all pondered since their arrival in London. Given the fact that their parents had left this life and everything it offered behind, none of them were completely sure.

For a time, Ella had felt as if they'd undone all their parents had wanted by coming to London. But the difficult circumstances had given them little choice. With their father gone and little money, there had been nothing left for them on Oak Island.

"I think so," Norah replied. "Above all, they would've wanted us to be happy."

"Are you happy?" Lena asked.

Norah turned to face her in time to see a shadow cross her sister's face. "For the most part. Are you?"

"At times." Lena frowned. "It's just that I don't feel as if I belong here yet."

Norah placed an arm around Lena. "I know. I feel that at times as well. It's not home." Yet she had to admit that since meeting Simon, she'd felt more settled.

Lena looked almost relieved at her admission. "Exactly. It is very nice, and I enjoy parts of our life. But…"

"It's difficult to describe, isn't it?"

"Yes." Lena's gaze sought Ella and Marbury again. "I worry if that feeling will grow worse with Ella gone."

"She's not really leaving," Norah said, though she knew exactly what Lena meant. "Still, it won't be the same without her in the house."

"No, it won't." Then Lena forced a smile. "I am very happy for her. For them."

"I think Grandfather feels the same as we do." Norah watched as a range of emotions passed over the duke's face. A mix of pride, sorrow, and joy. She knew exactly how he felt.

"That surprises me, given how he treated us on our arrival."

"True," Norah agreed. "This must be a painful occasion since he never got to see Mother marry. Her and Father's elopement must've been quite a blow to him."

"I'm sure you're right." Lena's smile became more genuine. "Why don't we offer our support?"

They joined him, each taking one of his arms. Their gestures of affection always seemed to startle him but in a positive way. This time was no different.

The Countess of Marbury gave the happy couple a warm embrace, as did Lady Havenby. Viscount Worley was there, as well, and kept the mood light with his humor. Still, Norah missed Simon and wished he had come. She would welcome the comfort of his presence.

Soon they returned home, where the wedding breakfast was being held. The guests who'd been at the church joined them for the meal. As was tradition, the bride was never congratulated. Only the groom was, implying that the honor was conferred on her for marrying him. Norah didn't appreciate the custom but knew how much Marbury loved her sister.

"Will you be leaving us soon for another of your adventures?" Norah asked Worley as they mingled with the guests while waiting for breakfast to be served.

"Not for several months, unfortunately. I am anxious to go, though."

"You always are. But from what Marbury has shared, you enjoy the homecomings just as much as the adventures," Norah teased.

"I won't deny it." Worley chuckled. "Why don't you and Lena join me on this next trip?"

"Where are you going?" Lena asked, much to Norah's surprise. Her sister had never expressed a desire to travel.

"To Mexico to visit an Incan site. It promises to be spectacular."

Norah gave a mock shudder. "I don't think I will accompany you. Greece, perhaps. But a jungle? No, thank you."

"I think it would be amazing," Lena said, her expression one of wonder. "Though I would prefer to begin my travels on the Continent."

"Would you really like to go to Paris and the like?" Norah asked.

"I would. Perhaps leaving here for a time would make it feel more like home when I returned."

Norah's heart ached at the thought. She couldn't bear for both Lena and Ella to be gone.

"Not anytime soon though." Lena smiled, seeming to sense

Norah's thoughts. "Have no worry that I'll leave you. Perhaps in a year or two."

Norah made no effort to hide her sigh of relief, causing Lena and Worley to laugh.

"If I had sisters like you, I wouldn't be able to leave so easily," Worley admitted. "It would be too painful to say goodbye. What of you, Norah? Do you want to travel?"

She considered the question. "Yes, but I want to travel with someone who would make the journey more enjoyable." She nearly caught her breath as Simon came to mind. Traveling with him would be a true pleasure. His knowledge of artifacts and historical sites would make exploring new places fascinating. She enjoyed his company, no matter what they did together.

The guests took their seats, then Davies and several footmen entered with silver trays of food to begin the meal, distracting her from her thoughts. Bacon, sausages, and thick slices of ham, as well as coddled eggs and toast were served. Coffee and tea were offered as well.

Once the meal was over and the dishes cleared, cake was served, along with flutes of champagne. Norah knew the cook had also prepared enough cake for the servants to enjoy.

Their grandfather stood, his glass raised, and silence descended. "Best wishes to the bride and groom. May they know that their future happiness is near and dear to the hearts of us all."

Everyone cheered, then took a sip. Norah couldn't help the lump in her throat. Though they'd known this day was coming, having it nearly over was another thing entirely. The thought of waking in the morning without Ella in the house was unfathomable.

She blinked back tears and focused on Ella's glowing face and the tender looks Marbury gave her. Ella was happy, and that was all that mattered. She'd been through so much and had been there for Norah and Lena to lean on for so many years. It was her turn to enjoy life rather than worry about her sisters.

Soon the time came for Ella to change and depart with Marbury. The couple would spend the night at his home and then leave for Paris in the morning.

Norah and Lena joined Ella in her room to assist her, though Dorothy, her maid, had everything well in hand. Norah walked over to the wardrobe and peeked inside, her chest aching at its emptiness. The sight made the moment all too real. Ella was leaving, and nothing would be the same.

She did her best to hide her tears as she smiled and laughed with her sisters, teasing Ella by calling her countess. Ella chuckled with them. As if by unspoken agreement, none of them mentioned the weight of saying goodbye that hung in the air.

Norah didn't want to ruin Ella's special day by sharing her thoughts, so helped as best she could, hurrying her sister along and teasing her that Marbury might leave if she didn't rush back downstairs.

"You look beautiful." Norah studied her sister in the mirror as Dorothy pinned a blue hat on her head while she sat at the dressing table. The fitted bodice of her pale blue gown flattered her slender curves and her fair coloring. The deeper blue overskirt was drawn back into a bustle, revealing several layers of the white lace underskirt. She still looked every inch a bride.

"Thank you." Ella pressed her hands to her heart. "I am so very happy. And I cannot wait for both of you to feel this way, as well." She rose from the dressing table and turned to take their hands in hers. "I love you both."

"We love you, too." Norah kissed her cheek, careful not to muss her appearance, followed by Lena. "Write when you can. We can't wait to hear all about your trip."

"Have a wonderful time," Lena added.

Norah held open the door, torn between wanting the painful moment over and wishing she could prolong Ella's presence. She and Lena followed her downstairs. Most of the guests had left, and Marbury waited near the foot of the stairs, along with their grandfather.

Fate had placed an odd twist in their path when Marbury had

come into their lives. The fact that he and Ella had fallen in love somehow reassured Norah that all was as it should be. That their lives were moving in the proper direction, even if they couldn't see the outcome. Would that prove true for Norah?

Marbury must've heard them, for he turned to watch Ella descend the stairs, his heart in his eyes. The love in his expression only made Norah want to cry more. But it also reassured her that Ella was in the best hands.

"You are so beautiful." He reached for Ella's hand. "Are you ready, dear wife?"

"Yes, I am." Ella released him to embrace their grandfather for a long moment. "Thank you for everything. I love you, and we'll see you soon."

"Indeed, you will." He cleared his throat, moisture in his eyes. "Take care and safe travels."

Marbury shook the duke's hand with both of his. Then, after one more hug for Norah and Lena, the couple were waving goodbye as Marbury's carriage took them away.

As if by unspoken agreement, Norah and Lena both flanked their grandfather on the front step, looping their arms through his. Rather than return immediately inside, the three stood there for a long moment, staring at the empty street.

"They'll be back before we know it," Lena said quietly.

"Yes." Norah nodded, needing to comfort herself with that fact. "But things won't be the same without them."

"No, they won't." Their grandfather glanced at each of them. "Thank goodness the three of you came to me. I am truly blessed."

Norah leaned her head against his upper arm, certain Lena was doing the same. "We are the ones who are blessed."

The duke smiled and drew a deep breath. "Would the two of you care to join me in my study? It seems like a good day to spend some time together."

Norah shared a surprised look with Lena, who answered for both of them. "We would like that very much. Do you have something in mind?" she asked as they turned as one to go inside.

"I received a new book that I ordered that I thought we might enjoy. It's a mystery set in Paris."

With a smile, Norah listened to Lena's excited reply, her heart filling just a little bit more. Life wouldn't be the same without Ella, but there was still much to look forward to.

They'd spend the rest of the day with their grandfather. Tomorrow was soon enough to resume their search for the stolen coin. Her heart quickened at the thought of seeing Simon again. Yes, so much to look forward to.

⚜

Chapter Twenty-One

SIMON STEPPED INTO Worley's carriage that evening as dusk fell, casting an orange glow in the sky. "I appreciate you joining me on such short notice."

He'd sent a message to the viscount that afternoon to ask if he was available to join Simon to follow Stockton. If the director was stealing artifacts from the museum, Simon wanted to know what he was doing with them. Following him seemed the only way to discover that when his desk had revealed little. The ledger list remained a mystery and the two artifacts in the crates were still in the storage room thus far, but Simon hoped they would lead to answers.

Worley had offered his carriage with the thought that Stockton wouldn't recognize it if he happened to notice them.

"Your timing was perfect," Worley said. "This way I won't have time to miss Marbury."

"How was the wedding?" Simon asked with a smile as the carriage rolled forward. He could imagine how lovely Norah had looked but worried how she was feeling with Ella leaving.

"Perfect, of course." Worley shook his head with an amused expression. "Marbury and his new countess wouldn't have it any other way."

"I'm sure." Simon clenched his jaw against the urge to ask after Norah. While he knew she was happy for her sister, Ella marrying was a significant change in Norah's life. As close as the sisters were, the adjustment would be difficult.

Worley considered him from across the interior of the carriage for a long moment, making Simon wonder at his thoughts. "Norah and Lena shed many tears this morning."

An ache filled Simon at his words. He glanced out the window at the quiet streets. The urge to reach out and offer comfort was overwhelming. Yet he didn't know whether that would be wise.

"Yes," Worley said as the carriage jostled them both.

"Yes, what?" Simon frowned in puzzlement, certain he hadn't asked a question. Though he could be absentminded, this hadn't been one of those times.

"Yes, you should see Norah soon. I have no doubt that she would appreciate your support."

Simon opened his mouth to deny whatever Worley was thinking, only to close it. What was the point? "You are more observant than most."

Worley chuckled. "I do tend to study others closely. I suppose it keeps me from thinking about my own concerns overmuch."

"Understandable." Simon didn't know Worley well enough to respond more to his comment. Regardless of the man's specific worries, Simon could certainly relate to the statement. His upset over the missing artifacts kept him from pondering his feelings for Norah too deeply, something he wasn't prepared to do. Not yet.

Worley continued, "Perhaps you should consider attending the Sutton Ball tomorrow evening. I know the Wright sisters will be there. I could suggest Norah meet you on the terrace briefly so you might have a word in private."

Simon smiled. "I would appreciate that."

They settled on the details and, once again, Simon was astounded at how much the upcoming chance to see Norah lifted his spirits. He suddenly felt as if he could accomplish anything.

"Now then, back to business." Worley shifted to look out the carriage window at the darkening scenery. "Stockton tends to eat soon after he returns from the museum. The few times Marbury and I watched him, he remained home afterward."

"I'm hoping that if he's behind the stolen artifacts, he'll need to take steps to sell them. Perhaps meet with a potential buyer or the like. Something out of his normal routine." Simon told Worley about the two artifacts left in the crates as well as the ledger paper on Stockton's desk with the same numbers that had been stamped on the outside of the crates.

None of that was proof of anything. But since Stockton remained the most likely suspect, Simon wanted to learn all he could about the man.

Worley smoothed a finger along his mustache as he considered the idea. "Determining a possible motivation would provide a better understanding and perhaps even a clue where we should look for proof."

"Money is the most common one. I suppose he might be in financial distress of some sort," Simon said. "But I'm not certain how we could investigate that."

"Is he close to any of the museum staff?" Worley asked.

"Not particularly. If anyone, I suppose it would be Emerson."

The viscount lifted a brow. "It might be worth having a discreet word if you think you can trust him not to say anything to Stockton."

"I will consider it." Simon had come to know the young man better over the past two weeks since he'd spent more time at the museum. They'd developed a bond of sorts and had enjoyed several meaningful conversations.

"If only we could speak with Stockton's friends to find out more about the man."

"I've never seen him with anyone, nor has he mentioned any," Simon advised.

"Those kinds of details were what Marbury and I hoped to discover. Doing so proved impossible when the man remained home the few evenings we observed him."

"I happened to speak with a neighbor of Emerson's who was

able to share helpful information when I first thought he could be involved. You might try that."

Worley nodded. "Excellent idea. I shall try it tomorrow afternoon before Stockton returns home from the museum."

The carriage pulled to a stop two houses from where Stockton lived. Worley pointed to a modest, two-story red brick townhome with a narrow garden lined with a wrought-iron fence. They watched for several minutes, but Simon soon grew impatient. "Shall we get closer?"

"As in look in the windows?" Worley asked with some surprise.

"We can't see anything from here." Simon reached for the door and stepped out.

"Humph." Worley followed, still seeming shocked by Simon's suggestion.

Night had fallen and hid them from view as Simon led the way to Stockton's home. Only one light was visible in a window toward the back of the house.

As quietly as possible, they entered the garden and neared the lit window. Simon peered inside, heart pounding. If Stockton caught sight of him—

The thought was inconceivable.

The room visible through the window appeared to be a study of sorts with a desk and two shelves lined with books. Stockton was nowhere to be seen. Simon had the faint hope of seeing one of the missing artifacts. But of course, that would've been too easy. Nothing hinted at Stockton's line of work, let alone the stolen items.

Disappointment speared through Simon. He wanted something—anything—to indicate whether the director was guilty. He simply had to find Norah's coin. He wanted that more than he could say.

The thought had him moving to the next window.

"Vanbridge," Worley muttered with a hint of exasperation. "What are you doing?"

"Trying to find a clue," he whispered. For once, he wanted to be the hero in someone's life. Even if it was for only a moment. He could imagine the way Norah would look at him if he handed her the coin.

"You won't be able to do that if you're caught."

Simon turned to look at Worley, the viscount's glare making him think twice.

"True." He needed to use his head, not his heart, in this matter. With a resigned sigh, he gathered his thoughts and his patience, then returned to the lit window with caution.

Hoping the darkness hid him, he raised up to look in the corner and caught sight of Stockton entering the room and pausing before the fire. He'd removed his suit coat and held a drink. He rubbed his forehead, took a sip, then set the glass on a nearby table before shaking his head. He rubbed a hand over his face and shook his head again.

Simon eased away to look at Worley. "He seems upset. Anxious even."

"Perhaps he's having second thoughts about his actions," Worley whispered. "Any sign of the artifacts?"

"No." Simon turned back to the window and peeked in again, only to realize Stockton had disappeared. "He's gone."

Worley eased back to have a better look at the other windows in the house. "A light came on upstairs. Perhaps he's retiring for the night."

"It seems rather early."

"Wait. The light's gone." Worley continued to watch.

Simon carefully looked in the study window again. His patience was rewarded when Stockton returned to the room. He sat at his desk, opened a drawer, and pulled out a small stack of papers. Simon dearly wanted to know what they were, but it was impossible to tell.

They watched for nearly an hour, but Stockton did nothing of interest other than reading and jotting notes.

As the hour grew late, Worley leaned close. "What do you

think? Shall we consider it done for this evening?"

"I suppose." Simon hated to leave without accomplishing anything. "It seems unlikely anything more will occur."

They eased away from the house through the garden and back along the quiet street. Light glowed from inside one or two of the nearby houses, but no one was about. It truly was a quiet neighborhood.

"I wish we could have a closer look at those papers he was reviewing," Simon said as they neared the carriage.

Worley shook his head. "In case you're thinking about it, we are not breaking into his home."

"No. Not this evening."

Worley's beleaguered sigh was nearly comical. "You mean not without additional evidence."

"Yes, that, too." Simon clapped Worley's shoulder. "Thank you for the company and for providing a voice of reason."

Worley nodded at his driver, then followed Simon into the carriage. "I'm sure you'd do the same for me if needed."

"It would be my pleasure. Each time I search, I have high hopes it will amount to something." Simon scowled. "I fear I'm never going to recover the coin."

"Marbury and I felt the same way when looking for David Wright's journal. Then when we least expected it, the situation quickly changed."

"I hope that is the case soon. I'm running out of ideas."

"Persistence is key. Along with patience."

"My patience is in short supply, as well."

"We have a plan for tomorrow at the very least. I'll return to see if I can speak with any of the neighbors while you talk with Emerson."

"It's better than nothing." Simon considered what more could be done.

"Amidst your investigation, don't forget the ball tomorrow evening," Worley reminded him.

"I won't." While anxious to see Norah, he also wished he had news to share with her.

"TRULY?" NORAH STARED at Worley in disbelief at the Sutton Ball the next evening. The idea of not only seeing Simon but having a moment alone with him was more than she could've hoped for.

"Truly." Worley smiled, his gaze searching hers. "Had I known how much this meant, I would've thought of it sooner."

Norah and Lena had both been out of sorts since the wedding the previous morning. They nearly hadn't come this evening, but their grandfather had shooed them out the door, insisting it would be good for them to think of something other than missing Ella.

Now Norah was pleased he had.

"What time is it now?" she asked, wishing she had worn her pin watch.

Worley pulled a silver pocket watch from his waistcoat. "You have a quarter of an hour to prepare yourself."

Thank goodness the meeting time was nearly upon them. Otherwise, she would've been hounding Worley every few minutes for a look at his pocket watch.

"Have I told you how much I adore you?" she asked the viscount, her spirits lifting.

"Not lately, but I forgive you for the lapse," he teased. "However, we must take care that no one notices. Your new brother-in-law would have my head." He glanced at Lady Havenby, who visited nearby with friends. "Need I remind you that you could face ruin if caught?"

"I won't be." She didn't want to risk ruin. However, having a few minutes with Simon was just what she needed. She wanted to know if there were any new developments with the coin, but that wasn't the only reason she longed to see him.

"If anyone is out there other than Vanbridge, you'll return

inside immediately. I'll wait by the door to keep watch."

She nodded, feeling confident that nothing would go wrong. The evening was young, and though the terrace doors stood open to let in the cool air, it wasn't so warm in the ballroom that people needed a breath of fresh air. "Shall we?"

Worley looked around as if to make certain no one watched them, but given the size of the crowd, it was impossible to tell.

After nodding at Lady Havenby, Norah took his arm, pretending he'd asked her to dance, and they slowly made their way across the room, edging toward the terrace doors. Already her heart hammered in her chest as if bent on escape. She closed her eyes briefly, realizing how much she cared for Simon. This was not simply a friendship. Nor was it a fleeting tendre. What she felt was so much more. In truth, it frightened her.

They were different in many ways. She enjoyed balls and parties and visiting with friends, whereas he would rather remain home. She appreciated history but didn't immerse herself in it. She'd always been certain she would never marry a man like her father, who was more enamored with the past than the present, let alone the future.

Marriage hadn't been on her near horizon. She wanted time to enjoy her life before taking a husband. Now she didn't know what she wanted.

"Miss Wright. Viscount Worley," Lady Clara said with a broad smile. "I hope you're both enjoying the evening."

"We are. And you?" Norah nearly groaned in frustration. She didn't want to be delayed by the lady when it was such a challenge to escape her. Norah needed to take care to make certain Lady Clara didn't see her step out to the terrace alone. She might follow. Or worse, she might feel compelled to bring it to someone's attention.

"I am." Lady Clara glanced over her shoulder to where her mother visited with another guest. "Though I hoped more people would attend."

Norah frowned, wondering who she wanted to come but

hadn't. "It's still early. Perhaps more will arrive. I'm surprised you're not dancing."

"As am I." Her disgruntled tone caused Norah to share an amused look with Worley.

"Is there someone in particular you hope to dance with?" Worley asked.

Lady Clara cast a flirtatious smile in his direction. "Perhaps a handsome gentleman such as yourself."

"Oh. Well." A faint blush coated Worley's cheeks, then he cleared his throat. Apparently, he didn't really want to dance with her.

Norah bit her lip, wondering how much time had passed. Was Simon already waiting outside, worried why she hadn't yet made an appearance?

"May I have the honor of a dance?" Worley asked at last, much to Norah's relief.

Lady Clara's face lightened as if he'd presented her with a special gift on Christmas morning. "I would be positively delighted." She cast Norah a sympathetic look, suggesting she was sorry for stealing him away. "If you don't mind, Miss Wright."

"Of course not." Though pleased to have Lady Clara's attention otherwise occupied, she hated to lose Worley's assistance in keeping watch. Yet it couldn't be helped.

Norah waited until the pair moved toward the dance floor and then eased toward the terrace doors, her desire to see Simon warring with her wish to be careful. With a last glance around, she slipped outside.

The terrace seemed dark after coming from the bright ballroom. No one was visible in the narrow pool of light. Her stomach sank with the fear she'd missed Simon.

Then a warm hand reached out from the dark to take hers, and her heart flew. "Simon."

"Norah." He breathed her name, making it sound wonderfully exotic. He pulled her close, his gaze sweeping over her face, seeming to search for anything that had changed since they'd last been together, though it had only been a few days.

His hand cupped her cheek, and she leaned into his touch, suddenly feeling that all was well with the world once again.

"How have you been since the wedding?" he asked.

Her eyes adjusted to the darkness, and she could easily make out his concerned expression. To think he realized how hard it had been to say goodbye to Ella put a lump in her throat. "It's going to be a difficult adjustment."

"I'm sure."

That he hadn't tried to dismiss her concern or placate her was more comforting than she could've guessed. "The house is so quiet without her. We're a little lost. Even Grandfather."

"How long will they be gone?"

"Two weeks or more, depending on how the journey goes." She leaned in, drawing some of his strength. She'd missed everything about him, from his scent to his kindness and so much more. "What of you?"

He offered a partial, one-shouldered shrug. "I'm well enough, though I don't have much to report on the coin." He told her about the crates, the situation still bothering him.

"Doesn't it seem odd that whoever is behind this didn't simply take the entire crate?" Norah asked. "It's almost as if they're toying with you. One item here. Another there."

Simon nodded. "I have considered the same thing. But why?"

"To damage the museum's reputation? Or perhaps yours."

"To what end?"

She pondered the question. "The only reason that comes to mind is to force you to close the museum. Could it be your cousin, Lady Mendenhall?" Then she shook her head as doubt filled her. "But why would she act now?"

"I agree. Which brings me back to Stockton or a competitor. I've visited a few of the more likely ones but haven't come to any conclusions." Simon scowled. "Perhaps it's time to stir the pot."

Something in his tone caused worry to skitter along her spine.

"How so?"

"I'm not sure. But waiting and watching hasn't gained me anything."

Norah rested her gloved hand on his lapel. "Do be careful, Simon. This could be dangerous."

He covered her hand with his. "I know. Thank you for your concern."

She glanced toward the ballroom, wishing they had more time. "Will you keep me apprised?"

"As soon as I have something to report." He moved to hold her waist. "Thank you."

"For what?"

"Stepping out here to meet me."

Her heartbeat sped at his intent expression. "I have been thinking about you," she whispered.

"And you've been in my thoughts." His gaze dropped to her lips and her breath caught. Then his hands tightened on her waist, and he drew her against his hard length, sending desire spiraling through her.

Unable to wait another moment, Norah raised on her toes and pressed her lips to his. His mouth was warm and perfect. Just enough mastery to make her knees weak. While kissing him was still a new and exciting experience, she trusted him to act with honor. To not press her for more than she was willing to give.

But she was willing to give him so much more.

Their kiss deepened as their tongues swept against one another. He shifted to wrap his arms tightly around her and liquid heat poured through her.

A sound penetrated the fog of her brain and, apparently, Simon's as well, because he jerked back to look at the terrace doors. "I should let you go before you're missed."

No don't, she wanted to plead but held back. He was right. "Will you come in?"

"I don't think so."

Disappointment swept through her. Yet his answer was a

reminder of one of their differences. Would those keep them apart?

She didn't want to change him or force him to endure social events when he didn't enjoy them. But neither could she see herself remaining home day after day and night after night. That had driven her crazy on Oak Island.

"What is it?" he asked, trailing a finger along her cheek.

She forced a smile. "Nothing." That concern was for another day. It wasn't as if he'd suggested they consider a future together. She needed to enjoy the moment and allow events—and feelings—to unfold.

Holding tight to the thought, she kissed him briefly, then drew back. "Thank you for coming to see me, Simon. Be careful."

He nodded, then eased into the shadows while she moved to the terrace door and stepped inside. A quick glance around suggested no one had noticed her absence.

Yet as she stood there watching the crowd, she realized the evening had lost its luster. Her enjoyment of the ball had left with Simon.

"Oh, dear," she murmured. She was falling in love with him.

Chapter Twenty-Two

THE FOLLOWING MORNING, Simon arrived at the museum before anyone else. He quickly checked the storage room, and the crates were still there, along with a single item in each of them. Relieved they hadn't been moved, he hurried up the stairs to his office and unlocked it.

While at the museum the previous day, he had managed to copy the information on Stockton's ledger page during the few times the director stepped away from his desk. Simon retrieved it from his pocket and sat at his desk to study the list. This wasn't so different than the stone carvings he enjoyed deciphering. It took time to find a pattern, but if he persisted, it often revealed itself.

Soon sounds could be heard in the rest of the building, suggesting employees had arrived to open the museum. Stockton tapped on the door Simon had left ajar.

"Good morning, my lord." He bowed, then adjusted his spectacles, seeming surprised to find Simon already there. "What brings you by the museum so early?"

"I wanted to have a closer look at the new artifacts for the Incan exhibit." He already knew the items had been taken to the exhibit area with the exception of the ones in the crates but was anxious to see Stockton's reaction to his request. Simon normally designed the bigger exhibits while the director handled adding artifacts to existing displays.

"Oh?" Was it Simon's imagination or did dismay tighten the man's features?

"Is that a problem?" Simon asked.

"Not at all. Whenever you're ready."

Simon rose from his desk. "No time like the present." Speaking with Norah the previous evening had done more to clear his mind than all the thinking he'd done on his own, and he was eager to move forward with his life.

Though he might not be ready to label his feelings for her, he couldn't deny them. Their heated kiss made him long for more. He'd even been tempted to attend the ball to prolong their time together.

He had woken this morning filled with purpose and determined to take action. He wanted the mystery solved and the artifacts returned. But he couldn't take steps until this situation was resolved.

If Stockton was the one stealing, he wanted to know now. He leveled the director a hard look as he moved toward the door, causing the man to take a step back. The man frowned, seeming confused before turning toward the stairs with Simon directly behind him.

"Do you have something specific in mind for the exhibit?" Stockton asked.

"Vaguely. It will help to see all the artifacts together first."

"Of course." Stockton hurried down the stairs as if time was of the utmost importance, something out of character for the man.

Good, thought Simon. The more he made Stockton nervous, the better. He'd be more likely to take a misstep. That might be all that was needed to provide the evidence he sought.

Stockton led the way to where the Incan exhibit would be placed. A large canvas curtain kept the area from the public's view. He drew back the canvas and held it aside for Simon to enter.

Simon studied the items, which ranged from clay pots to

statues to pipes. "Weren't there others?"

"I think this is all."

"No. I'm certain some things are missing." Simon made a show of looking over the items, picking up several to examine before setting them down. He turned to face Stockton with a brow raised.

"Hmm." Stockton adjusted his spectacles again. "I will check to see what the inventory list noted."

"I'll wait." Simon folded his arms over his chest to suggest his patience was limited. He wasn't about to let the director avoid his question.

"Very well." Stockton's mustache didn't hide his scowl. He was obviously displeased with Simon's demand. Especially since he so rarely demanded anything. "I will retrieve the inventory list from my office and then check the storage room."

Once the man left, Simon counted the pieces again. The ledger page had noted fifteen but only thirteen were here. Would Stockton return with the two items from the crates? Simon's hopes rose that he would know in the coming minutes whether the man was guilty. Unable to wait, he ventured down to the next floor toward the storage room.

He greeted the employees he passed, then paused in the doorway of the storage room to peer inside.

Stockton muttered to himself as he checked the numbers stamped on the crates before looking inside. The first one he looked through was empty, and he set it aside to look through another.

The director's search had Simon reconsidering his suspicions. He acted as if he were looking in the crates for the first time. Simon's breath caught as he picked up one of the crates that still held an artifact. He dug around in the straw and pulled out the artifact to stare at it in disbelief. "What on earth?"

Simon drew back from the doorway as he collected his thoughts, sifting through what he'd witnessed. It almost seemed as if Stockton was surprised by his discovery. Did that mean he was innocent?

With a sigh of frustration, Simon entered the room. "Find anything?"

"Yes, my lord. It seems whoever unpacked the crates failed to see these items in the very bottom. My apologies."

"Isn't there an inventory list so we know what should've been shipped?"

"Yes." Stockton gave him an almost sheepish look. "In truth, I was given a report that noted two items missing and was undecided what to do about it. I should've come down here to look myself."

"Mistakes happen. Please advise the staff to take more care." Simon's stomach tightened at the realization that he had the wrong man.

He'd been so certain Stockton was guilty when the man's only crime was that he was a rather inept director. Disappointment swept through him. While pleased to eliminate Stockton as a suspect, Simon was at a loss as to who else to pursue.

"Of course, my lord." Stockton carefully unpacked the small statues and held them aloft. "I'd forgotten how exciting it is to open these treasures."

Simon walked forward for a closer look. "Those are interesting. Let's take them upstairs with the other artifacts, and I'll share what I'm thinking for the new display."

They started up the stairs only to see Emerson rushing toward them. "My lord. Mr. Stockton. I have terrible news."

"What is it?" Simon asked.

"The Tumbaga Gold statue is missing."

Simon stilled in surprise with Stockton behind him. "Are you certain?"

"Yes, my lord." Emerson's distress nearly matched his own.

Simon muttered a curse under his breath as a mix of frustration and anger swelled within him. One step forward and two steps back.

"Show me," he told Emerson and hurried after him with

Stockton trailing behind.

The statue Emerson mentioned was a solid gold figurine six inches in height with an elaborate fanned headdress and simple clothing. It was one of the centerpieces of the pre-Columbian exhibit, which meant its loss was a major blow to both Simon and the museum.

That statue had been one of his uncle's prized possessions. When his cousin, Anna, heard of this, she would be furious. Never mind that he'd offered that she take her choice of any of the items her father had in his collection.

Guilt filled him. He should've kept watch over the museum the last two nights rather than staring in Stockton's windows and meeting Norah. Apparently, he needed to hire guards to patrol the museum at night to make certain nothing else was taken. Or had someone managed to steal the figurine during the day when no one was looking?

"I don't know how this could've happened." Emerson led them to the display. A lamp shone on the empty shelf in the glass case where the statue should be. No glass was broken, and, at a glance, the lock seemed intact.

A crushing weight descended on Simon, threatening to squeeze the air from his lungs. Once again, he was at a loss as to how to proceed. What more could he do to uncover who was behind the thefts and stop them from taking more?

LATE THAT NIGHT, Simon sank into the chair at his desk in his study, propped his elbows on the surface, and dropped his head into his hands, filled with despair. The time had come to admit defeat.

Four more artifacts had been discovered missing from the museum. That meant five artifacts had been taken in the last twenty-four hours, several of them quite valuable. No doors had been broken, nor any locks damaged. The police had been called, and Simon had personally spoken with each employee. None had seen anything or had any helpful comments.

The items seemed random with no connection that Simon could see. The statue Emerson had found missing in the pre-Columbian exhibit. A hammered, hand-forged medieval shield. A gold and ruby Egyptian pendant. An ancient clay tablet from the Bronze Age. A beaded copper bracelet from the Viking era.

Some large. Some small. Some expensive. Others only valuable to a collector. They'd come from different eras, different floors, different exhibits. Only one had been part of his uncle's original collection. The rest had arrived later, at various times from a wide range of sources.

Simon sat back with eyes closed, exhausted from the turmoil of the day. He and the employees, Stockton included, had searched the museum from top to bottom with the hope of finding the items stashed somewhere only to come up empty-handed. He felt sickened by the losses.

"My lord?"

Simon opened his eyes to see Fletcher hovering in the doorway. He knew the butler had noted his upset upon returning home. "Yes?"

"Mrs. Fletcher is wondering if you'd like your dinner now."

"No, thank you." He had no appetite. The thought of food made him ill.

Fletcher took a few steps closer, his brow furrowed with concern. "Have you received bad news, my lord?"

"You could say that."

Fletcher nodded solemnly and moved to the side table with the decanters and glasses. "Then, it's a drink you need."

"I don't think—"

Fletcher shook his head even as he poured amber liquid into a glass. "I know liquor won't solve the problem. But it won't hurt either. Spirits have been known to ease a troubled mind. Perhaps a drink will provide some relief."

He sat the glass before Simon and backed away.

"Thank you." Simon took a sip, but when Fletcher frowned, he took a deeper drink. The whiskey burned down his throat, but the warmth was welcome and released some of the tension in his chest.

Miles appeared in the doorway. Fletcher must've advised him that Simon was upset.

Simon heaved a sigh, oddly grateful for their presence. "I'm going to close the museum."

"What's happened?" Miles asked as he walked forward to join Fletcher.

Simon explained the additional thefts they'd discovered and the lack of clues.

"What about employing security?" Miles asked. "I could assist, as I'd certainly like to help catch whoever is doing this."

"I appreciate your offer and might accept it. Apparently, that's something I should've done earlier." Once news of this spread, his reputation and that of the museum's would be destroyed.

"There has to be something we can do," Fletcher insisted.

Simon shook his head. "At this point, I feel as if I've tried everything."

The thefts not only affected the museum's future but his own as well. While he'd been regularly asked to examine interesting finds in the past, that would grind to a halt after this. The likelihood of anyone trusting him with artifacts were nil.

He emptied the glass, enjoying the heat in his belly when the rest of him felt so cold. But it was only temporary, much like many of the pleasures in life—family, love, happiness. Fleeting and impossible to hold onto. "Three of the employees volunteered to keep watch this evening," he said. "Come morning, we'll dismantle the exhibits and remove the artifacts. Some will have to be brought here. We'll move the more unique and valuable ones first."

A well of emotion rolled over Simon. He couldn't help but think of how disappointed his father would've been. His uncle, as well, considering one of the missing items had been his.

He'd never felt more like a failure than in this moment. Just when he'd started to think the coming years might bring happiness, fate slapped him down again. It was as if he were being reminded not to make plans or raise his hopes for a happy future.

The first exhibit he'd dismantle would be Norah's. He would return her father's items, except for the coin. The thought had him glancing at the decanter with thoughts of refilling his glass.

"I'm sorry to hear it, my lord," Miles said with a shake of his head. "I remain at your service."

"As do I, my lord." Fletcher bowed deeply.

"Thank you both." Simon watched the two servants leave, then set aside the glass and stood. He needed to try to get some rest. Tomorrow would be a long day.

⇶⤛

"The Marquess of Vanbridge is calling, Miss Norah," Davies announced from the door of the music room where Norah was playing the piano. "Are you receiving?"

"Yes, of course. Please show him to the drawing room." Her heart lifted at the thought of Simon despite the early hour. It was too soon for callers. The realization gave her pause. Did he have news?

"As you wish." Davies nodded and retreated.

Norah stood, suddenly nervous, and not solely because of the unexpected visit. She hurried down to the drawing room, her feet moving quickly of their own accord. It was as if every part of her was anxious to see him.

She remained standing in the drawing room, her gaze fixed on the entry. She didn't have to wait long.

"The Marquess of Vanbridge," Davies announced with a dip of his head.

Norah's stomach dropped the moment she saw Simon's

solemn expression as he carried in a small wooden box. Something was terribly wrong. Aware of Davies looking on, Norah dipped into a curtsy. "Good morning, my lord."

"Miss Wright." Simon bowed, then set the box on a table, his green eyes bleak. "I have come to return your collection. Unfortunately, I'm closing the museum."

His statement squeezed the breath from her lungs. "I don't understand."

"I'm closing the museum," he repeated, seeming to think that if he said it again, she might understand. But she didn't.

"What happened?" She took several steps closer only to have him stiffen. "Simon?"

His rigid posture, along with the fact that he didn't meet her eyes, suggested something terrible had occurred.

He tightened his lips, seeming to brace himself for what he was about to say. "Five more items have been taken. I'm left with no choice but to close before anything else disappears."

"Oh no. How terrible." The words were inadequate, but Norah couldn't think of what else to say. "I'm so sorry."

Davies departed, for which Norah was grateful. She wanted a moment to speak with Simon in private, though she was beginning to doubt that would change anything.

"Simon." She took a step closer, hand outstretched to touch him.

But he stepped back. When he finally looked at her, the remoteness in his eyes shot a sharp pain through her chest. "Please accept my deepest apologies for the stolen coin. Of course, the museum will provide financial repayment for its value."

Norah stared at him, his words flowing around her but not making sense. Not when she felt like he was saying something else entirely. "That's not necessary."

His lips twisted to the side, suggesting his displeasure. "I would like to thank you for your assistance with the search, but our association has now come to an end."

Norah's heart grabbed. "Why?" As far as she was concerned,

what happened at the museum didn't have anything to do with their relationship.

"My time will be taken with closing the museum and finding homes for the artifacts. I doubt our paths will cross again."

Now her heart dropped to her feet. "I see." But she didn't. None of what he said made sense. "I'm terribly sorry to hear of the additional thefts, but closing the museum seems drastic, don't you think?"

"One of the items was my uncle's. My cousin will not be pleased. I have no doubt the countess will spread the news far and wide about the missing artifacts. Visitors will be few when they have reason to worry about their personal safety, even if the items weren't taken during business hours. If I don't take extreme measures now, there may not be any artifacts left. I can't risk that."

But what of us? Norah wanted to demand. His formal demeanor made her wonder if she'd imagined the affection between them. Clearly, she'd misunderstood what he felt for her. While her heart was held by the distant man standing before her, he didn't seem to feel the same. How could she argue when he was so determined to say goodbye?

"I'm sorry you feel it's come to this." Did he understand that she wasn't just referring to him closing the museum? She clenched her hands, nails biting into her palms with the hope she could hold back her emotions.

How ironic that when they'd met, she'd been so certain she wasn't ready to marry. Especially not to a man whose focus was on the past.

Reminding herself that she hadn't been ready for a commitment didn't ease her pain. Not when the ache in her heart consumed her both physically and emotionally, threatening to choke her.

"I wish you the best." His green eyes flashed with a hint of emotion, but it was gone before she could decipher it. "It was a pleasure becoming acquainted with you."

Her breath shuddered at the finality of his words. Then he bowed and strode out the door, leaving her to sink into the nearest chair, knees too weak to hold her.

She stared at the small box of her father's things, not wanting to think of the wonderful display Simon had created now empty.

Then again, that was how she felt. Empty.

How foolish of her to believe that a man like Simon could love her. He'd been bound to her by her father's artifacts, nothing more. Once again, she wasn't enough on her own.

Chapter Twenty-Three

"N ORAH?" LENA PEEKED around the edge of Norah's open bedroom door. "Are you ready?"

"Yes." Norah forced a smile, her heart impossibly heavy. Though tempted to remain in bed to nurse her hurt, she refused to do so. Just because Simon was giving up on discovering who was behind the thefts didn't mean she had to. Besides, having a purpose felt much better than wallowing in self-pity.

"I'm proud of you." Lena smiled as Norah collected her cloak and reticule.

"Whatever for?" Norah asked, genuinely puzzled.

"I know how upset you must be. Yet you're moving forward with the best intentions."

The sympathy in her sister's eyes brought a now familiar lump to Norah's throat.

Lena had come into the drawing room shortly after Simon left the previous day, and Norah had shared what happened.

"It wasn't as if we had an understanding," Norah said, all too aware of how hollow her protest sounded. "Simon might think the situation is over, but I refuse to believe that. He needs help regardless of whether he admits it."

She'd asked Lena to accompany her to a few more museums. Perhaps staying busy would help ease her aching heart, even if she had doubts whether their efforts would make a difference.

While she didn't truly expect to find anything, she had to try. Anything was better than sitting in her room, staring out the window, wishing.

Wishing Simon felt the same regard for her as she did for him.

Wishing he'd allow her to be a part of his life.

Wishing she were enough.

"I agree to the last part." Lena studied her as they descended the stairs. "Though I did think there was a hint of an understanding between you."

Norah shook her head. So had she.

"Are we looking for anything specific today?" Lena asked, seeming to sense it would be best to change the subject. "You don't expect to find Father's coin in one of the displays, do you?"

"That would be too much to hope for. We will be observing, in addition to speaking with the owners, if possible. Surely, we can form an opinion whether we think they could be involved."

Norah chose to ignore the look of doubt that crossed Lena's face.

In short order, they were settled in the carriage with Dorothy, driving toward the Special Antiques Museum. James, the footman, accompanied them as well. Though they'd visited many museums since arriving in London, they'd never been to this one.

"It feels strange to be doing this without Ella." Norah glanced at Lena, who gave a single nod of agreement and then blinked quickly. Norah missed Ella terribly and knew Lena did, too.

The museum owner greeted them at the door, but within the first few minutes, Norah was certain he couldn't be involved with the thefts.

With a round face, receding hairline, and a smile that invited one to smile back, Mr. Chorley looked like everyone's favorite uncle. His jovial demeanor and enjoyment of history made the tour a delight, though it felt like a waste of time, given her objective.

The next museum on her list wasn't far. The Museum of

Archaeological Findings was on Manchester Square and was one they'd visited last year. It was larger and more professional than the previous museum but certainly less friendly. The staff was formal and reserved, acting as if they were too busy with their duties to bother with visitors.

Norah and Lena decided against a formal tour and instead walked through the exhibits on their own, selecting only a few to explore. They strolled through the rooms, whispering in hushed tones to share opinions. The museum was enjoyable but lacked heart. It didn't bring history to life like Simon's.

The realization did little to improve Norah's spirits. Perhaps the search was a poor idea after all. Trying to help only kept Simon in the forefront of her thoughts. Had the time they'd spent together meant nothing to him? What of those shared moments when they'd seemed so connected? Then there were the knee-weakening kisses. Surely it was rare to have an emotional and physical bond.

Then again, apparently, she was the only one who had felt it. The thought caused her to scowl.

"What is it?" Lena asked.

"Nothing important." Not caring to explain how much she missed Simon or how much of her heart he held, Norah turned to walk to the rear of the room where an Egyptian exhibit stood.

The faint sound of voices could be heard from a corridor with several doors, one of which stood ajar. She halted, wondering if she should move away to give the speakers privacy. It sounded like a rather heated conversation, based on their tones. Since she couldn't make out their words, she continued her perusal of the artifacts until a name caught her notice.

"Vanbridge."

Norah stilled, holding her breath as if that would somehow help her better hear what they were saying. She eased closer to the corridor but kept her focus on the exhibit in case someone emerged and saw her.

"His uncle made my life impossible," the same male voice

continued. "Since I didn't have the opportunity to make the late marquess pay, it seems only fitting that the current one does."

The other person—a man—responded, but the reply was too quiet to hear.

She continued to listen, but the voices remained muffled, much to her dismay.

"Norah?" Lena moved toward her. "Shall we move on?"

"Not yet." Norah didn't explain, hoping Lena understood the pointed look she gave her. She wanted to see who had been speaking and if they said anything more.

Lena frowned, obviously confused by her odd behavior. She glanced at the exhibit, then looked back at Norah as if unclear what held her interest.

Norah waited, but the voices were too quiet to make out. Did she dare walk closer?

"I want to see who's back there," she whispered to Lena. Some of her urgency must've shown, for Lena nodded.

Norah drew a deep breath and then walked into the corridor, her focus on the one open door. Lena remained by the exhibit. Norah glanced inside the room as she walked slowly past and saw two men, both of whom turned to look at her.

She studied them briefly in an attempt to be able to describe them, if necessary, then continued forward only to realize the corridor ended just ahead, sending panic skittering along her spine.

"I'm sorry, but visitors are not allowed in this area," one of the men said. "Is there something we can help you with?"

Norah turned to face a tall, thin man with a distinctive widow's peak, hoping she didn't look as guilty as she felt. "We had a question about an exhibit and were looking for someone to ask."

"There isn't a written explanation of the artifacts," Lena added as she joined Norah. "It's rather confusing."

"I'm happy to help." The younger man, near Norah's age, with pale wavy hair and a slick smile, stepped forward and gestured in the direction from which they'd come.

Norah led the way and tried desperately to think of something to ask as she paused before the exhibit. "I hope we didn't interrupt an important conversation."

"Not at all." Yet the man's gaze shifted to the door where the older stood watching them. "We're happy to assist visitors with their questions."

Norah didn't bother to share her opinion that the staff was less than welcoming. "Is the owner of the museum here today?"

"Yes. That would be Mr. Evans, with whom I was speaking." He gestured toward the now empty doorway.

She nodded, her thoughts racing.

"What were your questions on the display?" he asked.

The more he spoke, the more certain she was that it had to have been Mr. Evans who'd said the things about Simon's uncle.

Only then did she realize the man was waiting for her question. She glanced at Lena, relieved when she asked about the discovery of one of the artifacts.

She didn't know if the information she'd learned was significant, but she had to share it with Simon.

⇒⟫⟨⟪⇐

"A Viscount Worley is in the lobby and requests a moment of your time, my lord," Emerson told Simon.

"Bring him up, please." Simon dusted off his hands from his work of packing the artifacts from the pre-Columbian exhibit into crates.

The work was tiring, mainly because it added to the overwhelming sense of failure that had shadowed him since the discovery of the additional five stolen items.

No other things had gone missing—as of yet. Whether that was because the museum was guarded at night or the fact that it had closed and whoever was behind the thefts had achieved what they wanted remained to be seen.

He should've sent word to Worley of the new developments. One more action he'd failed to take.

"What on earth is going on?" Worley asked after Emerson escorted him to Simon and left to return to his own work. The viscount glanced around the room, where several crates stood in various stages of packing. "Why is the museum closed? I had to pound on the door to gain someone's attention."

Simon heaved a sigh, but it did little to help release the tension simmering inside him. "Five more artifacts disappeared. I had no option except to close."

"Five?" Worley's brows rose in surprise. "That is upsetting. No leads?"

"None."

"The police?"

"Of little help." Simon shrugged. "They took notes on the few details we know and promised to look into the matter."

"So, you're just going to close and let it go at that?" The irritation in Worley's tone took Simon aback.

"Do you have a better suggestion?" Simon detested his defensive tone but couldn't help it. "We searched the museum for the items. We interviewed all the staff." He shook his head. "All for naught. I can't afford to lose any more pieces."

Worley glanced around, seeming to want to make certain they were alone, then stepped closer. "When you say 'we,' to whom do you refer?"

"Myself, Stockton, and Emerson for the most part."

"What happened to your suspicions of the director?" Worley's voice was barely above a whisper.

"He won't be in until later this afternoon." Simon explained the director's surprise when he discovered the two artifacts in the crates. "After that, I don't see how I can suspect him."

Worley stroked the tip of his mustache as he so often did when in deep thought. "I'm not so sure."

"How do you mean?"

"He's visited the Museum of Archaeological Findings twice in the past three days."

Simon considered the news but dismissed it. "No doubt he's looking for a new position."

"Isn't Vincent Evans, the owner, one of your main competitors?"

"Yes. All the more reason Stockton would seek employment there."

"On his second visit, which I just witnessed, he carried in a bulging valise and returned without it."

Simon frowned. Was there a chance he'd been right about Stockton all along?

"Did you have a chance to speak with Emerson about Stockton as we discussed?" Worley asked.

"Yes. Though it wasn't especially helpful. He doesn't know much about Stockton personally, nor whether his finances are in poor condition. However, Emerson has the impression Stockton doesn't care for me."

"I find that rather suspicious. Did he say anything else?"

"Only that Stockton thinks I'm undeserving of my good fortune." Simon shook his head, still surprised by the comment.

Worley frowned. "What good fortune?"

"Inheriting the title and my uncle's collection."

"Perhaps he should take a moment to count the number of loved ones you lost on your way to inheriting." Worley practically growled the words.

Simon appreciated that at least one person understood. He would've traded all of his inheritance to have his parents back.

"What does Miss Wright think of all this?"

"Norah?" Simon blinked at the sudden change of topic. Or perhaps it was simply the mention of her when he'd been trying so hard *not* to think of her. It shattered the fragile hold he had on his self-control.

"She has a fine head on her shoulders," Worley added. "I would've thought you'd seek her opinion on recent events. The two of you have obviously grown close over the past few weeks."

"The day after the five additional artifacts were taken, I took apart her father's exhibit and returned the items to her."

"And?"

Simon looked away, unable to meet his gaze. "I advised her that it was best if our association ended." He gestured toward the half-packed crates. "My time will be taken with finding homes for the artifacts. I don't plan to attend any events where I might encounter my cousin, the Countess of Mendenhall. One of the missing artifacts was her father's." Explaining his reasoning for saying goodbye to Norah made it feel logical. If only that took away the pain as well.

"You're just giving up?" Worley shook his head. "Closing the museum and returning to your reclusive ways. Throwing your hands in the air in defeat." He turned away and then spun back to cast a glare at Simon.

"What would you have me do?" Simon demanded. Anger took hold. Not at Worley but at the situation. Unfortunately, Worley was the nearest target. "Do you have a suggestion to help resolve this mess?" Sarcasm laced his tone as he glowered at the viscount. "I've followed every possible lead backward and forward. Nothing else has come to light."

"Don't give up. That's what I want." Worley folded his arms across his chest. "We need to keep pressing until we have answers."

"Keep pressing who?" Simon rubbed a hand over his face. "Do you think I haven't gone through all the details more times than I can count?" He couldn't sleep. He couldn't work. His life had been completely turned upside down. But worst of all was stepping away from Norah. "I don't know what else to do." He said the last part quietly, his anger having fled as quickly as it came. He looked around the nearly empty exhibit as a matching desolation filled him.

"Don't give up," Worley repeated. "I don't have the answer. But let us at least press forward. I will continue to follow Stockton. Do you know anyone at Evans's museum who would shed light as to what Stockton may have brought him?"

"I suppose I could ask Emerson to apply for a position there, too. If pushed, Evans might be bold enough to admit it if he has something of our pieces."

"Yes." Worley latched onto the suggestion like Simon had thrown him a rope to grab from a sinking boat. "Perfect. What else?"

"Retrace our steps and go over what we've already looked through." Simon felt an odd tangle of hope and despair. However, despair was definitely winning. He remained unconvinced that their efforts would prove fruitful. "I don't see how we can expect to find new information since we're covering the same ground."

"If I learned anything from working with Marbury to find David Wright's journal, it was that persistence is key. Perhaps we will notice something we didn't see before. Or whoever is behind this will become nervous when they realize we haven't given up."

"I suppose it can't hurt. But I'm not reopening the museum. I have guards scheduled to make rounds for the next week to make certain nothing else is taken until everything is removed."

"That makes sense. The last thing you need is additional thefts. None of Stockton's neighbors had anything of interest to say. I'm going to have my valet have a word with Stockton's servants. Maybe one of them has noted something unusual. I doubt they'll speak with me, but they might share it with a fellow servant."

"Good idea."

"Keep thinking, Vanbridge." Worley strode forward to clasp his shoulder. "I will do the same." His eyes narrowed. "I think you're making a mistake by not involving Miss Wright. She might have an idea we haven't considered. Think about it. I'll be in touch." With a nod, he was gone.

Simon sighed. He didn't need anything more to think on when his mind was already filled to the brim. Did he dare send a message to Norah? If so, what would he say?

He missed her with a deep ache. His life wasn't the same

without her. She was a warm, caring person who made him rethink his future plans.

He'd lost nearly every person he'd ever loved over the years. The thought of risking that again was nearly more than he could bear. But even more disturbing was not having the bright light of her in his world.

Chapter Twenty-Four

"ARE YOU CERTAIN he's here?" Lena asked as their carriage pulled up before Simon's museum less than an hour later.

"No." But Norah knew Simon well enough to think it unlikely that he remained home with all that had happened. If he was truly closing the museum, it would be a monumental task. "But he most likely is."

"Do you think he needs to know what you heard right away?" Lena asked. "Would it be better if you sent a message?"

Norah knew her sister worried that speaking with Simon would be upsetting. Lena was right. It would be. Even the thought of seeing him made her chest ache so much that she could barely breathe. But if what she'd overheard might help, she had to tell him as soon as possible.

James, the footman, opened the carriage door and assisted Norah to step out. She glanced at Lena. "You're welcome to wait. This won't take long."

"Nonsense. Dorothy and I will join you."

James knocked on the locked museum door several times before someone came to see what they wanted. Norah explained that she needed to speak to Simon regarding an urgent matter.

"Allow me to see if he's available," the young man said and hurried up the stairs.

Though tempted to simply follow him, as waiting seemed ridiculous, Norah remained in place. She wasn't brave enough to seek out Simon without his agreement. Not when he'd already bid her such a final goodbye. The thought knotted her stomach. Perhaps this hadn't been a good idea after all.

Before she could tell Lena, the young man returned to advise them Simon waited for them upstairs.

Reminding herself that this was business, nothing more, didn't help. She wasn't certain if she could talk past the lump of emotion that nearly choked her, part anger and part hurt. She hadn't forgiven him for telling her goodbye.

Lena looped her arm through Norah's and offered a smile. "We'll get through this together."

Norah nodded. Yet her steps slowed as their escort gestured toward the room where the pre-Columbian exhibit was. She wished she could wipe the turmoil surging inside her from her expression before she stepped inside. But based on the way she felt, that wasn't possible.

Would it be so terrible if he knew how she felt? Or would that only make him feel sorry for her?

"Norah?"

She jerked her gaze to Lena's, realizing she'd halted just outside the doorway, even as her thoughts whirled. How silly of her when she was the one who'd wanted to come here. This wasn't about her, but the missing artifacts. With a deep breath to regain her balance, she let go of Lena to walk forward where Simon stood just inside the room.

She drank in the sight of him. It seemed like it had been weeks rather than days since she'd last seen him. He looked wonderful, if tired.

"Norah."

Tingles ran along her skin at her name on his lips and the flash of emotion in his eyes.

"Did you receive my message?" he asked, one brow raised in surprise.

"No." She glanced at Lena before looking back at him. "We haven't been home for several hours."

His brow furrowed. "Oh? Then how did you come to be here?"

Norah licked her suddenly dry lips. Why was it that looking at him stole her thoughts?

She cleared her throat. "Lena and I happened to be at the Museum of Archaeological Findings and overheard something we wanted to share."

Now he looked truly perplexed.

"The owner, a Mr. Evans, mentioned you."

"Did he?"

"Well, not to us." She gestured between herself and Lena, well aware she wasn't explaining this in a coherent manner. "I mean, we overheard him speaking to someone else. He said he knew your uncle. And that he—the late marquess—made his life rather uncomfortable."

"Miserable, in fact," Lena added, for which Norah was grateful.

"And how it was only fair that you paid for it." Norah bit her lip.

Simon stared at her in surprise. "I have never liked Evans and assumed the feeling was mutual. But when I first considered him as a possible suspect, I wondered if my opinion was clouded because of that. Interesting. This certainly sheds new light on the situation."

"Though not always fair, we are often held responsible for our relatives' actions." Norah and her sisters had certainly experienced their share of bias from some of the people who'd known their mother and father. Not all of them had been pleasant.

"I appreciate you coming here." He looked as if there was more he wanted to say, yet he hesitated.

"Of course," Norah replied when he said nothing else. "I wish we were of more help."

"You've done so much already. Thank you."

Norah nodded, watching as Simon stared into the distance, suggesting he continued to sort through their news. She glanced around the room, hating how empty it already was.

"We're guarding the museum and will continue to do so," Simon said at last, following her gaze. "In fact, I'll be here this evening to watch over things. That will give me time to find a way to see if Evans is involved."

"I hope the situation resolves quickly." Then, before she made a complete fool of herself by saying how much she missed him and that she wished things between them were different, Norah glanced at Lena. "We should be going."

"Yes," Lena agreed. They both curtsied.

"Goodbye, Simon." Norah looked at him one last time, her heart aching when he said nothing more.

She turned and led the way down the stairs, her chest tight, making it difficult to breathe. Though she wondered about the message he'd mentioned, she couldn't imagine that it contained anything important, or he would've told her.

The faint hope that seeing him again would make him relent and suddenly profess affection for her snuffed out. That was it then. Their association was truly over. She clenched a hand in the folds of her skirt and hoped she could maintain her composure until she and Lena returned home.

SIMON STARED OUT the window of his office later that evening, uncertain what to do next. He hated this feeling. It was one that had followed him far too often since the death of his parents. A clear path forward wasn't visible, much like those terrible days after their funerals, while he'd waited to learn where he would go, only to realize no one wanted him.

He was at a loss on all fronts, starting with Norah.

She'd been standing right in front of him, but rather than speak what was in his heart, he'd watched her walk away. By now, she had surely read his message. What did she think?

Yet how could he take any steps forward with her—if she'd have him—when his life was in such upheaval?

He spun away from the window, done with the doubt. It had held him in its grip for too long. From this point on, he needed to claim the future he wanted. No more waiting for events to unfold. He intended to move forward, starting with resolving the thefts of the artifacts. Closing the museum wasn't enough. He wanted to find whoever had done this and hold them accountable.

The information Norah had shared was interesting but far from proof that Evans had taken the missing items. Yet, when he added in what Worley had seen, he had to suspect Evans and Stockton were working together.

Simon walked to his office door and studied Stockton's desk. The director hadn't yet cleaned it out in preparation for leaving the museum for good. Simon had asked him to remain on through the end of the month to help with closing and offered extra pay if he did so, and he'd agreed.

Stockton had been in earlier, but Simon had told him to take the remainder of the day off. Simon didn't want him there until he determined a plan. Miles and Emerson were watching the museum with Simon through the night. Simon hadn't told Stockton those details. It was another strike against the director that he hadn't bothered to ask who was guarding the place or whether he could help.

This would be a good time to look through the director's desk again. Instead of examining the papers, he needed to think about where Stockton could hide the missing items.

Though some of the artifacts would be difficult to hide because of their size, the coin could be tucked anywhere. Would he have already removed the items from the museum? Would he take the risk of keeping them in his home when, if discovered, they would prove his guilt?

The coin had been a turning point in the thefts as far as Simon was concerned. Its loss had made Simon begin to suspect the thefts were personal, directed at him. The clay pot didn't hold the same importance. Would Stockton keep the coin near as a reminder of his cleverness? Simon moved to the man's desk, considering the possibilities. Where hadn't he looked when he'd previously searched it?

Simon tried to put himself in Stockton's shoes and sat in his chair, examining the desk. The two lower drawers were unlocked, so unlikely choices. Simon patted his pocket and retrieved the pick he'd taken to carrying.

He unlocked the top righthand drawer, pleased in an odd way to know his skills at picking locks had improved. He removed the few papers inside, giving them little more than a cursory glance. Then he patted the interior of the drawer and felt along the sides and top, feeling rather foolish. Nothing seemed unusual there.

He returned the papers to their position, locked the drawer, and shifted his focus to the lefthand one. Blank sheets of paper were inside, making Simon wonder why the man would lock it.

Simon pulled out the papers and felt along the sides and top, pausing when his fingers caught on a folded piece of paper wedged in the back corner of the drawer.

It took several tugs to pull it free. The weight of it was enough to set his heart thudding. He unfolded it with care and could hardly believe his eyes as he stared at Norah's coin.

Damn. Stockton was guilty after all. An odd mix of elation and anger rushed through him to have at last found proof. But where were the rest of the missing items?

NORAH REREAD SIMON'S message, something she'd done numerous times over the past several hours while pacing her bedroom, still uncertain what it meant.

Dear Norah,

I fear I acted hastily when I ended our association and would like to offer my deepest apologies. Worley has convinced me that I gave up too soon. I intend to take action to resolve the thefts once and for all. But I wanted to say I'm sorry to you first. I should very much like to call on you next week once the situation at the museum is behind me.

Yours,
Simon

It had taken all of Norah's reserve to not rush back to the museum and tell him that she was the one in need forgiveness. She worried she had been overly persistent about her father's missing coin. She didn't want Simon to do anything rash. Norah need only remember what had happened with her father to be concerned.

One thing had become clear during the past few days—she loved Simon and wanted him in her life. His message written in a masculine scrawl suggested he cared for her as well.

The realization that she was prepared to set aside her original plan to wait several years before considering marriage had her sinking into a chair. Waiting that long to be with Simon felt impossible.

She turned the notion over in her mind. Yes, in the past few months, she'd finally felt like she was starting to experience life. She'd been certain marriage would take that away. She still wanted to experience new things—but with Simon. Living life to the fullest wouldn't mean nearly as much if he wasn't by her side.

Simon would never hold her back, even if he didn't want to always do the same things she did. But maybe they were good for each other. She would pull him out of his study and away from his work, while he would help her to slow down and enjoy the quiet moments. She didn't want to change him. Instead, she hoped to balance his life and thought he'd do the same for her.

Yes, he appreciated history almost as much as her father. But perhaps being together would encourage him to value the present and future as well.

A knock sounded at her door. "Miss?"

"Yes?"

Dorothy entered with a smile. "It's time to dress for the ball."

"Already?" Norah blinked, trying to remember what ball. The last thing she wanted was to attend a gathering when she longed to be with Simon.

The maid moved to her wardrobe and pulled out the blue gown they'd decided she should wear this evening. "This is a lovely one, don't you think? The color is so flattering."

"It's one of my favorites," Norah murmured as her thoughts raced. What if she stopped by the museum on her way to the ball? Just for a few minutes to ask Simon what he intended. To caution him to take care. She didn't want him to place himself in danger, especially not because of the coin.

After all, it was the memories of her father that mattered, and she would hold those close and cherish them always.

She wanted to tell Simon she'd continue to help with the search. She and Lena could go to Evans's museum again. Perhaps they could discover more. Having a suspect would surely make Simon's investigation easier.

Her thoughts circled with possibilities while Dorothy helped her dress and arranged her hair. Soon the maid finished and departed even as Lena entered the room, wearing a pale lavender ball gown with cream lace touches.

"Don't you look lovely," Lena said with a smile. "That is one of my favorite gowns on you." Yet as she studied Norah, her smile faltered. "What is it?"

"I have a request," Norah said, hoping to convince her sister to agree.

"Of course. What is it?" Lena's concern warmed her heart.

"I have to speak with Simon this evening."

"But Lady Havenby is meeting us at the ball. She'll worry if we don't arrive on time."

"It's about the message he sent. It won't take long." Only long enough to ensure he didn't intend to do anything rash. If something happened to him like it had her father—

"Norah." Lena's gaze held on her with intensity. "This isn't just about Vanbridge or Father's missing coin. Tell me what's truly bothering you."

Norah drew a quick breath. The mention of their father caused her heart to stumble. The weight of what she'd said to him the day he died threatened to crush her once again.

Lena took her hand and held it tight, her blue eyes steady though her brow was creased with worry. "It's all right. You can tell me. I've known something was wrong since before we left Oak Island. It has to do with Father?"

At that, Norah's eyes filled with tears. "I did something terrible. That last day. It was all my fault." The words came in a rush. She couldn't have held them back if she wanted to.

"What was your fault?"

"I argued with him that morning. I wanted to spend a few months in Montreal with my friend, Anna, and her family. But Father refused." Her breath shuddered as her guilt overwhelmed her. "I told him the search was pointless. That he hadn't found hardly anything all those years. That he loved those shafts and the hope of treasure more than he loved us."

Lena gasped, her eyes wide with dismay. But she still held Norah's hand. "Oh, Norah."

"I know." Norah's tears fell. "He died because of me. I'm a terrible daughter. A terrible person."

"No. No, you're not. He and Mother argued about that same thing more than once. I know because I heard them."

"You did?" Norah took the handkerchief Lena handed her and wiped at her tears. "I thought I was the only one who heard them."

"It did feel as if he put the treasure above us. You were brave to speak your mind. Each year since Mother died, his obsession grew. You did nothing wrong other than tell him how you felt."

"But if I hadn't pressed him, he might have not been caught in the collapse. He would've been more careful. The fact that he was angry with me—"

"It wouldn't have mattered." The pain in Lena's face hurt Norah's heart. "That didn't cause him to do anything differently that day. If anyone is to blame, it's me."

"Why would you say that?"

"I knew something was wrong, but I didn't know what. Still, I said nothing until it was too late." Lena squeezed her eyes shut and shook her head. "Living with that has been nearly impossible."

"Lena." Norah waited until her sister opened her eyes. "If I'm not to blame, then neither are you." She sighed as she considered that truth. "Father lost some of his perspective when Mother died. I felt like I had to try to make him see that. Realizing I wasn't enough to convince him to change was devastating."

"You mean that *we* weren't enough. Ella tried to warn him about that, too."

"I wish she were here." Norah sniffed. "I should've shared this with both of you months ago."

"It wasn't the right time then. It is now. And we'll share this with her when she returns." Lena leaned forward to hug Norah, and they held each other tight for a long minute.

"Thank you for understanding. I don't know what I'd do without you."

"You won't ever have to find out. Sisters are forever."

"Yes. Forever." Norah drew back, her heart lighter with one exception. "Can we please stop by the museum? Simon said in his message that he intended to take action to resolve the thefts. I worry he'll do something dangerous."

Lena's lips tightened. "I'm not sure if it's wise."

"It won't take long. I promise. Just a few minutes, and we'll be on our way." Lena's reluctant nod sent a wave of relief through her.

"Lady Havenby won't even realize we're late," Norah told her after they were handed into the carriage. Still, a shiver ran along her spine when she noted the concern etched on Lena's face. That made her worry all the more.

SIMON STARED IN disbelief at the hidden panel behind the lefthand drawers of Stockton's desk. If only he'd paid more attention when he'd searched the first time instead of focusing on the papers.

It had taken time to see the drawers were shorter than they should've been. After several minutes of prying, the wood panel behind them popped free. Inside were three more of the missing artifacts.

"Damn," Simon muttered as he unwrapped the clay pot from a thick cloth. He was anxious to see what the other two wrapped bundles contained.

The scuff of a shoe on the stairs reached his ear. He stilled as the hair stirred on the back of his neck. Ridiculous when it had to be Miles or Emerson coming to see him.

His stomach fisted at the sight of Stockton on the landing. The man jerked to a halt at the sight of Simon, his gaze taking in the cloth-wrapped items on his desk.

The director's eyes went wide, his nostrils flaring in surprise. He stared at Simon, and his mouth moved as if he were deciding what to say.

"What is it?" a voice asked from behind Stockton.

Simon leaned back in the chair as if he had all the time in the world. As if every muscle in his body weren't bunched for a fight.

"We have an unexpected complication," Stockton said, then stepped aside so the other man could join him.

"Come to collect a few things?" Simon asked, gesturing toward the artifacts.

Vincent Evans glared at Simon, his mouth twisting with irritation. "You weren't supposed to be here this evening, Vanbridge."

Chapter Twenty-Five

"NORAH, SOMETHING'S NOT right," Lena whispered as the carriage rolled to a halt before the museum. "I'm certain of it."

Her statement heightened Norah's nerves. She had a similar feeling, though she couldn't say why. "All the more reason we need to go inside. Simon could be hurt."

"James, can you please accompany us?" Norah asked the footman when he assisted them to step down.

"Of course, miss." He unhooked the carriage light and held it aloft. His tall, broad-shouldered form was reassuring, though it didn't lessen Norah's growing concern for Simon.

After requesting their driver to wait, they hurried up the stairs to the front door.

"I thought to knock, but…" Norah reached past James for the door, somehow unsurprised to find it unlocked.

"That's not good," Lena whispered.

"Perhaps the two of you should wait here while I have a look," James suggested, his voice quiet.

"We'll come with you." If Simon was hurt or in danger, surely more of them would be better than less.

"But—" James began, but Norah shook her head.

"We are coming, too." She glanced at Lena, who nodded, despite the worry pinching her features.

James stepped inside with the light held high. A faint knocking sound echoed from the rear of the museum, bringing them to a halt. "Shall we follow the sound?" he asked in a whisper.

Lena shared a look with Norah then shook her head. "We should go upstairs."

Norah didn't question her. This was eerily similar to when they'd found Simon hurt not so long ago. On shaking legs, she followed James up the stairs, all of them being as quiet as possible. Doing so in ball gowns with the rustling yards of fabric was no easy feat.

Soon, muffled voices drifted toward them, and the glow of a light was visible from the floor where the offices were. With a worried glance at Norah and Lena, James set the lantern on the stairs and edged upward, one step at a time with the sisters close behind him. When they neared the top, Norah tugged on James's suit coat to stop him, wanting to listen to whomever was speaking.

"If you'd been home where you were supposed to be this evening, this wouldn't be necessary." The man's voice was angry and vaguely familiar.

It took only a moment for Norah to remember where she'd heard it—at Evans's museum. He'd been angry then as well.

"Terribly sorry to inconvenience you." Simon's dry reply caused Norah's knees to nearly buckle with relief. Thank goodness he sounded unhurt. "Then again, I'm not the one who has been stealing," he continued. The bite in his tone made it clear how angry he was.

"Not stealing, exactly." Norah was certain that came from Stockton. "Merely hiding a few things for a time."

"Pardon me if I don't see a difference," Simon countered.

"One does what one must," Evans replied.

"Are you the one who hit me?"

"I believe that was one of my overzealous men. They didn't expect to find you here that night. Stockton let them in to haul out some of the artifacts he'd set aside."

"You mean stole," Simon argued.

"As I said, one does what one must. Besides, you and I both know you shouldn't be in this business." Evans's words nearly had Norah gasping in outrage.

"Why is that?" Simon asked.

"You shouldn't have inherited to begin with," Evans replied. "You are a marquess by accident. Nothing more."

"True," Simon agreed. "Several accidents, in fact."

"Both your father and your uncle's interest in history was nothing more than a hobby. The late marquess didn't have his facts right half the time."

"It was enough that he and my father enjoyed learning about the past, much like the people who visit the museum. He never attempted to profit from it like you."

Norah wanted to shout at Simon to stop disagreeing since the odds were not in his favor. He would only anger Evans more.

"Do you have any idea how much you've cost me by spreading the ridiculous notion that discoveries should be shared with the native people?" Evans's angry voice echoed in the building, even louder than before. "They weren't the ones who found treasure or paid to have it excavated."

"But it was their culture that created it. Why shouldn't they share in any financial gain?"

"Your attempt to be fair-minded is ruining business for all museums."

"Museums shouldn't be run like a business, but rather a philanthropic venture. I can see we won't agree, but that's hardly a reason for the gun. Put it down. Now."

A gun? The word stole Norah's breath. Knowing Evans had a weapon raised the stakes considerably. How could they possibly disarm him?

The element of surprise was on their side, but she needed to think of how they could best use it. An idea came to mind, and Norah started up the remaining stairs, only to have Lena grab her arm.

Her sister's fierce expression and the shake of her head did nothing to help Norah's nerves.

"Trust me," Norah mouthed, hoping her sister understood. A distraction was in order, and she could easily provide it.

Lena reluctantly released her, though her lips remained pressed tight with disapproval.

Norah leaned close to James. "Wait a few moments. Then grab the taller man if you can."

He nodded in agreement.

With a deep breath, Norah climbed the last few stairs and kept walking.

"Good evening, gentlemen." Stockton was on her left and she stayed closer to him, giving Evans a wide berth since Stockton seemed less likely to grab her.

Though she knew Evans held a gun, seeing the pistol in his hand was still a shock. Especially since it was pointed at Simon.

She glanced at Stockton and Evans, pretending surprise at the sight of them but continued toward Simon. Simon's eyes darkened at the sight of her as if he couldn't believe she was there—or perhaps wished she wasn't.

"Miss Wright." Simon's tone was fraught with tension.

"When you asked me to meet you here, I didn't realize you were planning a party." She smiled brightly at Evans, then Stockton, both of whom seemed confused by her appearance.

Perfect. Now was the time to act. With luck, James would realize that.

A shadow moved behind the two men, and she sent Simon a pointed look. It took him only a moment to understand.

James grabbed Evans from behind while Lena pushed Stockton in the back, sending him stumbling forward. Simon lunged toward Evans and shoved the gun toward the ceiling, then struck the man several times. The three men struggled briefly while Stockton regained his balance, his expression frantic as he watched the battle.

Then he reached for Norah, eyes wild as he took hold of her

arm. She didn't think twice and fought him, using elbows and fists to break free.

"Damn woman," Stockton cursed and reached for her again, his efforts complicated by the brawling men.

Lena joined the fray, and the two sisters pummeled the director back. Norah refused to give him the chance to aid Evans.

She needn't have worried, for when she turned to look, Simon punched Evans squarely in the jaw and stomach, then wrenched the pistol from Evans's grasp. At last, James managed to subdue Evans.

"Halt, Stockton," Simon demanded. "It's over."

The stout man's chest heaved, the swatch of hair he normally combed over his balding head flapping alarmingly to one side. "It wasn't supposed to happen like this."

"What was the plan?" Simon asked, pointing the pistol at the two men while he gestured for Norah and Lena to move behind him.

Stockton swiped at his hair, then ran a hand over his face, his distress obvious. "When Mr. Evans approached me with a proposition and a well-paying position a few months ago, I couldn't refuse."

"Shut up, Stockton," Evans demanded.

The director glared at Evans. "No one was supposed to be hurt." Then he turned to Simon with mounting anger. "You showed so little interest in the museum. Why would I put all my efforts into improving it when you didn't care?"

"That's not true. I trusted you to keep things running smoothly."

"Business was already going downhill, so I took the clay pot with the hope of speeding it up. But you didn't notice for some time, which gave me the idea of making you think your absent-mindedness was worse than you realized. Then came the unveiling of the Wright exhibit." Stockton shook his head, casting an annoyed look at Norah and Lena. "That increased visitors significantly. Evans offered me a reward to take the coin and insisted that when word spread of the thefts, business would plummet, forcing you to close. But it didn't work. If anything, people grew curious, and we had even more visitors."

"So, you took more artifacts," Simon said as he reached for Norah's hand and eased her close. Her heart settled at the contact, her relief that he was unharmed easing her fears.

"I am not a thief." Stockton lifted his nose, suggesting the term was offensive to him. "It was Evans who forced me to do it."

"I didn't force you to do anything," Evans argued. "You took my money with glee."

"What man doesn't dream of a better life?" Stockton's question didn't gain him any sympathy.

"Where are Emerson and Miles?" Simon asked, his expression wary.

"Locked in the butler's pantry," Stockton advised. "When I arrived, I told them I had found the missing items and wanted to show them. Then I locked both in there before letting Evans into the museum."

"That's the knocking we heard," Lena said.

"We'll free them," Norah offered. "Where is the key?"

In short order, she and Lena took the carriage light downstairs and unlocked the door to release a relieved Emerson and Miles. Emerson took Norah's carriage to fetch the police while Miles hurried upstairs to assist Simon and James.

"Lady Havenby is going to be very worried," Lena said.

"It can't be helped." Norah wound her arm through her sister's as they climbed the final flight of stairs. "But she'll be delighted to be among the first to hear of the excitement this evening."

"It's been too exciting for my tastes." Lena gave a mock shudder.

"And mine." Norah couldn't completely dispel the hot ball of worry in the pit of her stomach when she remembered the sight of Evans pointing the gun at Simon. "Thank goodness it ended without injury."

They rejoined the men to find that Evans and Stockton's hands had been bound, thanks to rope from the storage room. Miles and James escorted the two men downstairs to await the police. Simon stood near Stockton's desk on which the gun sat, along with a few wrapped items.

"You will be pleased to see what I found." Simon held up their father's coin, and Norah gasped in surprise as he gave it to her. "My apologies for the upset it caused you to have been missing for this long."

Norah shared a smile with Lena. "We're very happy to have it back." She studied Simon. "Please tell me you're not still going to close the museum."

"Indeed," Lena agreed. "That would be terrible."

"Perhaps not," Simon said with a frown. "I will have to give it further consideration."

Norah was dismayed that he didn't immediately change his mind. "Your exhibits provide a unique look into the past. I have no doubt the museum has stirred an interest in history in many others."

"It's true." Lena reached to touch his arm briefly. "I hope you keep it open." She glanced at Norah. "We should continue to the ball before Lady Havenby sends word to Grandfather. I will wait for you downstairs."

Norah nodded, relieved to have a few minutes alone with Simon, and turned to face him. "You're sure you are all right?"

Simon held her gaze. "Yes. Are you?"

"Fine, thank you." She hesitated, uncertain what was going through his mind. "I would like to return the coin to you with the hope you will not only reopen the museum but include the exhibit of my father's work." She offered it to him.

He took it with a surprised smile. "Very well. I promise to take good care of it."

She moved a step closer, wondering how to share what was in her heart.

"Norah, why did you come this evening?" Simon asked as he put the coin in his pocket. "When I saw you come up the stairs, my heart nearly fell from my chest."

"I wanted to speak with you about your message. To make certain you weren't planning anything dangerous." She looked into his eyes, so grateful he hadn't been hurt. "I'm happy I did. Seeing Evans point the gun at you was horrifying."

He drew her into his arms and held tight, his warmth seeping into her. "I am sorry to have placed you and your sister in danger."

"You didn't." Norah leaned back to meet his gaze. "While I never particularly liked Stockton, I never dreamed he'd do something like this. And Evans." She shivered in the circle of his arms. "What a horrible person."

"Indeed." He trailed a finger along her cheek. "I suppose you must leave now."

She gathered her courage, still wanting to know what he was thinking. "Yes, but about that message."

He gave her the slow smile she adored. The one that lit his eyes until at last curving his lips. "Now that the mystery of the thefts has been solved, I am free to tell you what's in my heart. I love you. I adore everything about you. From your boldness to your kindness. Your intelligence and appreciation for history. Your sensitivity and compassion. All of you."

Then he kissed her with such passion that it left no doubt as to how he felt. She melted against him, loving the feel of his hard strength against her. He was so handsome and kind. So perfect— perfect for her.

"Simon." She was nearly breathless when he drew back. "I love you, as well. The clever way you think." She touched his temple. "Your caution and reserve. The way you view the world and those around you. Your thoughtfulness. When I'm not with you, I'm wondering about you."

"I seem to have that same affliction when it comes to you," he said. "I thought not to marry. What Evans said was true. I wasn't supposed to inherit." He frowned, the pain crossing his face causing her heart to ache. "I lost so many loved ones that I never intended to allow anyone else to touch my heart again. It's too painful. But now I see that not having you in my life would be far worse. Please tell me that you'll consider spending the rest of your life at my side. Would you marry me?"

"Oh, Simon!" The well of emotion rising within her made it nearly impossible to speak. "I had thought to wait a few years before marrying. I am only beginning to enjoy this new life and was certain a husband would push my dreams aside. But now I know I wouldn't enjoy new experiences without you. I love you, so."

He kissed her again, making her feel cherished and loved. Nothing felt so right as when he held her.

"You have made me very happy. May I call upon you tomorrow?"

"I would love that."

"Perfect. How do you think your grandfather will take the news of our plans?"

"He'll be pleased for us, though we may have to ease him into it. Especially since Ella has just left."

"I will try to be patient."

"But not too patient." Then she wrapped her hands around his neck and lifted on her toes to kiss him once again, her heart full. After a long moment or two—perhaps three—she eased back. "I'm sorry to have to leave you."

"As am I. But I will need to speak with the police. Until tomorrow?"

She nodded. "Tomorrow and every day afterward, I hope."

"Yes. Always."

SIMON BLEW OUT a relieved breath when the police hauled away

Evans and Stockton a short while after Norah and Lena departed. He knew there would be more questions come morning, but they could wait.

"Thank you, Emerson, for everything." He reached to shake the man's hand.

"I only wish I could've done more, my lord." Emerson scowled as he shared a look with Miles. "I'm appalled we didn't see through Stockton's ruse and got locked in the pantry. He told us he knew where the missing artifacts were and, in my excitement, I walked into his trap."

"As did I." Miles was also clearly disgruntled.

"He played tricks on us all," Simon said. "Though there is something I would like you to consider doing."

"Anything at all, my lord." Emerson's easy agreement reassured Simon he was doing the right thing.

"Would you consider taking the position of director of the museum?"

Emerson's mouth fell agape. "Truly?" He blinked several times. "I don't know what to say."

"Say yes," Simon suggested with a smile. "I need someone I can trust to oversee things, make certain the artifacts are safe, and that the visitors enjoy viewing them."

"Yes." Emerson beamed. "The pleasure would be mine. You won't regret this, my lord."

"I'm sure I won't. Shall we meet here in the morning to see about cleaning up the mess and putting exhibits back together?"

"I look forward to the challenge." He shook Simon's hand once again, then Miles's. "I wouldn't have wanted to share that interlude with anyone else, sir," he told the valet.

"You are a fine gentleman, Emerson," Miles said with a bow. "I look forward to seeing you again soon."

Emerson grinned, then turned to Simon. "Are you sure there's nothing else you'd like done tonight, my lord?"

"Go home and get some rest. We'll have a busy day tomorrow."

Emerson bowed and departed.

Simon clapped Miles's shoulder. "I'm sorry you were in danger."

"There was no danger for me. Only embarrassment," Miles insisted. "I knew you would deal with whatever Stockton and Evans did with success. You've been training for months."

"The boxing?" Simon considered that as he locked the front door behind them. "I suppose it's true. Then again, Miss Wright's footman was of great assistance."

Miles shook his head. "You would've done well enough without his help. That much I know for certain."

"Thank you for your faith in me, Miles. I appreciate it." The two men walked to the nearest cab stand in silence, an idea coming to Simon. "I realize the hour is late, but I wonder if you would assist me with something."

"Of course, my lord."

Simon grinned. "There's no time to be lost."

Chapter Twenty-Six

LATER THAT EVENING, Norah finished a dance with Lord Crampton and dipped into a curtsy before taking his arm to be escorted back to Lady Havenby. The lady had insisted Norah and Lena stay at the ball for a time so she could make certain they were both well.

Norah thought it was so that they'd be on hand to answer any questions she thought of about their earlier excitement. Lady Havenby adored being the first to know—and share—gossip tidbits. The sisters had asked her not to tell others for a time but knew she wouldn't be able to hold her silence for long.

Time slowed to a crawl for Norah. She wanted the evening over and done. Tomorrow couldn't come soon enough with Simon's visit to look forward to.

"A pleasure as always to dance with you, Miss Wright." Crampton, a gentleman a few years older than she, with a round face and pale hair, studied her as they neared Lady Havenby. "You seem especially quiet this evening. I hope all is well?"

"My apologies for being such poor company." She forced a smile, not knowing what else to say. That she only wanted to dance with Simon? That she didn't feel like speaking with anyone except him? While true, she didn't want to be rude. Crampton was a nice enough gentleman. He just wasn't Simon.

"You're never that," the lord assured her.

"Thank you for the dance." She nodded as he left her with Lady Havenby. Lena had finished dancing, also, and stood nearby with friends.

"Whatever is wrong?" Lady Havenby asked in a whisper. "Your dour expression will turn away any gentlemen who might wish to dance. If you're so unsettled after what you and Lena endured, perhaps you should return home."

The lady had seemed both shocked and fascinated by their tale, hardly able to believe that the once reclusive Marquess of Vanbridge had been threatened with a weapon earlier and engaged in a brawl to save them all.

"Yes, I believe I should." Norah was nothing if not relieved at the suggestion. All she could think about was Simon. She considered explaining her feelings for him but wanted to hold the secret close to her heart for a little while longer.

"Truly?" Lady Havenby looked terribly disappointed.

"I'm sorry. My thoughts are elsewhere. I'm just not myself after this evening's events." Perhaps she should tell her how she felt about Simon. "You see, someone has caught my affections," she began.

"Oh, my." Lady Havenby stared at something over Norah's shoulder.

Awareness swept over Norah, sending tingles along her skin. She gasped, then slowly turned, hoping beyond hope that who she thought might be there would be.

And he was.

"Simon." He looked so handsome in his formal evening attire that her heart threatened to leap from her chest.

"Good evening." He bowed, his gaze taking in Lady Haven-by.

"Our hero has arrived." The lady beamed brightly as if she had always thought of Simon as one.

Simon only blinked before shifting his attention to Norah. "Forgive me for being late. I didn't want to miss the opportunity for a dance."

"Yes, please." Norah couldn't extend her hand fast enough.

He took it, tucking it into the crook of his elbow with care.

Lady Havenby clapped her gloved hands in delight. "I believe I understand now the true reason for your distraction. Enjoy your dance."

"I can't believe you came." Norah felt as if she floated at his side, her happiness complete. "Is all well?"

"Yes. I'll visit with the police again in the morning. But after you left, I could only think of you." They waited as the dancers cleared the floor. "It seemed ridiculous to be home when I could be here." He turned to face her, his warm green eyes holding on her. "With you."

Norah drew a long, slow breath as her heart filled with love. "That is exactly how I was feeling. And now here you are. I can hardly believe it."

"I am the luckiest man in all of London." He led her onto the dance floor as a waltz began.

She stared into his eyes as they circled the floor, moving in time to the music, certain she'd never been so happy before this moment.

"I'm so proud of you, Simon."

"For what?"

"You solved the problem of the thefts. Despite all the odds against you, you persevered."

"Only just. I quit, if you remember."

"A temporary setback."

"Because of you. The thought of never seeing you again was inconceivable."

"It's how we react to what life hands us that matters. Since your parents' deaths, you have overcome one hurtle after another. You are an amazing man." She smiled at the uncomfortable look on his face. "I have been thinking about your uncle and his obsession."

"Oh?"

"My father had an obsession, as well. With the treasure on

Oak Island. He placed its importance above his family's."

"I would guess he didn't see it that way."

"How do you mean?"

"He surely thought of it as a way to provide for his family. To prove to your mother that she made the right choice when she left her life to be with him."

Norah considered that. "You may be right. I told Lena about his final day. How we argued that morning."

"And?"

"She seems to think that our argument wouldn't have pushed him to do anything out of the ordinary. Perhaps she's right. She'd heard my parents argue about Father's fixation with looking for the treasure in the past. If those discussions didn't cause him to act foolhardily, an argument with me probably wouldn't either."

"I would agree. I'm pleased to think you're coming to peace with that." Simon came to an abrupt halt, and Norah nearly stepped on his foot.

She looked past his shoulder to see Viscount Ludham behind him with a smirk on his face and an embarrassed lady standing nearby. "Vanbridge, when will you learn to dance?"

"Ludham." Simon's eyes narrowed as he turned to glare at the man. "You are the one who bumped into me."

"Impossible," he argued, his words slurring slightly, suggesting he was the worse for drink. "I am an excellent dancer. You should stay in that dusty old museum of yours where you belong." He looked at Norah, his gaze raking over her, making her long to look down to see if she was properly covered. "I'm certain Miss Wright would prefer you did."

"Actually, the lady and I are enjoying our dance," Simon countered with an edge to his tone. "Mind your own business, Ludham."

"Or what?" The viscount stepped closer, his chest thrust forward.

The dancers nearby had stopped, as well, and watched with interest.

"Or I'll be forced to remind you what good manners are." Simon straightened his shoulders, clearly not intimidated by the taller man. "Apologize to the lady for bumping into us." He gestured toward Norah.

"You must be jesting." Ludham frowned, suggesting he was unable to believe Simon wasn't rushing away.

"Care to join me outside so we can settle this?" Simon raised a brow, daring him to agree.

"Do take care, Ludham," Norah said with a smile at Simon. "He disarmed someone with a gun a few hours ago. Vanbridge is no one with whom to trifle." She knew Simon would prefer not to share the details, but she couldn't resist given the circumstances.

"A gun? Truly?" The viscount's incredulous expression was nearly comical.

"Absolutely." Norah took Simon's arm. "He's a pugilist, you know, in addition to being an excellent dance partner. The marquess has skills beyond yours in many, many areas."

Only too late did she realize how her last statement could be interpreted even as Simon chuckled. Heat filled her cheeks, but she didn't correct her words. Simon was indeed excellent at kissing. She had no doubt he would be equally as skilled at other aspects of married life. In fact, she could hardly wait to find out.

"Beg your pardon," Ludham muttered, seeming to take Norah's warning to heart.

Simon turned to face her, the heat in his gaze scorching. "Do excuse us, Ludham. We have a dance to finish." Then he drew her into his arms and returned to dancing without missing a beat.

Norah couldn't resist one last glance at Ludham, who stared after them while his dance partner stalked off the floor.

"Well done, my lord," Norah said to Simon. "It's past time someone put that man in his place."

"Happy to be of service." Then he eased her a little closer as they continued around the floor.

The feel of his arms around her as they twirled to the music made all else drop away until the waltz ended. She curtsied as he bowed, then he offered his arm to escort her from the floor.

"I think you'll be pleased to hear that Emerson has agreed to become the director of the museum."

"You're keeping it open?" Norah was thrilled. "Oh, that's wonderful news. He will be perfect in the position."

Simon nodded as he guided her out the open doors onto the terrace. Lamps provided warm pools of light, but he moved toward the shadows. "I'm hoping you will allow me one more kiss before we part for the evening."

"A kiss from the marquess, the man I love?" Norah placed her hands on his chest as he drew her close. "That would be delightful."

And it was.

Epilogue

Four Months Later…

SIMON PACED HIS bedroom, robe flapping against his bare legs. He had never been more nervous in his entire life. This was his wedding night, when he would at last make Norah his.

But he hadn't told her the truth—that he was inexperienced with intimacy. What if he did something wrong and ruined everything?

Of course, he'd done some research on the subject, but the descriptions he'd found made for awkward reading. The dry words didn't begin to describe the desire he felt when he was with Norah. They'd had several passionate encounters that convinced him how much he wanted to make love with her. But he also wanted it to be perfect.

If only he knew how to do that.

She'd looked so beautiful in a white silk wedding gown this morning with a rosebud tucked into her hair beneath her veil. The brief ceremony had been perfect with her grandfather looking on, along with her sisters, Marbury, Worley, and other friends. They'd had a wedding breakfast at the duke's residence with everyone in fine spirits. He knew she worried about Lena being left with their grandfather, but Lena had teased that she was looking forward to having some peace and quiet for a change. That had eased Norah's concern, along with Ella's promise to visit Lena and their grandfather often in the coming days.

The museum was doing well after reopening, and Emerson had proved to be an excellent choice as the new director. Stockton had chosen to move to America after offering evidence against Evans, who'd been forced to close his own museum, as he was standing trial for his actions.

Fletcher and the rest of the staff had been beside themselves with excitement that Simon and Norah had married and greeted the new marchioness with enthusiasm when they'd arrived after the breakfast. Norah had made certain extra cake was prepared for them so they could help celebrate the happy day.

Simon continued his pacing, realizing he wasn't even certain how much time he should give Norah to prepare for bed. He walked to the connecting door and listened. Nothing but silence reached him. Surely that meant the maid had departed and Norah waited for him.

With equal measures of anticipation and worry, he tapped on the door, then opened it and stepped inside.

The room was filled with candlelight and the warm glow of the fire. Several vases of flowers were set about the room, lending a sweet fragrance to the air. But it was the woman who stood before the fire in a nearly sheer white gown who captured his attention.

His nerves fell away when she turned to face him with a smile. "I was beginning to think I needed to come and get you."

"My apologies." He took her warm hands in his. "I didn't know how much time you might need to prepare."

His gaze swept over the plunging neckline that left a swath of pale skin visible. The curves of her breasts were clearly visible and caused his mouth to go dry. The tips of her breasts pressed against the taut fabric and suddenly, his knees threatened to buckle, even as his manhood stiffened.

"You are beautiful, Norah."

Her genuine smile suggested he'd said the right thing. Hopefully his luck would hold, and he'd also *do* the right thing.

He trailed a finger along the soft skin of her cheek, then touched a long strand of her unbound hair that nearly reached her waist. "I love you, my marchioness. Forever and always."

"Perfect." She reached up to place her hands on his neck, her body pressing against his. "Because I love you, dear husband." She bit her bottom lip, and his cock stiffened even more. "May I share a secret?"

"Of course." His breathing became more labored, even though he wasn't doing a thing except holding her narrow waist. The heat of her body was nearly as compelling as the rest of her.

"I cannot wait a moment longer to make love with you." She lifted to kiss him, her tongue seeking entrance as her soft curves moved against him.

He wrapped his arms around her, taking the lead in this erotic dance they shared. He cupped her bottom to lift her against his stiffness. Her soft gasp of pleasure reassured him that he was on the proper path.

"Nor can I." He released her bottom and eased back to move a finger slowly up from the flare of her hip to the dip of her waist. After a moment's hesitation, he continued upward to the tip of her breast to draw lazy circles around it.

"Simon." She braced a hand against his chest as if unable to keep her balance.

Excellent, he thought. That was exactly how he felt. He wouldn't trade the feeling for the world. Eager to continue his exploration, he drew aside the deep neckline to reveal her breast with its pink tip and touched it with a finger, fascinated to see it tighten in response. Just like his own body did.

"Norah?"

"Yes?" Her voice was breathless and barely above a whisper. She tipped her head back, seeming to thoroughly enjoy his touch.

"I, too, have a confession to make."

"Oh?"

He nearly smiled as it seemed to take all her concentration to form words. He liked to think that was his doing.

"I have never made love to anyone before." He watched her expression, hoping she wasn't disappointed.

To his pleased surprise, she smiled. "Good. That makes two of us and proves we're even more perfect for each other."

What could he do but kiss her again? His fingers continued their exploration of her breasts, quickly learning what pleased her. He drew back and bent low to kiss her neck, following the deep neckline down, then took a taut nipple in his mouth, thrilled when she arched into him.

"Oh, Simon. That is lovely." Her hand ran through his hair and then found its way inside his robe, causing it to fall open. She ran her hands along his chest, then even lower, to the flat planes of his stomach.

His cock stirred again, hardening even more if that was possible. He knew without a doubt that he needed to move quickly lest he spill his seed before they even made it to the bed.

With that in mind, he drew up her nightgown and caressed the firmness of her bare thigh. The curve of her hip was something he wanted to examine more closely but that would have to wait. For now, he let his fingers wander to the curls at the apex of her thighs as he continued kissing her.

Her body trembled against him, her breath coming quickly. Unable to resist, he explored her very center, pleased to find her folds already slick. Her hips thrust against his hand, and he nearly lost his mind.

He couldn't wait any longer and lifted her into his arms to carry her to the bed where the covers were already turned down. He set her on the bed and paused a moment to appreciate the sight of her long blonde hair fanned across the pillows.

"Beautiful," he said again, then shrugged off his robe and tossed it aside.

"Oh, my." Norah lifted onto her elbow and reached for his manhood. "I didn't expect…it to be…so much."

He gave a half chuckle mixed with a groan as those soft fingers grasped his hard length. After only a few of her exploratory strokes, he pulled away her hand. "You've nearly undone me, my love."

"I should like that." She looked up at him, seeming to be fascinated by the idea.

"Not yet." He eased onto the bed beside her to kiss her again as he roamed his hand over her body, taking his time, then found her dampness once again. He wanted to make certain she was as ready for him as he was for her.

When her hips started a rhythmic dance, he nudged aside her knee to settle between her legs with his manhood pressed against her center, and his elbows holding his weight. Nothing had ever felt quite so perfect.

"Are you ready?" he asked as he looked into her eyes.

"More than I can say." The complete trust and faith reflected in her eyes made his heart swell with love.

He kissed her even as he made her his, thrusting into her with one smooth motion.

"Oh!" She stilled, her body stiffening in response to his invasion.

"Hold tight." He hoped like hell that her body adjusted as he'd read it would. What if he'd gotten this part wrong and there was something more he should've done to ease his way inside her?

Before the worry gained ground, Norah shifted beneath him and a pulsing need to move had him drawing a deep breath with the hope of keeping still. Then she tightened her arms around his neck and drew him close for a kiss before she slowly moved her hips.

"Oh, yes," Norah whispered between kisses.

"My sweet wife." Thought dropped away as his body took over to move with hers in a rhythm as old as time. Need built layer upon layer until he didn't think he could bear any more. He simply had to touch her again and lifted on an elbow to caress her wet folds.

"Simon!" She stiffened beneath him, her body pulsating as she found her release.

With a groan, he followed her, holding tight as an explosion of stars swept him away. He shuddered against her, certain nothing would ever be the same again.

"Simon, my darling." She pressed kisses over his face. "I love you so much."

"And I love you more than words can say." His heart overflowed as he kissed her once again.

At last, he shifted to her side, settling her against his chest. "You have changed my life for the better, Norah. I don't know what I would do without you."

"You'll never have to find out." She wrapped her arm around his chest. "We are now one in every possible way. Forever."

He smiled and reached for her hand to kiss the delicate skin of her inner wrist, loving the way she shivered in reaction. "Forever and always."

He'd said it before and intended to keep saying it to remind himself how lucky he was that this beautiful woman had barged into his life so unexpectedly. Then he closed his eyes, his happiness complete.

About the Author

Lana Williams is a USA Today Bestselling Author with over 35 historical romances filled with mystery, adventure, and sometimes, a pinch of paranormal to stir things up. Filled with a love of books from an early age, she put pen to paper and decided happy endings were a must in any story she created.

Lana spends her days in Victorian, Regency, and Medieval times, depending on her mood and current deadline. She lives in the Rocky Mountains with her husband, and a spoiled lab, and loves hearing from readers. Stop by her website and say hello! There, you can find links to connect with her on Facebook, Twitter, or Instagram.

Website: lanawilliams.net
Facebook: LanaWilliamsBooks
Twitter: LanaWilliams28
Instagram: authorlanawilliams